SO
SLOW
THE
DAWNING

SO
SLOW
THE
DAWNING

by
INGE
TRACHTENBERG

W · W · NORTON & COMPANY · INC ·
NEW YORK

COPYRIGHT © 1973 BY INGE TRACHTENBERG

Library of Congress Cataloging in Publication Data

Trachtenberg, Inge.
   So slow the dawning.

    I. Title.
PZ4.T757So [PS3570.R23]   813'.5'4   72–8970
ISBN 0–393–08538–4

To Ali, In Memoriam

SO
SLOW
THE
DAWNING

FLOWERS ALONG THE ROADBED

For ten Pfennige you could buy a whole sheet of paper angels. Large ones and small ones, bust or full length. They were separated by perforations, gummed on the back, and when you licked them the taste of the glue made your tongue tingle. The large angels had wings made out of nice white goose feathers. I used to pretend that I had such wings, and that I could fly next to trains I was in, and that I was picking the flowers which grew along the roadbed. I was a skinny child, stork-legged and very blond.

Berlin. In the late 1920s.

We lived in a big apartment house, in eight sunny rooms. Petunias and geraniums grew in green flower boxes on the balcony in front of the dining room. The other rooms had glass shelves in the double windows on which pots of flowering plants stood; Emma watered them each day with a pewter watering can which had a long, thin spout.

I collected cacti. Some bloomed yellow, some had fat, purple petals, most of them were simply prickly. They were as nothing to the beauty of the flowers that grew along the roadbed of the railway. The blue cornflowers, the orange poppies, golden-rod, and brown-eyed Susans; colors out of Montmartre. . . .

Actually, of course, I was inside of the train.

With my sister, Renate, and our mother and the Fräulein.

All the way from our station in Charlottenburg out to

the Grunewald, I would press my nose against the window and watch the flowers rush by. I would glide just a little above them, beating my wings slowly, majestically, flying easily at the speed of the train. Casually, I would reach down and pluck a flower here and there. A few yellow wheat stalks too.

The bouquet grew and grew. . . .

"Get ready," Mother's voice would intrude. She was standing up already. "Here comes the station. Now for some fresh air."

Fresh air was very important. We took the excursions into the Grunewald, we walked to our dancing and piano lessons, we "breathed deeply" at Mother's behest. "A breath of fresh air" was an essential part of each day.

Once, when Renate was thirteen and I was eight, we planned a terrible revenge on Mother because she had sent us out into a November drizzle. To that end, we removed our identical red scarves and mittens and the navy berets we wore. We also unbuttoned our navy double-breasted coats and stepped into puddles. But coming home, properly soaked and bedraggled, we found that Mother was out playing bridge. She didn't see us, nor did we catch pneumonia.

Our battle with Mother went on constantly, relentlessly, though without any real malice on our part. It was simply the thing to do—fight Mother. Half the time, I suspect, Mother had no idea that she was being fought; our lives didn't really touch that much.

In the mornings when we were going to school, Mother was still sleeping. It was Emma who would slam the oatmeal on the round dining-room table and slop the boiling cocoa so that there would be brown puddles in our saucers. The oatmeal was cooked especially to fatten me up, but I emptied it regularly into the toilet bowl. Instead, Renate and I gorged on the fresh rolls which Fräulein Clara fetched each morning before we were up.

And we sneaked into the cupboard where the honey was hidden. It was meant for Sunday only.

Frl. Clara walked us to school until we were quite big, and she picked us up again. Dinner was at two o'clock, and we would find mother at her desk doing the household accounts. She always smelled delicious and she always asked, "How was school, duckies?" But she didn't listen to our replies. We tested her. "School stinks; Frau Klempner made in her pants!" "That's nice. Wash your hands; dinner is ready."

Three afternoons a week we returned to school for needlework, religion, and art. On the other days Mother took us shopping. To the tailor, Mr. Phillipe. To the bootmaker on the Kurfürstendamm; Mother was proud of us, we had long, narrow feet that could not be fitted with ready-made shoes. And we went to the underwear lady, who embroidered suitable things on our batiste slips. Fat yellow ducks and, later, tiny forget-me-nots for me; I never graduated to the appliquéd love knots that Renate already had on her lingerie.

School day or not, at five o'clock Mother went to the café. Except, of course, on bridge afternoons. At the café— Dobrien's, Leon's or the Jause Haus—the ladies met. On the rare occasions on which we were invited along, it necessitated the wearing of white stockings and patent leather Mary Janes and our good, camel-colored suits. Or even the plum velvet dresses. In short, it was a dubious pleasure for us in spite of the vanilla ice cream served in heavy silver sherbets.

Supper was served to Renate and me on trays in our nursery. We considered it our favorite meal because we could read while eating.

We called each shopkeeper Fritz.

There was the Vegetable Fritz and the Soap Fritz and the Wurst Fritz. I loved going with Emma to buy a pound of *Schmierseife*, literally "smear soap," from the Soap Fritz. It was green and had the most heavenly smell as it was ladled out of the wooden barrel and slapped, glistening and sticky, into heavy white oiled paper. I also liked going to the Wurst Fritz; he gave out samples.

Best, though, were the stalls in the open market which came to our neighborhood twice each week—the Herring Lady, enormous in a gray, woolen man's sweater with holes at the elbows, who promised that her herrings had eyes as blue as mine. The Pigeon Lady, whom I couldn't stand because of the way she would grab the fluttering birds out of their bamboo cage and twist their necks—all in one motion. The Cheese Fritz with his enormous knife behind the huge Swiss cheeses, and the lovely, cool smell under the tarpaulin where the Fish Fritz had his tank that was full of carp swimming about.

Across from the *Bierstube*, the pub, at the corner of our street, was the apothecary, the Medicine Fritz. His store was full of wondrous things and a high jar of round cellophane-wrapped sourdrops stood on the counter. I used to get happily lost gazing at them, anticipating the tart taste, wondering which color to pick. Once Mother bought a *Punktroller*, which was a thing like a rolling pin, covered in hard rubber, punctuated with little rubber nipples. On Thursdays and Fridays Mother used it to roll her thighs; the masseuse came on the other days. I looked forward to being old enough to roll my thighs as well.

As to the Bierstube, I only visited it once. I was eight years old; I needed to buy a stamp. I had secretly written a letter to Renate's beau because they had quarreled.

"Dear Walter," I had written, "please make up with Renate. She loves you and so do I."

Buying the stamp was nice. It was dark in the bar, and it smelled of beer. A lot of big men joked with me. "Na, Fräuleinchen, aren't we a little young for beer?" I curtsied and said politely that I just needed a stamp, I wasn't allowed to drink beer. Opening a careful fist, I let the Pfennige tinkle to the tin bar. "Na *gut*, there you are, little frog," the barkeep said and handed me a stamp. I curtsied again. "Danke schön. Auf Wiederseh'n."

Unfortunately, Mother and Father met Walter's parents at Kempinsky a couple of nights later. That's where all their crowd met after the opera. For caviar and champagne or Moselle and Rhine salmon. Walter's mother had the letter along; it was passed around. Among the exclamations of "how sweet" and the "adorables," I imagine that my father's face must have darkened. The next morning I received my one and only spanking from him —for having no pride.

Of course there were double standards in those days.

Little girls had to have pride, but grown-up ladies could do anything. We were perfectly aware of that. Didn't we hear them when our parents gave parties? And hadn't I met Father and Frau Rotkorn in the broom closet?

That broom closet!

"Ellen, I'll put you in the broom closet!"

"Ellen, the broom closet!"

"Ellen!"

The terror in the darkness, the ominous shapes all around me, impossible to believe that those fingers reaching for me were only limp mop heads. Cowering with my hands over my ears, mouth wide open—"Fräulein, Fräulein, I'll be good. Let me out, I'll be good . . ."

How strange it was then to see Father there with Frau Rotkorn. Emma had sent me for the mop because a gentleman had thrown up in the bathroom. Careful to leave the light shining in the corridor before opening the door of the hated place . . . and Father laughing and putting a finger to his lips and winking at me. Frau Rotkorn didn't notice the intrusion; the party was loud.

Things were always different when Father was at home. It was not often; he traveled on business with a wine and liquor line and in the summer he liked to take a cure at a spa. But those rare times! He would have breakfast with Renate and me and know about the oatmeal in the toilet bowl and the honey. And he would order grandly, "Emma, eggs for the girls!" even though we were supposed to have only one egg per week.

And when Father was home our parents sometimes woke us up late at night when they came back from a party. They woke us to hug and to kiss us, and for no reason, and because they were a little drunk. Once they put on a masquerade. Father in garters and undershorts, wearing a formal shirt and his tall silk hat, and Mother in a slip with her big ostrich-feathered chapeau. What a show that was—Father tapping his silver-headed cane, Mother doing kick-ups; marvelous.

Also, when Father was home, there were the Jewish holidays. Wearing the selfsame high silk hat and striped pants and a black coat, he would lead us to the synagogue. Renate, Mother, and I sat upstairs among the women. I folded my hands piously; the Hebrew sounded so strange and beautiful, but Mother and Renate were a little impatient. "Why must the services be endless? Repetitions, nothing but repetitions." "Psst," I hushed. Afterward, at home, the table was set with the best dishes, and the old candlesticks shone, and the long loaves of holiday bread were hidden under an embroidered cloth. "My grandmother embroidered that," Father said each time. We all stood behind our chairs while he lifted his glass and sang the blessing. Mother raised her eyebrows and made faces. Of course her irreverence drove me right into more earnest prayer.

"And bless the wine and the bread and Renate and Papi . . ."

Sometimes I punished Mother by not having her blessed.

Sundays were best if Father was home.

He had a way of whistling that was a remnant of the days when he had been the goalie for the Würzburger Kickers, the famous soccer team. At least Father said that the team had been famous. His stories of the exploits of the team were only matched by his stories about his outfit in the war, and for both I was his main listener. As to the whistling; it was somehow up and down, musical, the way old-fashioned horns used to sound, the kind with the rubber bulbs. Father gave this whistle on Sunday morning as a signal that he and Mother would now welcome our visit. Dropping whatever we were doing and storming into their bedroom, we would pile on top of them in their half-dark bedroom. The heavy purple draperies would still be drawn, Mother's silk hose, garter belt, and panties would be scattered on the chaise longue which stood, on graceful turned legs, at the foot of their bed. It was also purple, upholstered in velvet, and there were tiny lace pillows piled on it. Best was the smell, musty and sweet, warm as Mother's hair. A little cigarette smoke, perfume, and maybe a dead bunch of violets on the glass top of her dressing table. Mother always wore fresh violets pinned to her black seal coat.

Father, his face scratchy, would immediately start tickling and wrestling; there were flailing elbows, giggles and screeches, and sometimes tears. Until Mother said, "That's enough. Ring for Clara."

Clara and Emma would both come, each carrying an enormous tray. By that time the curtain had been drawn, Mother had made a grab for her scattered underthings and stuffed them under a pillow, had brushed her hair and her teeth, while Father, always keeping hold of slipping pajama bottoms, had lurched around the room looking for his cigarettes, and had then brushed his hair as well. He would do that standing in front of his bureau, and since he needed both hands to brush with his two military brushes, he would lean against the bureau edge to keep his pants up. It was of great interest to us, and once we were actually rewarded by the pants really slipping down at some careless motion Father made. Renate turned quickly away; I am said to have shouted, "Oh, oh, Father's things are just like the ones on the man in the park." Of course I was referring to a statue of Apollo. We played catch around it.

Later, we went for a walk. For the Sunday walk, contrary to weekday excursions, we got all dressed up with white kneesocks and white cotton gloves. Uusually we took the route toward the Grunewald, along the Hundekehlenallee to the Roseneck—lovely suburban streets—to the edge of the woods. Mostly, Father and I marched ahead, while he told me about the time when, buried alive by an exploding French shell, he was finally dug out and had spent the rest of the war in a field hospital. Or about the midnight patrols he had led, the hand-to-hand combat he had been in—demonstrating with blood-curdling yell how, knife in hand, he had charged. Mother and Renate, catching up with us, would also watch, Mother shaking her head. "Ach, Ernstl, not again." But if we really got far enough ahead to be out of her sight, Father would give me lessons in drill. "Hup, two, hup, two . . ." And if I made a mistake, his drill sergeant voice would bellow, "*Du Rindvieh!*" in thick Bavarianism.

At other times, Mother and Renate prevailed. Then we went parading down the Kurfürstendamm. This was their pleasure; they stopped and looked into every store window, and even Father was inattentive to me, though I tried to bring the conversation back to our topics. He was busy lifting his hat—"Grüss Gott, Guten Tag"—to passing acquaintances.

But regardless whether we had been in the forest or on the Kurfürstendamm, on the way home Mother led the way, driven by a strange unease. "Let's hurry, she'll spoil the roast," and when we sighted our street Mother would actually speed ahead, certain that our Sunday dinner was in peril. Then Father took Renate under one arm and me under the other, and we would mimic Mother in anticipation. She would meet us at the door. "I just saved the roast," she would say. Mother never disappointed us.

Of course, after the big dinner, our parents napped. In fact, that was the end of our Sundays together; when they awoke later they vanished into their adult world. Coming to kiss us good-by, they were mere specters—beautiful, lovely smelling . . . unreal. Mother's hair was ash blond and heavy, pushed softly around her face, and she was always warm to the touch and soft—velvets and feathers. When she looked like that we forgot that she was angry so often when Father was away. As for him, he would hoist me high and catch me surely. I was always excited when I was around him; he was handsome, slick and blond, he had steel-blue eyes and a mustache, and he stood tall.

Excitement left when Father was off again.

Life dimmed a little, the colors faded. But I accepted that; it was the way things were. There were times for everything.

Until 1933 when everything changed.

I still kept on flying next to trains, beating my feathered wings, but the goldenrod had dried a sere brown; it waved in a sharp wind.

Bachelor buttons, their blue faded, broken in stem.

Dead the brown-eyed Susans.

And all the petals blown off the poppies.

Icy winds and black branches poking skeleton tentacles toward a desolate sky.

There were no bouquets to pick, the wheat had long since been harvested, threshed, and ground. I was dressed in my brown sweater for flying, the sweater I had taken out of mothballs with the beginning of winter.

I suppose I was prepared.

Though the change came gradually, as other seasons.

I

On the first day of school it is customary in Germany to give a child a *Zuckertüte*, a sugar bag, actually a cornucopia made from cardboard, covered in shiny foil paper and filled with sweets. The idea was that these sweets, carried to school, would sweeten the start of learning. My bag was almost as tall as I, pink foiled with white paper lace around its neck; angels were pasted all over it.

Mother had accompanied me to school herself on that first morning. The two blocks to the big red building on the Sybelstrasse seemed endless. Finally, finally, I was to be a big girl like Renate. Maybe I would even be a "sensual creature" like her. Judging from Father's smile when he pinched Renate's cheek and called her that, it was a good thing to be. I don't remember the moment when Mother left, but I recall sitting at my desk, clutching my Zuckertüte and seeing Frl. Schmiedecke for the first time. She had china-doll pink cheeks and black, shining hair and nice gray eyes; I loved her instantly and felt safe enough to let go of the sugar bag. Frl. Schmiedecke was also soft voiced, not at all like the mean teachers Renate spoke of. I yearned toward her— Dutch boy-cut hair and blue eyes fixed on her, sitting at my desk, knees together, back straight, hands folded on the tabletop; I'd be a very good girl.

However, it soon became obvious—even to me—that I wasn't cut out for this role. I was a troublemaker. I had to talk when talk was mortal sin, and I had to sing just a little too loudly, but mostly I had to yell out in class; the other kids were so stupid. "You goose, everyone knows that," I shouted, and Frl. Schmiedecke made me the first example. Into the corner I went, face to the white stucco wall, and I closed my ears to the snickers and also to Fräulein's voice. "All right for you, old Schmiedecke, I won't love you anymore, that's all. I'll only love Mother and Father and Renate and my grandparents and Tante Gert and the Wurst Fritz . . ." on and on. Much comforted by the number of people I had to love, I finally emerged from this public humiliation unscathed. Later on, however, I did adopt restraint as a necessary expedient.

Against the black mark of my deportment stood the bright star of being smart. Not particularly intelligent, but plain school-smart. I knew things. I had information gleaned from years of hanging over Renate when she did her homework. I knew the capitals of all European countries, the names of authors and composers, where Brazil was, and what H_2O meant.

During the year when Goethe was being memorialized on the occasion of the 100th anniversary of his death, I had helped Renate to memorize the endless verses of the poem "Der getreue Eckart"; in the process I had learned them by heart as well. Frl. Schmiedecke, proud of me, arranged for me to recite it during the Goethe Feier, a solemn assembly of heavy rhetoric about his meaning in the German scheme of things, his contribution to *Kultur*, to the world. The occasion was considered too adult for the lower grades to participate in, so my appearance was a great honor. Fittingly, Mother dressed me in my fraise silk dress and my Mary Janes. She even came to hear me. I wasn't really overwhelmed by all this, but I was concerned about not wrinkling the dress and keeping my knees together as I sat up on the platform with the other dignitaries. Nor did I forget my lines. I stood up there and looked out at all the faces, and I had a very good time.

"O wären wir weiter, o wär' ich zu Haus'" . . . all about the Furies who come to drink the beer the children had been sent to fetch, and how old Eckart reassures them.

"*Und lasst ihr sie trinken, . . . Dann sind sie euch hold, die Unholden*"—let them drink the beer, and they will be gracious to you. And the children give drink to the Furies and upon reaching home their tankards have been filled again; a lovely miracle.

We loved mythology. All those heroic gods, all this raw power, all these heroic deeds performed in the service of the Vaterland. It was no less than my own father's philosophy: you come home from the war either victorious or on your shield, dead. Yet, I was glad that Father had only been buried alive and wasn't dead. Or maybe I didn't really understand that we hadn't won the war. It was all very confusing.

We still played dying with wooden sticks, pointed, but we already said, "Ack, ack." Frenchmen shooting Germans, or trying to. In the end we Germans always won. We were reared by a history book telling about the monster Treaty of Versailles. The illustration in our reader showed a peaceful village street, a peasant woman standing in front of her cottage, holding a letter. A white babushka hid her hair so that she was neither old nor young, but her expression was puzzled. Across the street we saw the mailbox. The caption under this picture explained that the woman could not mail her letter because the mailbox was in France. "Poor Alsatians," I said; they lived so peacefully, these good Germans on both sides of the street. Until the French rent them apart.

"Ack, ack . . . gotcha, Frenchie!"

"But if the French are our enemies, why must we speak French?"

"That's a good question," Father said. He was not much of a linguist. Mother gave him a withering look; she hadn't forgiven him yet for the way he had opposed our getting the mademoiselle. It had been the time when Frl. Clara's old mother had gotten sick and Clara had to go home to Oberstauffen to nurse her.

Mother had decided that we would get a mademoiselle in the meantime, in order to be forced to speak French. For some reason the fiction always existed that we could speak French if only we would. Mother maintained that she had reared us bilingually, and anyhow, every cultured person spoke French.

Mlle. Renée turned out to be a middle-aged lady with dark frizzy hair in an untidy bun, very black eyes, and a wart on her chin. She ran with tiny steps on sandpiper legs, and she wanted to learn German. It really worked out very nicely. When Mother was around she and Mademoiselle conversed in fluent French, and we kept quiet the way children should. When Mother left, we taught Mlle. Renée German—with enormous amount of giggling, with screeches and small-clawed hands clasped over her mouth when she made a mistake. I suppose in the process we acquired a little French too; anyway, Renate did. It was she who had really undertaken Mademoiselle's German training and often, she had to explain matters to her in French.

The earliest stories of my childhood are concerned with Renate standing over my crib, letting me tear at her hair. My earliest memories are of things she and I did together—the meals, the games, the conspiracies against Mother. Wetting our toothbrushes because Mother made Frl. Clara check whether we had brushed, or when company came and brought candy, biting into each piece to find the ones with marzipan, Renate's favorites, or the cream-filled ones I liked. All the other pieces we turned carefully around to hide where they had been bitten, and then we presented the box to Frl. Clara; she didn't mind. Sometimes though, we received a whole pound of nougat. It was quite a problem because we both loved it. I hoarded my portion carefully, nibbling only the stingiest amounts to make it last longer, while Renate immediately stuffed herself with her part. And when hers was gone, she would ask, "Can you spare a piece?"

"You shouldn't have eaten yours so fast," I would say self-righteously.

"You're right; I'm a pig," humbly.

What could I do? Grudgingly, I would share my

nougat. Yet, I understand how it was for her. She loved candy too much to be disciplined. It was simply different for her than for me—the same as she had to luxuriate long in hot, scented baths and liked silk and used hand lotion. She was five years older than I, she had long legs and long hair and a wide mouth with full lips. "She isn't pretty like Ellen," I had heard a lady say, but I had known that I was not being complimented. Renate had something that was more important than "pretty," and while I did not know what it was, I was glad anyhow. Especially since she often played with me.

Mostly, Renate was patient with me, even later when she had to drag me along on walks with friends or to birthday parties. At Rosa Weiss's party I gave her a bad time when I asked during spin-the-bottle, "Have you gone to the bathroom today?"

Everyone, except Renate, thought it was cute; I was five years old. It was one of the few occasions when Renate tattled on me, and I was scared that Mother would be very angry because I knew perfectly well that I had been naughty. But Mother only laughed; she was insensitive to both my misdeed and to Renate's embarrassment.

Mother often missed these points; punishment was a haphazard affair in our lives depending on Mother's moods rather than on actual transgressions. Yet, we kept the fiction alive that our parents were strict in the sense that other people's parents were strict. "Oh Mother will kill me, absolutely kill me" if my grades weren't perfect.

Really though, we knew that Mother didn't care about grades; it was perfectly obvious. But she lauded the conventional virtues:

It was good to be scholarly, wise, honest, obedient and kind.

It was right to love God and one's parents, and even one's enemies.

And you absolutely had to be clean and neat.

However, we were pretty sure that none of that was

taken too seriously with the possible exception of the part about being clean and neat.

As to Mother's "attacks," as we called them, when punishment came flying upon us, it used to burst on us suddenly, terribly. Storms of towering dimensions—"Your room is a pigsty," a screech.

"Oh God, what have I done to deserve such children?" a wail.

We would leave for school, beaten puppies. "What have we done now?" I would ask. Renate would put her arm around me.

"Who knows?" she would shrug, and I would feel better.

Later, when we were older and it had gotten worse, we became cynical and learned how to deal with it. Renate became a magnificent liar; I, a fighter of issues. But it made little difference how we reacted, when it was time for a storm it would rage forth, a natural phenomenon which awed us in spite of ourselves.

Mother always maintained that she told us "everything." This euphemism for sex education made for very sketchy knowledge. When we saw a pregnant lady, mother pointed her out to us and said, "Look, she is carrying a baby under her heart."

This produced no exact image in my mind, but trying to get the conversation over with, I would quickly say, "Oh, I know all about *that!*"

Renate laughed. "I bet she doesn't understand a thing," she remarked, but Mother took me at my word. "Of course she does!" She believed that such knowledge was *comme il faut*, like speaking French. "I don't believe in fooling children," she went on. "These ridiculous stories about finding babies under cabbage leaves or about the stork bringing them . . ."

I interrupted. "You mean the stork doesn't bring babies?"

Renate crowed. "I told you!"

Mother shrugged. "Oh well," she said. "We'll talk of it again."

My best friend was a small girl named Inge Herlinger. She always wore smocked dresses which her grandmother embroidered for her in beautiful colors. Her parents were divorced; Inge and her mother lived with her grandparents. Inge never talked of her father, which I thought odd, but I didn't dare ask her about it, not even after we heard that he had died. It was just one of the things about Inge.

Then there was Romi Braun and Katrine Simon. We were all in the same grade. Among the subjects that comprised our curriculum in school was one called Religion. Of course it was the study of the Christian religion and we Jewish children were excused from it. I suppose that was how Romi, Katrine, Inge, and I were first thrown together. We received our Jewish Religion mandatorily in the afternoon. The teacher, Herr Phirsigbaum, wore high black boots and had a beard; we didn't think much of him. Though we were told that we owed Religion the same respect that we were to give to other school subjects, we never took it very seriously—it was a time for fooling around, and there were boys in Religion, pupils from the neighboring boys' school. Of course that redeemed these afternoon sessions in our affection!

Once a week we met, the four of us, and knitted and sewed for the poor children in Africa. I had trouble with the thumbs in the mittens I knitted. Inge embroidered things on bibs, dresses, and infant sacques, which her grandmother ran up on the machine for us, Romi made aprons, and Katrine never finished the endless scarf she kept working on.

"I dropped another stitch," she would wail, but not too unhappily; her distinction was that she was a good soccer player; even her brother let her play. I would take the knitting out of her hand—"Ach, you're so clumsy," clucking over the tangle, though kindly; a girl who could kick a ball as far as Katrine could not be expected to know how to knit too.

We were always encouraged to think of the poor *Auslands Deutschen*, Germans living in alien lands such as America or Africa or France. These displaced citizens were the ones who would be glad to have the spinach I didn't want to finish, and they would be happy to have nice long brown wool stockings that I said were itchy. I did feel sorry for them, of course, but I also thought that they must be pretty stupid.

Every once in a while the question came up whether we should allow other children to join our *Kränzchen*, literally "a little wreath," and there was especially the discussion about Steffi Levy. Steffi was the fifth Jewish child in our class, but we thought she was odd. She could read Hebrew as fluently as she read German, and she had curly black hair, cut short instead of the customary pigtails or Dutch boy–cut smooth blond head. We had seen her father, who had the tailor shop on Wilhemsdorferstrasse. He sat in there, all hunched over like a hunchback, and he was small and curly and dark like Steffi, and someone had told us that he spoke with an accent. Steffi had been born in Berlin as we were, but still, she was a foreigner, wasn't she? And not nice. Kind of sharp-tongued. "Crazy," we thought. Mother said that the Ost-Juden were that way.

"But why? What makes them different?"

"Oh the Jews who come from Poland and Russia are so, well, you know, so Jewish."

"But we are Jews too."

Mother laughed. "That's different. We are Germans; Jewish is only a religion."

"Then is Steffi Polish? Her father comes from Warsaw, I think."

"No. Jewish."

"I don't understand."

Mother shrugged. "Anyhow," she said, "you know the Poles are dirty and poor."

"But Steffi is clean."

"Really Ellen! You stick to your nice little friends; why don't you ask Christa to join your Kränzchen?"

Christa had moved in below us and was in our class. We discussed it at our next Wednesday.

"My mother said we should let Christa in," I said.

"She's stuck up," Romi protested.

"Because she is noble," said Katrine.

"What's noble?" asked Inge.

"When your name has a *von*, like Christa von Adelsberg. It's like a king or something."

"Not that high. More like a duke."

We thought about that, then Inge ventured, "Maybe she doesn't want to join."

"Why shouldn't she?"

"Because we're Jewish."

"That's just a religion," I crowed.

"Yes, but she's noble."

I laughed. "She isn't so noble; she's nice." Yesterday she had given me a bite of her sour pickle.

Christa was glad to join. She could knit very well, and she showed me how not to get my thumbs crooked. She also knew really keen stories about Africa, her father having been in charge of a diamond mine there.

"Then, when you lived there, you were a poor Auslands Deutsches child," I marveled.

Her eyes were very blue, and she had a way of tossing her long braids when she laughed and getting red in the face. She knew what I meant.

"My mother always said I had to eat my spinach because of the poor children in the homeland who didn't have enough to eat during the depression," she answered.

We all thought that was marvelous. It was probably the first time in our lives that we could actually and concretely punch a hole into our parents' pious talk.

"But why did your father come back here to Germany if everything is so poor?"

"He said that things are changing."

We thought that Herr von Adelsberg must be right about that; certainly we weren't poor.

2

Christmas trees smelled better when I was a child.

Maybe because real candles were used, pungently dripping hot wax on fat green needles—the singed smell, the forest smell. Then of course there were apples and cookies and marzipan, and goose in the oven and red cabbage. Or maybe it was just the excitement.

On December twenty-third we fixed the Christmas plates for the superintendent and his family. Their name was Feuerhahn. Literally translated that means "firecock or "fire-rooster." He was a small, mean man, but of Frau Feuerhahn I remember only her sweater, big and green; she wore it winter and summer. Their daughter Mimi was my age, but smaller than I. She had oily dark-blond hair, the bangs on her forehead separated into almost individual carpet fringes. Her eyes were small and close together, her nose tiptilted, and her ears stuck out between the greasy hair. I thought she was beautiful because her ears were pierced; she wore tiny corals in them. Mother laughed at me when I wanted to get my ears pierced too. "Only common children have their ears pierced," she said; it was lower class.

Ordinarily we had little to do with the Feuerhahns. True, each time you came into our building the procedure required Herr Feuerhahn to look through the small glass window in his door to check who was there before buzzing the door open. In that way I guess we saw him daily, but it is unclear to me now why I should have been so afraid of him. Yet I was; he ranked together with the chimney sweep dressed all in black, the policeman with his gun, and the presence in the broom closet in my roster of horrors. These were the phantoms that would "get me," and if I forgot it, Fräulein would remind me, "Ellen, I'll tell Herr Feuerhahn . . ."

But at Christmas it was different.

After helping Mother fix the Feuerhahns' plates with apples and nuts, with a rare and exotic orange and a marzipan pig which had a shamrock in its snout, and after putting ribbons and star stickers on the box with my outgrown dresses, Renate got to tie the big red bow around the neck of the *Schnaps* bottle.

"Otto, Otto, look who's here!" Frau Feuerhahn gave the joyful cry.

And he would come, and all was smiles, and "Na, ach, ja, ja, na ja!" and Renate and I curtsied and wished a Merry Christmas and curtsied again. In the elevator going back up we didn't look at each other; it had been kind of embarrassing.

Still, Christmas was wonderful.

The year I was ten years old my grandmother introduced Chanukah. That was Oma, my mother's mother, the one everyone called the *shiksa*, though not to her face.

As I got the story, she had met Grandfather when he was but a lad, an apprentice in a store. She is said to have said on seeing him—in fact, on watching him pack a carton—"That Jew will go far!" Later, they got married. She was the daughter of a prosperous landowner, a kind of gentleman farmer, and she took marrying the Jew seriously enough to take instructions and become a Jewess. For which her father disowned her. I thought it odd that everyone called her a *shiksa* in such a contemptuous tone because she was the only one in the family who lit Shabbath candles each Friday night, and she prayed a lot in Hebrew. Grandfather, on the other hand, didn't seem to care.

"Pah, nonsense, *Schnaps* for the masses," he grumbled when Oma stood by the window reading in her black siddur.

Later, Grandfather left the Jewish community; I think it was in a quarrel over the Jewish income tax from which institutions and religious houses were maintained.

However, Grandmother had been right about one thing: Grandfather went far. And with her help. From one shoe store to a string of them, to a fine department store in Leipzig. But by the time I really knew him, he was retired. I said to Inge, "My Opa is a millionaire, he gives me five Marks every month!"

He did, indeed, and twenty-five Marks on every birthday. Later, as I grew older, he gave me secret loans when I needed money to have my bicycle fixed without telling Mother that I had been in another accident. He also brought me cubes of sugar, wrapped in café house wrappers, which he called rabbit's bread, and during the warm weather when the monkeys were in their outdoor cages, he took me to the zoo a lot. He was a life member of the Zoological Society, which entitled him to his own and four auxiliary passes, and on fine days he had his skat game at a stone table right across from the monkey cages. "Him and those other retired skat fiends!" Oma said angrily; she never went to the zoo, not even to sit at the outdoor café where there was music and dancing as well as a wonderful view of the Lion House.

On the evening we learned about Chanukah, Oma brought the Menorah and little candles and a picture book of the Chanukah story. Also a small umbrella which I had admired in a store; I thought that Chanukah was wonderful too. But when she explained that, being Jews, we should celebrate Chanukah instead of Christmas, I was indignant.

"But Christmas is better . . . the tree . . ."

"You see, we Jews don't believe in Christ, and Christmas is the celebration of Christ's birth."

"You mean there was no Christ?"

"Well, we just don't believe that he was God's child."

"But he was a man?"

"Oh yes, and he was a Jew."

"Well, then, why can't we celebrate his birthday anyhow, if he was a Jew?"

My mother laughed and hugged me. "The child is right, we can have both."

Grandmother shrugged. "You're confusing the children," she said to her daughter.

"Oh mother!" Notes of impatient disdain.

Later Renate and I discussed it. "Mother is mean to Oma," I said.

Renate thought it was because Oma was a *shiksa*.

We usually had a good holiday. Mother felt compelled to "do something" with the children during our vacations. Only sometimes it was not convenient.

The year I was eight years old we were sent to a camp in Nordfriesland, about an hour by horse-drawn wagon from the North Sea. We made this trip to the shore every day. The great thing about the horse and wagon was that Karl, the boy who fetched the horse from the meadow, was my friend. He let me tag along, and I sat on the split-rail fence while he put the halter on the horse. Then he would lead the big, square creature next to me, I would climb aboard, and Karl would lead us back to the barn to hitch the horse between the shafts of the wagon.

The wagon had benches all around its sides. The older children sat on them; we little ones were in the wagon bed, bucking and pitching and rattling, raising our voices in screaming song, and joining in the enthusiastic cheer the old kids gave when the horse would raise his tail, dispatch a steaming load, and give us a quick, embarrassing look at the chopped-meat sight of his insides.

Arrived at the shore, we raced down to the beach to see whether there was any water. At ebb time the ocean was so far out that on some days we had a long way to go to get wet. But what a delight that run toward the water was, the squeegy sand underfoot, the shallow holes half filled with warm brine, mirroring vast skies, inhabited by shrimp and other tiny creatures. And

then finally, the lapping waves—and always the delicious fear
. . . the tide will turn, the water will come back; I'll be
caught. . . .

There were plenty of stories about children who had
been caught too far out by the turning tide; and we were told
about them. The point made, we wouldn't have dreamed of going
off alone, away from the others; it was dangerous.

Renate had her first boyfriend, the famous Walter. I
fell in love with him too. He treated me terribly; I was the pest,
always hanging around. "Go wash," he said, and once, when I
had forgotten my bathing suit when we came to the beach and I
went into the water in my panties, he surveyed me critically, his
eyes sliding over my bony chest, and said, "You ought to be
ashamed of yourself!" I was. And I hated camp. I was only eight,
too young for all the best things—the kissing games, the giggles,
the secrets. Renate had disappeared into another world, the world
of "big girls"; she was caught up in all that excitement, she didn't
fight the system that separated us.

Back home, Mother said that she would never let us go
back; it was a disgrace how dirty I was, and I was covered with
hives. I argued that camp had been great, that I loved it, but
secretly I thought that it was nice to be clean again and to have
Renate back in the same world with me. The night we came
home a dish of nougat squares stood on our night table between
our white, inviting beds. Mother had put them into a little fili-
greed silver basket.

The next summer we went to visit our Tante Ruth in the
Harz. That year Father had persuaded Mother to take a cure with
him at Bad Kissingen; they would join us later.

Our Tante Ruth, my mother's sister, lived in a small
town at the foot of the Harz Mountains. She was married to a
little man with carroty hair and freckles. Their daughter, our
cousin Nanny, was likewise red-haired and freckled.

Tante Ruth, whom we knew from her visits to Berlin,

where she came whenever she quarreled with Onkel Kurt, had a habit of giving love-bites which rather hurt. Except for that we liked her fine. Consulting with Mother on what to do about the biting, we had come up with a great idea. In our finest block letters we had printed *BEISSEN VERBOTEN* on large pieces of cardboard. Mother thought it was funny, but Tante Ruth didn't. When we disembarked from the train wearing these signs around our necks she couldn't have liked it less. She never did have a sense of humor and was cross all summer, but we didn't really care. There was her white stucco house in the big garden with raspberry, currant, and gooseberry bushes, and her dog, Axel, who ate frogs while we shouted enthusiastic encouragement. Our cousin, Nanny, who was exactly in between our ages, took us all over the cobblestoned village and introduced us to her friends. They all talked funny, and most of them were barefoot; it was wonderful. Onkel Kurt was fine, too, except that he tried to stuff us with "good, fresh country cream"; we were his Auslands Deutsche children; poor, starved city mites.

One of the great boons of the little town was that we were permitted to ride bicycles every place. I loved the bumpy feel of the big cobblestones. Sometimes we visited Onkel Kurt in his dark emporium. He stood all day behind a wooden counter cutting lengths of cloth from huge, flat bolts, talking to the farmers' wives, who called him the Fabric Jew the way we talked of the Wurst Fritz, grinning his red smile, teeth stained. And we rode out into the country, and I could get off the bike and pick all the flowers I wanted; they were exactly the right kind. But they were usually dead by the time I got them home and into water.

Berlin was hot and dusty when we got back.

"I wish I could always live in the country," I said.

"Ugh," Mother said. "No stores, no theater, no people . . ."

"There are so people!"

"Farmers!" She shrugged, then she laughed. "And aunts that bite!"

I suddenly felt bad for Tante Ruth, sorry about the sign that had hurt her feelings. "Well, at least she stays home with her child," I said. "She doesn't go running to spas." Right away, I was scared; that had been pretty fresh. But Mother was in a good mood. "Come on, Ellen," she answered, "you wouldn't really want to live with Tante Ruth all the time, even in the country; would you now?"

I rushed into her arms. Of course I wouldn't.

3

My father came from a long line of wine merchants.

Accordingly, drinking had real status in my childhood. When I was discovered in my nightgown sitting on the grazed party–dinner table, emptying out the dregs of all the wine glasses —at four years of age—it made my father jubilant. "She's got the palate!"

Wine was tasted at dinner with long, slurping sounds, followed by smacking sounds, followed by an expression of thoughtful reverence before the pronouncement was made. "A small flower, slight, but pleasant."

I became a celebrated authority the time I said, "A yellow snapdragon, full of honeybees."

Renate, who knew me better, whispered, "You faker."

"Well, it was sweet," I defended myself to her.

Downstairs, in the cellar, where each tenant in the building had a locked storage area, Father had his wine cellar. He took us downstairs with him when a new shipment came. Handling each bottle lovingly, he read the exotic labels—Hergesheimer Spätlese, Schloss Wachenheimer—round-bellied bottles, slim ones, and he told us the story of each wine. He told us how they were aged and bottled, and who of his customers drank them, and about good wine years and mediocre ones. He placed each carefully into its diagonal rack, and from the very back he took a slim green bottle full of cobwebs. "Don't ever wipe cobwebs off; they are part of the mystique," he said, and, "Wine must breathe, uncork it ten minutes before pouring it."

It was beautiful to see how he uncorked the wines before a dinner party. The sherry for the cream soup, the Moselle for the fish, the Bordeaux for the roast duck, the sauterne for the lemon mousse. With the coffee, cognac was served and crème de chocolat or crème de menthe for the ladies.

"Drinking is an art," Father said.

Peeking through the door, I saw him lift the first glass —candlelight in sparkling cut glass, Father's elegant fingers holding the slender stem . . .

"*Prost*, my dear guests, to the wine!"

Father had a much younger sister, my Tante Gertrude, who lived in Nürnberg and was married to a pediatrician, our Onkel Wolfgang. Of course everyone called him Wolf, which was rather funny because he was a mild, dreamy, and absent-minded young scholar. His hair was always too long; it fell over his forehead and Tante Gert would push it back for him. "He can't think of mundane affairs like haircuts," she would say. In really great crises Onkel Wolf would be consulted by telephone; Mother considered him the last authority on pediatrics. Of course Renate and I claimed that Mother called him at the drop of a hat, but in spite of that I liked these consultations because I had the opportunity to say hello to my Tante Gert at the end. "Hello, *Schatzele*," she would say, and the tears would shoot into my eyes. I hardly ever saw her, but the love was strong between us.

It was she who gave me the insights that illuminated all of Father's stories, put them into their simple frame of provincial dignity and goodness. The family had observed orthodox ritual until, during the war, it became impossible to obtain kosher meat; then they had lapsed. Shortly afterward my grandfather died. Father was at the front, in the middle of the battle of Verdun; Tante Gert was a child of eight. She had told me often how she had sat in her mother's lap. "Mama, Mama," she had cried, "I know God punished us for eating *trayf!*" But her mother had said that that was impossible because God was good. Just the same, Tante Gert had become an agnostic, and I was sure that there was a connection.

Father had met Mother in Berlin when, a dandy—spats and silver-knobbed cane and foxtrot—he had simply swept her off her feet, and out of another marriage. "He took me for a walk," Mother had told us, "and when there was a loose cobblestone in the street, he carried it to the side of the road and said, 'That's the way I shall clear the road for you all my life.'"

It was a pretty disconcerting thought—one minute he was the country lad, rough and boorish and curly-haired, a good son. "My father took me on the road when I was sixteen, I wanted to help him, he wasn't well, and I had enough schooling." And the next minute he was this slick-haired Berliner. I never learned the story in between from him—the dissolution of the family business and of the family, was there a bankruptcy? A scandal? Anyhow, Father was headquartered in Berlin, traveling the provinces, selling wine and liquor from a firm not his family's. *Commission* was a really meaningful word when I was a child.

Mother's first marriage had been arranged by a marriage broker. I was intensely curious about that, though it was also embarrassing when she spoke about Herr Sokolovski. She did so quite frequently, always angrily. She had been eighteen, the marriage had been a good match, Herr Sokolovski, a prosperous businessman about fifteen years older than she.

"But why did your parents want you to marry so young?"

"My mother couldn't wait to get rid of me."

Grandmother had preferred Tante Ruth. For that, Mother idolized Grandfather. When we were small we knew him better than we knew Grandmother because, like his daughter Ruth, he came to stay with us when he and Grandmother quarreled. Later, after he was retired, they moved to Berlin, and we made Grandmother's acquaintance too. It always seemed impossible for me to connect her with the harsh presence our mother had conjured up out of the stories of her childhood. The beatings and the stinginess, but especially selling her daughter into an unhappy marriage. Grandmother's cheeks were dusty white velvet, the nicest cheeks to kiss, and she smelled of spices, and dinner at her house was always small roasted chickens, crisp, brown, delicious. I had little jokes with her, and I always felt that, somehow, my mother must be wrong. Yet, there was the arranged marriage—I had visions of my mother sold into slavery. Especially after seeing him.

One Sunday we were at the beach at the Wannsee when Renate spotted him. He was her father, she went to see him one Saturday out of each month. It was completely unreal for me—wasn't she Father's little girl, the same as I was? Of course. When I struggled to understand, "Well, which one do you love best?" Renate was impatient with me. "Really, Ellen, of course I love Papi best."

Our father was Papi or Paps; hers, Vati. That time, at the beach, it burst out of her. "Ach Gott, there is Vati."

A tall, corpulent man, dark—he walked through the sand, away from us, with heavy steps. His back was fat, his shoulders bent.

"Did he see us?" Mother exclaimed.

"I don't know."

Father laughed. "Go say hello to him, Reni." He called her Reni when he was very tender.

"Must I?"

Her eyes were dark. Suddenly I saw that she looked like . . . no, not really. But so different from us. Quickly, I took her hand. "I'll go with you," I said.

"No, you don't!" Mother jerked me away from Renate, who started slowly after her father, her shoulders very slumped.

Renate had been two years old when father and mother met, a child with huge bing cherry eyes; she had had a nurse-maid, Rösli, who was young and pretty.

"Young and tender and crackly!" Father said, laughing.

He lived across the street, flirted with the young nursemaid from his window to hers. "But she was modest, always pulled the shades down."

One day he had seen how she had stuffed Renate into her warm winter coat and leggings. Anticipating that she would soon emerge with the child, he stormed out of his apartment and waited in front of the house across the street. He had been right, Renate was being taken into the fresh air—by Mother.

"I was lost," Father would sigh when he talked about it. "Simply lost."

I felt that this was the proper type of romance—prince and princess, dancing in white satin, lace, fur . . . tired blue violets wafting sweet sadness. In my judgment, that was the way to marry. Not by arrangement.

Father said, actually, he only married Mother to get Renate.

"You mean Rösli, don't you?" she would snap.

He would laugh.

Rösli was fired while Mother was pregnant with me. Mother said one of the best things about Frl. Clara, who replaced Rösli, was that she had pride. "Yes," Father agreed, with a small wrinkling of his mustache, "she's a sober, worthy person."

"What's wrong with that?"

"Don't get excited. Nothing, nothing."

Father also said that he must have been out of his mind to marry Mother with such an entourage. "My God, I was twenty-six years old. A wife, a child, a nursemaid, a cook, a housemaid, the laundress . . ."

Mother sniffed. "I didn't know then that one can rough it."

"Rough it!"

"It isn't easy to manage with two in help."

"Not counting Frau Bauchenhorn."

Frau Bauchenhorn came twice a week, Tuesday and Thursday, to do the laundry. Looking as unlike the proverbial laundress as possible, she had skinny white arms, yellow hair screwed into a bun on top of her small head, and she was tiny. She stood by the stove on top of a wooden packing case in order to be able to reach the huge pot, and she stirred the boiling laundry with a wooden stick. Later Frau Bauchenhorn carried the huge basket downstairs into the basement, down the kitchen stairs, down six floors. Holding the basket with thin, strong arms, her belly pushed forward for extra support, she walked lightly. In the cellar wash-kitchen she scrubbed the laundry in the big tub on a corrugated iron board. Then she rinsed it and hung it on the line that was reserved for us on Tuesdays.

When I was small I loved to watch Frau Bauchenhorn get ready to go home. She was so tiny when she stepped out of her starched white uniform, still crisp after a day in the steam and toil of a big wash. Winter and summer, she wore brown woolen bloomers down to her knees and a woolen vest that was yellowed. She had a big laugh, too big for her smallness; it billowed out, provoked by anything I said, from under the rose-sprigged flannel slip she was slipping over her head. Then came the best part of the ritual.

She would pull big pins out of her bun, and her hair would tumble down—an incredible mantle of soft, sparkling gold, totally unexpected each time, an incongruous princess glory around her lined and tired face. "You're beautiful," I would exclaim, and her laugh would boom.

I told Father about the hair. "Too bad she's old," he said.

"I thought they were never too old or too young for you." Mother had that tone in her voice again.

"She's forty-five if she's a day."

"We'll be forty-five too, one day."

"Oh never, not you." He kissed her hand.

"Will I ever be forty-five?" I asked, pushing between them.

"You?" He looked me up and down with grave mien.

Then he burst out laughing, grabbed me, and hugged. "Put on some weight and you'll be a femme fatale," he said.

"What's that?"

"A gorgeous woman."

"Gorgeouser than Mother?"

"Oh much!"

With a small silver brush, into a thin silver tray, Mother was brushing crumbs off the tablecloth. The crease was between her eyebrows. "It wouldn't surprise me! Nothing is holy to you," she said.

"Too bad we haven't got sons; you'd feel easier."

"Who knows with you!"

"Oh come on!"

She flung the tray and brush down. Crumbs scattered, fly specks on the white tablecloth. And rushed from the room. Father shrugged.

Yet, I always felt that they were in love. Why else should she be so unhappy when he was away?

Father's habit of taking a cure at a spa every year was necessitated by his bad stomach. I used to think that it was the result of a stomach shot he had received during the war. "They had to draw the pus out of me with a ladle!" Father had said. Every time the soup tureen came to the dinner table and Mother served with the big silver ladle, I pictured the doctor at the field hospital. It was a big disappointment when I finally found out that Father's only war wound had been a shrapnel splinter in the calf; plus nerves, of course. It seems that the being-buried-alive story—a caved-in trench in the battle of the Marne—had really happened. So I suppose that one could consider the bad stomach as stemming from the war. Father turned absolutely green every time he was upset, had diarrhea to match Mother's "attacks," and his heartburn was famous. He went through cures, medicines, diets; there was an especially interesting time when he passionately drank only herb teas and ate nature foods, and there was the year of the self-hypnosis.

Father also said that he was psychic. He said that he discovered it when he was lying shell-shocked in his hospital bed. The Herr Doktor Major had tried to hypnotize him out of the shakes.

"He stared at me, and I stared right back!"

Father's steel-blue eyes demonstrated for me. That stare. I held my breath, listening to him. "Then he said that he couldn't hypnotize me because I was too strong; in fact, he said that I had great psychic power!"

After that, Father said that he had become the Major's assistant hypnotizer. Of course, all this was only hearsay because, in the meantime, Father had given it up. "Mother made me."

It seems that he had developed his psychic powers to rather a fine point—finding a friend lost on his first visit to Berlin. "I just concentrated and saw him get on the wrong streetcar, so I took a taxi, caught up with the streetcar, and there he was!" Shrug, simple. As a party game he found hidden objects, read designated lines in books, looked deeply into ladies' eyes and knew their secrets—his audiences were amazed. He used Mother as his medium, holding her wrist delicately between forefinger and thumb. "I read the message in her pulsebeat when she concentrated on what I should do," he explained to me.

"But why did Mother make you give it up?"

"It was too dangerous," Mother would interrupt. "He didn't know what he was doing in his trances, and I was pregnant with you."

It seemed too bad. I would have loved to have seen it. But even without actually seeing it, it influenced me greatly. I felt he knew everything about me, could read my mind, was a little dangerous. He liked that. Effects, drama—he called them practical jokes; they were more—the time I came into the dining room, where he stood motionless.

"Papi, Papi? What's the matter?" I was eight or nine.

He stared at me and then pitched forward to the floor. I ran to him. "Papi, Papi . . ." He didn't move, breathed heavily.

his eyes were closed, I thought his eyelids looked peculiar. White ice climbed into my chest, I knelt by him.

Then he opened his eyes and grinned. "Just wanted to see what you would do." Reaching for me, hugging me. "So you love the old father?"

I tingled, couldn't warm up. After he had jumped up and unlocked his cigar cabinet, I still sat on the floor. He selected a long, slender, light brown cigar. "Smoke?" he asked me, smiling.

"No, thank you," I said gravely.

The cigar cabinet was really a small glass-doored book-case, though one shelf did hold Father's humidor. There were maroon cotton curtains behind the glass, and it was kept locked because the books on these shelves were not for us. Renate first discovered where the key was hidden, and in one night, the bed-lamp under her cover, she read *Die Morphinistin*, a book about a lady drug addict. I tried hard to stay awake, nagging.

"What does it say? Tell me, tell me." But finally I fell asleep. The next morning Renate said that it hadn't been very interesting. There had been no love scenes at all.

"Who wants to read their old books, anyhow?" I said. It was several years until I found that I did.

Mostly though, things were locked up because of the maids. The linen closet was locked, Mother's jewel case, the silver chest, the liquor cabinet, and the door of the sideboard where the honey and jams were stored. Mother had an enormous bunch of keys which she was always mislaying. "Where are my keys? Who took my keys?" Clara, looking flustered, "I don't know, Gnä' Frau, honest." "Emma, have you seen my keys? I know I left them right here in the kitchen." Light blue eyes torn open to full width, "Honestly Gnä' Frau, I haven't seen them!"

I ached for them. The keys always turned up in Mother's other handbag.

Mother's real name was Selma.
We found this out when we were already quite big.

"But why does Paps call you Eva?" I asked.

"I hate Selma!"

"Selma, Selma . . ." I tasted the name on my tongue, shrugged. "It's not so bad."

"Your mother is an Eva; the first woman," Father said.

"Selma is a cow's name," said Mother.

Later she told us that she had been twelve when she and Ruth had been taken to see the farm. The cows had stood in clean stalls. Each had an enameled nameplate nailed to the split-rail stall door. The biggest cow was Selma.

When Renate and I were really furious at Mother, we talked of her as Selma. We didn't dare do it to her face, but it was satisfying just the same.

4

Ten was a landmark; ten candles and one to grow on, it made a lot of sparkling light in the birthday ring. There was no doubt in my mind that having two digits in my age lent me added importance. This was further borne out by the fact that I received a camera of my own, symbol of maturity, of trustworthiness.

The real difference that year was the party though. Usually we would have frankfurters and potato salad at children's parties. But the year I was ten, to mark the exclusive occasion, we had cold roast beef with remoulade sauce and string beans vinaigrette. I was fully conscious that this was a grown-up menu and very proud to have it served at my celebration, and I never told Mother that all the children sighed with disappointment when they saw it. I sympathized with them—to me, too, it seemed that party fare for birthdays should be stable, that one should know what one had to look forward to. I know that I was always hoping that it would be frankfurters, though the problem with them was that you could only take one at a time, and while it may still have been all right to take another when the dish was offered, you absolutely had to say no, thank you, the third time around, regardless of how much you wanted another.

I didn't cry once during my party. Up to then it had been a family joke that, due to overexcitement, I christened each birthday party with tears. Not that year. I escorted the children who had been called for by their Fräuleins to the door, I said all the grown-up things: "Thank you for coming," "Your present is just beautiful," "Get home safely!" I was holding the excitement in, I was behaving like a lady, I had made it without tears! But when the door closed after the last child and I wandered back into the dining room and stood looking at the grazed-off table, at the crumbs and the stain where Romi had spilled her cider, at the crumpled napkins—and at the all-overness of my party, a great sadness possessed me; I burst into tears. But since no one saw me, it did not count.

Of course today, looking back, my tenth year is marked as the year in which Adolf Hitler came to power in Germany. It is all jumbled in my memory with our getting our first radio, a big brown box that was put on top of the cigar cabinet, with seeing the zeppelin sail over our house, and with our hero worship for President Hindenburg. We had visited the site in East Prussia where a huge monument commemorated Hindenburg's successful battles. Now he was president of Germany, an old man with a big white mustache, and he wouldn't let that paperhanger come to power.

Yet, when that event took place, Father wasn't sure that it was such a bad thing for Germany. Adolf Hitler had promised bread and order; Father was in favor of bread and order. Over the radio we listened to his shrill voice and to the waves of roared "*Sieg Heils*"—I, for one, had no premonition of bad things to come. Grandfather was the only one who spoke really scathingly of the Führer; in fact, he likened him to another character he couldn't stand, "*Der Kerl Roosevelt in Amerika!*" But since Grandfather was always ranting against political figures, it meant less than nothing to us. What did we have to do with them anyhow? Just more grown-up talk; it didn't touch our world.

On May 1, 1933, there was a great celebration to hail the Führer. Frl. Schmiedecke wore her white lace blouse that had black velvet ribbons threaded through the eyelet. We were sitting still, waiting for her to give the order to line up, so that she could march us down to the auditorium for the festivities. We didn't particularly relish the prospect because assemblies of this sort always meant having to listen to endless speeches, but we had been told that we were to come back to school in the evening and would then be supplied with torches and allowed to march in a torchlight parade. We looked forward to that.

Frl. Schmiedecke stood silently in front of us for quite a long time. We felt a little uneasy, what was she waiting for? Then she started to speak.

"Children, I expect that you will be on your best behavior; this is a solemn occasion." Another long pause, then, "Romi Braun, Katrine Simon, Inge Herlinger, Ellen Westheimer, Steffi Levy, please get up."

We rose. She looked at us, her face was red; it was queer.

"I am sorry, girls."

We waited.

"You have to go home."

We stood some more, really bewildered now. I raised my hand.

"Yes, Ellen?"

"We don't have to go to the auditorium?" I asked.

"No," she answered.

"Why not?" I blurted.

Her mouth tightened, the flush deepened. What had I done?

"I don't know. These are my orders!" She spoke angrily.

We stood a little longer, then Steffi moved out of her desk and walked to the coat hangers that lined the west wall of the classroom. She took down her sweater, and the rest of us followed her. In the doorway, Romi turned back. The class had not moved, Frl. Schmiedecke still stood in the same place.

"Yes, Romi?" she prompted.

"Seven o'clock tonight?" Romi asked.

"No, you are excused from that too."

We closed the door behind us. In the hall, Frl. Mannheimer's class, the third grade, passed us. Two by two, they marched down the corridor, Frl. Mannheimer following behind. Seeing us, she stopped. "What are you doing here?" She had a raspy voice, big warts on her chin, and bulgy eyes; we called her The Toad, happy that she wasn't our teacher.

"Frl. Schmiedicke said that we could go home." Inge spoke for us.

"Ah yes, the Jewish children!" Then she laughed.

We waited.

"So go already, go on, go home," The Toad said and ran after her children. Her big behind bounced.

Down the stairs we went, twice we squeezed against the bannister as other classes marched by, then we were in the front hall and then out of the door. Outside, we stood together; there were no Fräuleins to pick us up, what should we do? Then Steffi said, "You see, it's started already!"

"What's started?" I asked.

"The anti-Semitism."

"The what?"

"Anti-Semitism. Don't you know anything? When they hate Jews."

"You're crazy."

"No, I'm not; my Papa said Hitler will throw out all the Jews."

"He will not."

"He will so."

"Well, not us." I settled it. "My father was a front fighter in the war."

"Yes, mine too," Romi said.

"Come on, let's walk home," Inge urged.

Steffi was the only one who had to go to the left, the rest of us moved off in the other direction. "That Steffi is a goose," I said.

"But The Toad said that it was because we are Jewish," Inge said.

"Oh The Toad! What does she know?"

"Hey, this is great, to walk home alone."

We stood and watched the traffic carefully before crossing.

"I'm going to tell Mother that I don't need Fräulein anymore; it's silly the way she treats me, as if I couldn't cross by myself," I decided.

The others agreed. Romi's house came first, then Katrine's. Inge and I walked the last block to our buildings.

"I would have liked to go to the parade tonight," Inge said when we stood in front of her house.

"Me too; I've never been."

It felt queer to come home in the middle of the morning. I rang the bell. It took a long time for Emma to open the door because Frl. Clara was out marketing.

"Are you sick, child?" Immediately, Emma's big hand went to my forehead.

I laughed. "No, lucky; no school!"

I could hear the radio screaming in the living room, Mother was in there. She was sitting in Father's leather chair, filing her nails. Her eyes widened when she saw me.

"They sent us home," I yelled. "Romi, Inge, Katrine, Steffi, and me, and we don't have to come back tonight; we are excused."

A funny thing happened to Mother then; her face kind of sagged, her mouth going down, her eyes wide open, she looked like I did the time I had watched myself cry in the mirror. Then she put her hands over her face and sobbed. Reluctantly, I went closer, stood in front of her. "What's the matter? Why are you crying?"

She sobbed louder. Again I thought, "Just like me," but I felt angry too; mothers shouldn't carry on. Gingerly, I put out my hand and patted her shoulder. She grabbed me and held me tight.

"My blond girl," she said, "my blond girl . . ." Over and over.

I held myself as stiffly as I could; it was very unpleasant, her wet face and her red eyes and a drop on her nose. Finally I couldn't stand it any longer and wrenched loose.

"Oh Mother," I said, just the way she sometimes spoke to Oma. I ran into my room.

It was a sunny, beautiful day. I watered my cacti, and then I went and sat in the kitchen and helped Emma pull the strings off the beans. I liked the sound when I snapped them just before dropping them into the big pot. Emma was making lamb stew.

"Put in lots of potatoes," I urged. "I love them when they taste all lamby and smooshy." But Emma got nervous because she was late putting the stew on, and she chased me from the kitchen. I wandered around some, but didn't want to go near Mother. Finally I called to her, "Can I telephone Inge? I already had my two." Mother called back, "As an exception." I was allowed two telephone calls a week; Renate had four because she was older. Inge said that she had just been on the verge of coming over, her Oma would take us roller skating right away. "Oh great!" I even found my skate key in the drawer where it belonged.

On the way home I met Renate.

"Did you have school today?" Maybe only we had been lucky.

She shook her head. "Don't tell Mother."

"I wrote a poem today," Mother said at dinner. Her eyes were bright.

"What about?" Renate asked.

We were always polite about Mother's poetry, though it embarrassed us; it was full of moon and love and beauty. When we were alone we made up parodies and giggled about them.

"It's called 'They Sent My Blond Girl Home Today.' " She looked at me expectantly.

"Can I be excused? I don't feel so good."

"Oh Ellen!" she said.

I bolted from the room. Later Renate came and asked

what was the matter, but I couldn't tell her. All I said was, "Mother is impossible, really impossible."

Renate shrugged.

Then we heard Mother call, "I'm going now. Auf Wiederseh'n!"

It was five o'clock, time to go to the café.

In July I wrote a poem too. A farewell poem for our beloved Schmiedecke. Secretly we talked of her as Hildegard; how nobly she compared—after four years of being our teacher—with the screechy-voiced art instructress or Frl. Mannheimer, the substitute. We had experienced even worse—Frl. Karlemann. She wore shirtwaists pinned high on her neck with a swastika pin, and she had a pince-nez. She would stand in front of us—"And since your own teacher has weakly succumbed to a tiny little bacillus, I have been entrusted with the unpleasant task of pushing some learning into your empty heads!" Then, in a roar, "Open your books, page eighteen!"

Frl. Schmiedecke had been different. And now we were into our last days of school, the last ones in elementary school before going on to the Lyceum in September. In the end, though, I couldn't bear to give her my poem because it was too mushy; instead, we chipped in with the whole class and bought her a big pot of cyclamen. Frl Schmiedecke liked it very much, she said that cyclamen were one of her favorite plants, and that she would take good care of it, and each year when it bloomed, she would think of us. Then she shook hands with each girl. Most of us cried. But she hugged only Steffi Levy.

It was funny about Steffi. I had become friendly with her too. Ever since that Wednesday . . .

Wednesday was singing, first period. Our classroom was painted white, windows all across the east wall, the blackboard north, and on one side of it were the maps, on the other, nailed to the rough plaster, the huge flag, red around the swastika. This new addition rather brightened things—you could stare at the black symbol and get a feeling of abstraction rather like in a maze. There was a summer drone in the school, composed of chalk smells and dancing dust motes, an unheard hum of almost vacation time.

All thirty-six of us rose when Frl. Schmiedecke came in.

"Good morning, Frl. Schmiedecke."

"Good morning, children."

We stood at attention.

"You may sit down."

We collapsed with various noises, contortions, squeezing into our desks, opening the tops, and getting out the music books, relieved to be moving, making sounds after the minute's discipline. The desks were arranged in pairs, in three rows across, six rows deep. Inge was my deskmate, Romi and Katrine were right behind us.

That morning Frl. Schmiedecke was flushed and absent-minded, and we took advantage with extra noise and banging and even dared to talk to each other a little. It was nice but unusual, and as such, a little disquieting. She was acting strange, Frl. Schmiedecke, just sitting at her desk, staring, with her head turned to the window.

"What's the matter with her?" Inge whispered.

I shrugged.

And then there was the sharp knock of her ruler on the desk. "Girls!"

Silence followed instantly, completely.

"Open your books, page twelve, 'Dieser Kuckuck der mich neckt.'"

Relieved, we obeyed. Soon we were singing about the cuckoo who mocks from the depth of the green forest. Frl. Schmiedecke beat time in the air with her ruler, standing before us in her green dress with the ecru lace collar around her white neck. And then in harmony, row A and B and C, always twelve of us calling cuckoo, cuckoo, cuckoo, mocking the others, trilling the simple, sweet notes, eyes on Fräulein—and when the ruler stretched horizontally toward us, almost like a blessing hand, softly, we subsided—only row C very low, calling cuckoo, cuckoo, cuckoo . . .

"That was splendid!" Frl. Schmiedecke was smiling now, and I felt better. Inge noticed it too. "Her broken heart has healed," she whispered to me, but Frl. Schmiedecke was back on the job.

"Inge Herlinger, you have a lot to say. Why don't you come up here and lead the class in 'Wir treten zum Beten.' "

Inge blushed scarlet and shuffled to the front. She took the ruler that was handed to her, raised it, looked at us pleadingly. But we laughed. Well, it was funny when a child tried to act like a teacher. Inge returned to her seat, chastened. Then Frl. Schmiedecke led us off herself, singing softly, articulating the words clearly.

> We stand before God
> We pray to the Just One
> He lets not the evil
> Enslave the righteous one
> Blessed be his name
> He forgets not his flock.

We sang earnestly, the old hymn resounding, making the chalky schoolroom air dance, and June sunshine lay outside. Anyhow, I liked singing about God. He seemed a fine old gentleman, and sometimes I wished that I knew more about him. I was thinking about that when I realized that we had swung into "Deutschland, Deutschland," the national anthem. I joined in enthusiastically; it was a song for shouting.

> Deutschland, Deutschland
> Above all
> Above all in the world

I sang, I yelled, responding to the ruler waving in the air, the fellowship of all our voices, the rhythm . . . the ruler cut us off.

"You're not singing, Steffi?"

There was silence.

"Stand up, Steffi Levy."

She stood, her face down, hidden by tangled curls. I twisted around in my seat to see her better; she was three rows behind us.

"Look at me, Steffi."

She raised her face high. Her chin stuck forward, she was very pale and her eyes shone. I saw that her hands were clenched and felt my stomach contract; she was crazy.

"You weren't singing, Steffi?"

"No."

"Why not?"

"I'm not allowed to sing that song."

"Not allowed to sing the German anthem?"

"My father said . . ."

"Not allowed to sing 'Deutschland, Deutschland über alles'?" Frl. Schmiedecke's voice had risen. I shivered; I guess we all did.

"My father said only God is above all."

"More important than one's homeland?"

"Yes."

Silence again. Frl. Schmiedecke looked at Steffi reflectively. The red had receded out of her cheeks. We held our breath.

"So you refuse to sing that song?" Her voice was very calm.

"Yes I do."

"All right, see me after class."

We collapsed. Balloons pricked by pins, tires by nails, we all collapsed.

"Let's sing the 'Horst Wessel' song next," Frl. Schmie-decke said to the class.

I joined as loudly as the rest. It was the Nazi anthem, another song for shouting.

"By the way," Fräulein said after we had finished, "by the way, from now on when I come into the room in the morning and you get up, don't say 'Good morning, Frl. Schmiedecke' anymore. Say '*Heil* Hitler' and raise your right hand like this." She showed us. "Understood?"

"*Jawohl*, Fräulein," we shrilled.

The bell rang then, and she left the room, saying for the first time, "*Heil* Hitler." She raised her arm. Her face was red again.

I took my sandwich out of my desk and unwrapped it. Cautiously, I peeked under the rye bread to see what was on it.

"Do you have liverwurst?" Inge said.

I stared at the bread.

"Do you?" she repeated.

"I don't know," I said at last. I dropped the sandwich and struggled out of my seat. I banged my hip in the haste I felt; it seemed suddenly urgent, I had to talk to Steffi right away.

That had been the beginning. Twice after that I played with her during recess.

"What are you starting with her for?" Inge asked.

"She's really nice."

"I thought you said she's crazy."

"Well, she is, but she's nice too."

5

 $\mathbf{F}$ ather had decided to take all of us to Bad Kissingen.

The Opel was new that year. A small gray car, not very pretentious; Father had felt that his Mercedes was too classy to drive up to some of the provincial hotels he visited on business. Mother wasn't wild about the change, but it was one more thing that she sighed over in a resigned fashion—like only two in help and not having a mink coat.

Grandmother, however, thought of any automobile as the height of luxury, and that day when Mother had met her at Reimann's, the café Grandmother went to—Mother's crowd met at Dobrien's—she had practically yelled, "Is the Oppel outside?" and in a voice absolutely calculated to be overheard.

Father roared when he heard the story.

"Her mispronouncing it really topped it," Mother wailed. " 'The Oppel!' Oh my God, I could have died; I have never been so embarrassed."

Father was still laughing.

"The pretentiousness, the ignorance . . . to boast about that car, that miserable Opel."

"Now Eva, let's not start on that; the Opel is a good little car."

Mother sniffed.

All this was forgotten when we started off the next morning. It was the first summer vacation without Fräulein; I felt very independent.

Suitcases stowed away, Renate and I in back, Mother in front wearing her pink suit with the matching hat and the jersey scarf to protect her hair, and Father behind the wheel. Before we were out of the Droysenstrasse, Renate and I were singing. Soon Mother joined in, her small soprano true, then Father. As always, this dissolved us. To say that Father had no voice was a vast understatement. His singing, loud and deep, covered a multiscale of tones; it could squeak and boom, mostly it reverberated as if a pitchfork were being banged on a rusty rain barrel. But he liked to sing.

That day, Father decided to break the trip in half, and in the afternoon we stopped in the Thüringer Mountains in front of a hotel which looked like a Swiss chalet, brown chocolate, green window boxes with red geraniums, galleries with fancy carvings all around.

Since Father was tired from the drive, he took a nap. He could stretch out on a bed and be instantly asleep; he was breathing deeply already before Mother and we left the room.

"Let's get some fresh air . . . all those gasoline fumes . . ."

We made the bored faces that we thought appropriate at the mention of air, but we were glad to get out into the open, to stretch after the long ride.

Only a few steps beyond the hotel we came into the deep green valley, ringed gently with gradually and greenly rising hills, layered against a background of mottled steel-gray and purple. And in the distance, the black mountains, mountains from which the sun struck sparks, all dark purples, black-greens, and charcoals. It was, this walking in the green heart of the valley, as if the clover we trod on was velvet, as if we were centered in the core of an emerald. Even Mother, great verbalizer that she was, always pricking us with her endless "looks" and "sees," even Mother knew enough not to talk. We just walked through fat meadows and along a path of pine needles and through a small wood of sun-flecked birches, and I left the small wildflowers alone and wanted nothing. The quiet afternoon was serene; we crossed a tiny bridge over a clear brook, and then Renate started to hum, and with the purplish shadows coming down, we finally turned back toward the hotel.

The scene in the dining room denied the peaceful mood we had shared. It bustled! Red cheeks and dirndls and mugs of foaming beer and pigs' knuckles and Father making the waitress blush. I, as always, happily overwhelmed by a big menu; Thüringer dumplings were famous, what would I eat with them? But Renate, who had hummed so sweetly just a little while ago, was quiet now. I had noticed lately that she changed her mood like that. That, suddenly, her nostrils could turn white and her lips be a pink that was almost unbearably delicate.

"What will you have, Reni?" Father asked.

"Potato salad."

"And what else?"

"That's all I want."

"Potato salad? What kind of a meal is that?"

"It's all I want, Father; I'm not hungry."

"Nonsense! Eva, make the child eat something decent."

There was a pall over the meal then. I knew why she wanted only potato salad, didn't I? And sometimes she was so unhappy. Was I old enough to have to share it?

I missed Fräulein.

We didn't talk about it until next morning when we stood by the rail of the lookout. Breathless from the climb, triumphant to have succeeded in our plan to leave before Mother and Father would be awake, to have beat the sunrise. The mountains that had been black from below were mouse gray now, and we were furry inside of them and watching the piercing silver rays rising from behind, washing silver into gray, tinting blue into mauve, splashing light toward the sky.

"Last night," I said and cleared my throat, "I know you ordered potato salad because it was the cheapest thing on the menu." It came out too loud.

"That's not true." Renate spoke loudly too.

"Papi isn't poor; we don't have to be that modest."

"I know."

"Why do you get so unhappy?"

"You wouldn't understand."

"Yes I would."

Renate stepped away from the railing and sat down on a weathered bench. I stood before her, fierce with love. "Tell me!"

"Everything is easy for you; he's your father, but he isn't mine."

The shock of her words made my voice quaver. "That's crazy."

"No." Her eyes were dark and her hair; I thought of Herr Sokolovski and felt guilty.

"You're his girl just like me."

"No."

"Did your Vati say that?"

"No, Mother . . ."

"Oh Mother, you know how mean she can be."

"But she was right. Yesterday, before supper, when we were washing up, she said Papi is so good to me."

"Why shouldn't he be?"

"I am not even his real child . . . and he is so good to me."

"That's no reason to be unhappy, you goose." My eyes were smarting. Renate had dug her fists into her eyes. I wanted to touch her, but didn't.

Suddenly, all was milk white around us. I turned back to the view, and there below I saw veils of white lift from sunny green. "We missed the sunrise!" I cried angrily.

Father treated us nobly at breakfast. He ordered grapefruit, which was a great luxury.

I told about our climb, Renate was quiet. Mother was feeling cross that morning; we had kept them waiting for breakfast, she had wanted to get an earlier start, the beds had been awful, she said that she had been worried about us. "Why are you sulking?" she snapped at Renate.

"Leave her alone!" both Father and I, as from one mouth.

"Well!" Mother said.

"I want to have a talk with you," I announced as Father and I were stowing the overnight bags into the car.

"*Jawohl!*" He clicked his heels and saluted me.

"No, seriously; about Renate."

He frowned. "I've noticed; what's the matter with her?"

"Do you love her?"

"What?"

"Do you love her like your little girl?"

"She's my big girl."

"As much as me?"

He was laughing again. "Oh more, much more."

I shrugged; there was no discussing anything serious with him.

I tried Mother while Father paid the hotel bill and Renate was talking to a girl she had met who also adored Hans Albert, the movie star.

"Why do you always talk to Reni about Papi not being her real father? Why must you always talk of that old Herr Sokolovski?"

"You are getting impossibly fresh, Ellen; I just don't know what to do with you anymore."

"You are making Reni unhappy."

"Renate is adolescent," she said and turned away.

In the car, Renate knit on the red vest she was making. She was smiling to herself, humming. She had once told me when I asked why she sometimes looked "so funny" that she was making up love stories in her mind. I presumed that this was what she was doing now. So I started to sketch the back of Father's head—the quarter of his cheek I could see and his hand on the wheel. And while Mother and Father talked quietly to each other, I decided that it was all nonsense, anyhow.

"What's adolescent?" I asked loudly.

Mother turned around to us. "Don't you remember when we had our little talk and I told you?"

"No."

At Bad Kissingen they showed us where the sanatorium was. "Right down the street from you, here!" Then Mother went along to settle us in at the pension. We had a long room and big brown beds and high feather quilts.

"I don't like the way it smells!" I didn't know why I was whining.

Mother was in a hurry. "Frau Schleifer will look after you, and tomorrow after breakfast you may come to visit us," she said.

Frau Schleifer had something the matter with her eyes. I did not know which one to look at, which one looked at me; they certainly didn't both act together. Renate took my hand.

"We'll be all right, Mutti. Have a good time."

"Yes. Good night, duckies."

She kissed us and rushed off.

At the sanatorium, things were very gay. The first morning when we came to visit, we found our parents on the balcony. Mother wore long black satin pajamas with bell bottoms, Father was in his blue silk robe with the striped ascot. We were introduced to several ladies and gentlemen, and I envied Renate, who did not have to curtsy any longer. Herr and Frau Fichtel were there too. They were friends of our parents' though they were much younger. We thought that Luz, a clear-eyed blonde, was wonderful; she was almost as tall as Rudi. "The beautiful Rudi," Mother described him even though he was an Ost-Jude. Yes, he was—wavy black hair, very blue eyes, white teeth with which he laughed a lot. He was also called The dashing Rudi, Father said, because he had been a racing driver and still considered car racing his hobby. He had taken Mother on a hair-raising spin. She said she'd never, never get into a car with him again, but she said it in a thrilled tone of voice. Another thing that made him interesting was a trace of an accent with which he spoke. "He certainly doesn't sound Polish," Mother said, shaking her head. "His people must have been very cultured; they probably only spoke French. You know, some Ost-Juden were really very fine people. My first parents-in-law knew a family . . ." She had launched into the saga of their riches.

"I don't know what they see in the parents," Renate had grumbled after we first got to know them. "They are intelligent and modern, not superficial and silly like the rest of the crowd." Luz and Rudi were both lawyers, which was also unusual, and last winter Luz had invited Renate to come to her office, and now Renate wanted to be a lawyer too. So we were happy to see them there at the sanatorium among all the strangers. Rudi kissed us, and Renate blushed, and everyone laughed, and Father took me on his lap and let me sip of his champagne, and made much of me, but I struggled off; I hated his show-off manners. We left soon afterward, promising to look for them in the *Kurpark* later.

My first sip of the healing water caused a violent coughing fit. It tasted of rotten eggs and smelled the way a kitchen match reeks after it has been blown out. Just the same, I paraded around with Mother and Father, holding the tankard-type glass by the handle. Especially after Renate met Herr Grün. At least it was something to do. Father bowed to all the people they knew, and Mother smiled at them charmingly, even if she was just in the middle of scolding me. And all the people smiled and bowed back, and the band played marches and polkas, and the air was balmy with a heavy smell of blooming chestnuts.

Herr Grün wore a yellow tie, had black hair, shiny as my patent leather shoes, and a big black mustache. His suit was nipped in at the waist and belted and beige with a maroon check.

"He looks like a gigolo," Mother said.

"What does he want with Renate? She's just a child," Father grumbled as we watched Renate parade by with him. Renate blushed when she saw us. I filled them in.

"He's twenty-four years old, and he says that Renate is very mature for her age." (I did not mention that Renate had told him that she was seventeen.)

"What does he do, where does he come from?"

"He's from Nürnberg, and he works for his uncle who makes motorcycles."

"What's that emblem he wears in his lapel?" Father asked after we had passed them on the next round.

"It's his party badge."

"He's a Nazi?"

"He had to join, but he thinks it's all nonsense!" I knew everything.

Father stopped in the middle of the path, pointed his tankard at me and shouted, "I want this to stop!"

Mother said, "Oh Ernstl . . ."

I wasn't present at their confrontation, but Renate explained it all to me, and of course I could see that from then on she would have to meet Herr Grün secretly. He took her dancing.

Each evening, after we had eaten our supper, Renate and I went to visit our parents to say good night. They would just be up from their nap and getting ready for the evening. Mother flushed and loose-haired, Father freshly shaved and smelling of 4711. I would have liked to linger, but Renate rushed us through the procedure. Yes, we had eaten supper. Yes, we locked our door when we went to sleep. Kiss, kiss, and we walked along the deeply carpeted corridor to the elevator, clanked down and out through the lobby and into the summer night. I remember the heavy scent of jasmine settling cloyingly upon my chest as we walked back to the pension.

A few minutes later Renate would be gone, and I would lock the door and try to pretend that I was grown up. There was no reason for the awful feeling in my belly. One good thing though, I became quite a correspondent that summer. I wrote faithfully to Oma and Opa, to Tante Gert and Onkel Wolf, even to Tante Ruth, and of course, to all my girlfriends. Father said that the stamps would bankrupt him.

"Since when are you such friends with Steffi Levy?" Mother asked, turning the sealed envelope I had given her to mail over in her hand.

"Oh, she's really so nice . . ." I started, but Mother had to leave for the hairdresser.

I shrugged; it was just as well, she wouldn't have understood. The fact was that I was writing a lot of letters to Steffi, all about how scary it was when Renate was gone at night; somehow, I thought that she would know what I meant.

Renate was always home at eleven o'clock. I would be dozing when I heard our secret knock. Then I flew out of bed, unlocked the door, and felt how the mountain rolled off me; I was able to take deep breaths again.

And then, one night, Renate did not come home at eleven. Startled out of the light sleep in which I had awaited her, I became aware of feeling odd. I looked at the clock; it was almost midnight. I sat up, I listened, I stared at the black hole that was the open window. Was it always that quiet at night? The air, fragrant, but chill—I pulled the covers over my shoulders and remained sitting rigidly upright, listening. Wild pictures were trying to push into my mind—Renate lying murdered, strangled; "Don't ever go with strange men"—I forced myself to count the slats in the shutters. If there were more than twenty Renate would be back before twelve. But a far-off clock chimed twelve times, and she was still not back. What should I do? Should I call the sanatorium, what would I say? No, a few minutes more—I would hold my breath, I would count to thirty. A half minute. And again, three quarters of a minute. My heart beating wildly, the breath exploded, terror mounted, pulsed in my ears, louder and louder. I almost did not hear the familiar knock.

"You won't believe what happened," Renate cried, completely ignoring the fact that I had returned to bed and gotten under my cover without saying a word. She threw herself into the brown Morris chair. Her hair was disheveled, her cheeks scarlet. I forgot my anger and sat up. "What? What happened?"

Renate had been at the Blaue Taube with Herr Grün. They had sat in the courtyard near the dance floor. Otto Grün's nose buried in his *grosse Weisse* when the music started again. Suddenly someone had stood by their table, bowed and said: "May I have this dance?"

"But you were with Herr Grün," I said in astonishment.

"Yes, but he kind of asked Otto, and Otto nodded and said sure, and only then did I see that it was Rudi."

"Rudi! Rudi Fichtel?"

"Yes."

"Where was Luz?"

"She wasn't there. He was with another man. He said that they had just been walking and stopped in for a glass of wine."

"Is he a good dancer?"

"Divine!" She leaned back and closed her eyes, she breathed deeply and she smiled to herself.

I began to feel funny. "So what did he say?"

Renate did not answer at once. After a while she got up and began to undress. With her blouse pulled over her head, her voice muffled, she continued at last. It seemed that he had lectured her, what was she doing there, who was that fellow, and what was she thinking of, being with a guy who was not Jewish, didn't she know anything? "Do your parents know that you are out with this man?" She had made him promise not to tell. Renate interrupted her narrative to pour water from the blue flowered jug into her tooth glass, to brush her teeth. But with her mouth full of white foam, she turned to me and said, "Oh Ellen, he's so wonderful."

"What's so wonderful about all this? Papi told you the same thing. And anyhow, he's a good one to talk; Luz isn't Jewish either."

"She isn't?" Again Renate stopped in the process of rinsing her mouth.

"No, I heard Mother say today. She said that they have their problems because this Law Society or whatever it is, wants to expel Rudi, and Luz is afraid she has to resign too. Or something."

"That explains it."

"What?"

"He said that I should listen to him, that this is no time to get involved with a Gentile, that he knows."

"But all you did was to go out to dance."

"Yes, but that's how it starts, he said." Suddenly she laughed. "He talked to me as if I were about to elope."

"He's crazy." I stared at her, she was putting the pink lotion on her pimples. "He said all this while you were dancing?"

"Oh no! We didn't talk at all while we danced. Oh, he is marvelous." Renate whirled around the room. In her striped pajamas, her hair braided for the night, she looked suddenly like just Renate again. I felt relieved and also annoyed. "You are not telling it right," I complained. "When did he say all those things if you didn't talk?"

"Later. While we danced he said nothing. And Ellen, he held me close."

I compressed my lips. I wasn't going to dignify this conversation with another of my comments until she told it to me properly.

"Only just before the music stopped he said to go home immediately and to wait for him in the garden. He practically ordered me."

"When was that?"

"Oh about ten. I told Otto that I had a headache."

"Then all this time you were sitting in the garden here?" I looked toward the dark window, recalling my terror.

"Yes. In back under the trellis. There's a bench . . ."

"Yes." I knew where. Behind the rose hedge, shaded under a weeping willow; I had read there one morning when I had awakened early and sneaked out. There had been a heavy odor of roses and the grass had been silky under my toes.

"He sat me down under that tree, and he took my hands, and he talked and talked."

"Well, I hope you'll listen to him."

She was in bed. Lying with her head right in the middle of the pillow, her hands on her chest; she did not answer.

"Are you praying?" I asked.

She started. "Huh?"

"I asked whether you were praying."

"Praying? No. Why should I pray?" her voice dreamy.

"Why shouldn't you pray? It's night, you're going to bed. Remember: 'Now I lay me down to sleep . . .'?" I made my voice sarcastic.

"Do you think Luz loves him very much?"

I threw myself on my other side. "Put out the light," I said.

6

Renate and I went to a new school that fall.

Until we returned from Bad Kissingen, I had thought that I would join Renate at the Goethe Lyceum now that I was finished with elementary school. But Mother and Father told us that Jewish children could no longer attend state-run schools.

"Why not?"

"It's a new law. They are already enforcing it in some parts of the country; I would as soon anticipate the Berlin decree than have to change you later." Father wore one of his rare stern expressions. He was stroking his mustache and looking straight ahead. Suddenly, I didn't dare to ask more questions, though I had not understood what he meant.

"But where will we go?" Renate asked.

I started to feel better, realizing that wherever it was, I would be with Renate.

"A school named Liebfrauen Ober Lyceum." (Dear Women Upper Lyceum).

"Just what I always wanted to become, a dear woman." Renate looked angry.

"It's an order of Catholic nuns," Mother explained.

"Eeeks, nuns! Must we go to an old nun school?" I cried.

"It's that or a Jewish school."

"Then let's go to a Jewish school."

"Don't be silly; you have to get a decent education."

Romi, Inge, and Katrine were going to the Liebfrauen Ober Lyceum too. So was Renate's friend Kate. Steffi, of course, would go to the Theodor Herzl School.

"But my parents say that they have no discipline in a Jewish school. It's like it was in Jewish Religion class; you know we just fooled around there," I said to Steffi over the telephone.

"My father says you German Jews are all anti-Semitic," she replied.

"Oh come on, Steffi; that's silly."

"No, it isn't. Why can't you come to my house?"

I was silent. Mother and I had been arguing about that. She had said that I could have Steffi over, but I was not to go there.

"But why not? Steffi is my friend now."

"I don't know the people."

"Then get to know them."

"They are not our kind."

I had started to cry. "You're awful, just because her father is a tailor."

"It isn't that."

"Yes it is. You're snobby."

"Don't be fresh."

Discussions always ended by my being told not to be fresh.

Christa would go to the Goethe Lyceum. Our next Kränzchen was strange; we were about to go off in different directions, and Steffi was there. We had jelly doughnuts and hot chocolate but it was strange. We admired Steffi's beautiful needlepoint; she was making a pillow for her grandmother in Poland.

"But we are making things for the poor Africans."

"Charity begins at home," Steffi said.

Romi and I met in the bathroom. "You see, she is crazy," she said.

"What's so crazy about making a pillow for your grandmother?"

"The Ost-Juden only think of themselves."

"Because they are poor."

"I wish you hadn't made us have her at the Kränzchen."

We washed our hands for a long time, making white gloves out of the suds, stripping them off, foaming them on again.

"Please be nice to her," I said then.

"All right, but I'm glad she isn't going to the Liebfrauen with us."

In spite of myself, I agreed.

It was a long walk from the corner where we all met—Katrine, Romi, Inge, and I, and Renate and Kate. The big girls walked ahead, we followed. After the long Bahnhofstrasse, we cut through the Lietzensee Park. The park had two parts, sepparated by a broad avenue. We had to pass all through the first part, cross the avenue, and about halfway through the second we took an exit that was exactly across the street from the new school. The best thing about the walk was running down the broad stone encampment that was at the side of a waterfall in the first part of the park. The water gushed down to flow into a lake further below, and there was just enough danger of slipping and falling in to make it exciting. But on that first morning we were all a little subdued. In fact, Renate waited for me and took my hand to cross the avenue, and again later, to lead me into the school. The Lyceum did not look the way we knew schools to look. It was housed in two narrow, adjoining four-story apartment buildings—blond brick and with window boxes in which raggedy petunias waved on that September morning. But once inside, it was a real school, with milling children, and only the fact that the bustling, shouting teachers were nuns made it strange.

Directed to our room, we sat, hands folded, in our seats, and when the nun entered we rose with all the other children.

"*Grüss' Gott*, Sister."

"*Grüss' Gott*, children."

Everyone remained standing. Then I saw that they all folded their hands—fingers pointed to make steeples—the way angels look in paintings, and bowed their heads. I did the same, trying to peer up to catch Inge's eye. She was two seats across the aisle from me, but she wasn't looking.

"In the name of the Father, the Son, and the Holy Ghost," Sister said, and the children joined in.

I closed my lips. A hot feeling in my stomach made me very uncomfortable. Then I closed my eyes too. "Dear Jewish God," I thought. "Good morning."

On the way home we all agreed that it hadn't been too bad. Recess was great. We were led across the street and walked in the park. Of course we had to stay in line and couldn't run or play, but at least we could talk while we ate the sandwiches we had brought from home.

In German class we had been told to write an essay about a vacation. I had written about a visit to the heath where the heather was blooming, an ocean of burgundy waves under a blue tent. The German Sister had picked it out and read it to the class and said that it was poetic. I was pleased with myself. Romi said I was showing off again, and Inge laughed, but I thought of the time I had said that the wine was a yellow snapdragon. The Sisters were obviously no different from other adults.

They were all named Maria, which we thought was very funny, just like all the Fritzes. Sister Maria Theresa was our homeroom teacher, who also taught German. Sister Maria Celeste was the French mistress, and Sister Maria Magdalena taught math and geography.

Renate said that her day had been great. "You have no idea how much nicer the Sisters are than the teachers were at the old Goethe."

"Still, it's funny," I objected. "All that praying."

They had prayed before each class; I had gotten tired of saying hello to God.

Mother was at her desk when we got home. "How was it?"

"Awful," we said as from one mouth.

"That's nice. Wash up now. Dinner is ready."

The Sister who taught gym in school always used me to demonstrate the exercises; that is, the ones she could not show us herself. Though she was pretty good. Hanging in the air, making her way, hand over hand, across the horizontal ladder—a huge bat with a red face and steel-rimmed glasses. Sister Maria Katarina, getting off the mat after demonstrating push-ups, dusting off her brown habit, the rosary dangling.

"Come on, girls, move smartly. God loves healthy bodies."

Which was an opinion I thought that the other nuns did not share. Certainly they acted as if bodies didn't exist.

We had two girls in our class that year who were big and had bosoms already. They had been left back, and we giggled about them, but not because they were dumb. A note I wrote to Romi, saying "Imagine Rosa naked, flop, flop!" was intercepted and Romi, Katrine, Inge, and I ended up in the dark office of the Mother Maria Superior. The terror we had felt on our way down to her awful presence was heightened in the green atmosphere. Plants grew dense and tall in front of the window, it was humid and quiet while we waited for her.

"But what did Inge and I do?" Katrine kept asking in a whisper.

Romi was crying and angry at me. "You always do these show-offy things," she wailed sotto voce.

As for me, I had my familiar iceberg feeling, all cold and sharp inside, a raggedy landscape of desolation.

Then she came in, a tall gray nun, silently gliding, hovering, touching Romi's hair. Romi just kept on crying. The rest of us sat in silence, and the Mother Superior sat down too and looked at us for a long time. To my surprise, when she started to speak, she said nothing about the note or its contents. Instead she reminded us that the Catholic schools were the only ones in Germany that took Jewish children, and that therefore we had to be extra good, to deserve the privilege.

"Will you promise to be really, really good, children?"

We said that we would be.

Filing out into the corridor, so strangely still at that moment, Romi still sniffling, Inge said, "Wasn't she kind?"

"No!" I said it angrily and loudly.

"Psst!" they hushed me.

Of course I didn't tell Mother, but she overheard me tell Steffi on the telephone.

"But it isn't nice to eavesdrop!" I cried.

"Never mind that! You know, Ellen, you are lucky that you weren't expelled for such a note."

"Oh Mutti," I broke out, suddenly glad that she knew. "She was so creepy, so disgustingly holy, so nunny."

"You know she was absolutely right."

"No she wasn't. She would have been if she had been mad about the note; I mean, about passing notes in class, or about writing dirty things, but all she wanted to do was talk about the Jewish thing; what has being Jewish to do with it?"

"Don't change the subject, Ellen."

"I'm not, Mutti; she was happy, happy to have an excuse to say that to us."

"Don't be silly."

"I hate nuns!" I was crying. I cried a long time. When I stopped, I looked over at Mother where she sat before her dressing table mirror. She was buffing her nails again, with the little chamois gondola thing. Her face was calm; it was as if she hadn't heard me cry. In a conversational tone she said, "Funny, Renate likes the nuns." She shook her head. "It's really peculiar, two children reacting so differently."

Suddenly I was furious. Renate too! Everyone was against me. "Well, I hate them!" I shouted.

I stood in front of Mother, my fists on my hips. Now Mother looked annoyed. "No you don't," she said in her brushing-away-flies voice. "They are very kind women, very devoted."

Steffi was the only one who understood.

"It must be awful," she said, shivering in sympathy. "Ooh, they must be so creepy."

We were drinking cocoa at a stand at the Hochmeisterplatz. We were allowed to walk any place without Fräulein now, and the freedom was wonderful. I looked back at the summer, at missing Fräulein and being afraid, with a superior smile; I had been a child then.

"Let's go to your house," I said suddenly.

"Are you allowed to?" Steffi asked.

"No."

Our eyes locked; hers were very dark, shining too brightly, she did have crazy eyes, but she was my friend.

"You are welcome," she said.

"Let's go! Race you to the corner." Off I went.

First we stopped to say hello to Herr Levy. He didn't actually sit on his wooden table with his legs crossed the way the tailors did in story books, but otherwise he looked like a tailor, small and slight and bent, and with the tape measure hanging around his neck and a thimble on his finger and the white chalk marks on his dark trousers and rolled-up white sleeves. What I didn't know from just observing him through the window was that his eyes were huge and gentle, completely different from Steffi's flashing look; they were gray and had long lashes. His mouth, too, had a soft look, and he shook hands with me with a warm, dry hand, and the accent I had been braced for, expecting it to be harsh and staccato, the way we talked when we made fun of foreigners, that accent was soft, a melodious singsong. More foreign really than I had expected, yet . . . nicer.

I curtsied and was polite. He said typical father-things,

but his hand hovered on Steffi, touching her face, her hair, stroking the roundness of her cheek. I felt his anxiety, saw myself suddenly in that dark little store, a stiff blond doll, like the blue-uniformed one on the black horse that I had at home—an uhlan.

They lived in the *Hinterhaus.* We crossed the courtyard behind the tailor shop and entered the backhouse. It was just like any front house, except narrower, darker, the stairs steeper, and of course there was no elevator. I babbled about how nice it was for her father to be so close to his shop, not to have to travel to work, I bet he could even come home for dinner. Steffi was silent, fiercely so. I tried to shake the sense of being tested, the feeling of nervous humbleness when, finally silent myself, I climbed after Steffi to the fifth-floor landing.

Steffi had a key and unlocked the door. Again, I had to come up from under my preconceived notions of poverty. It didn't smell of cabbage, it didn't look "threadbare but clean," there wasn't even any awful flowered linoleum on the floor. Instead, the living room into which we came immediately from the tiny foyer was sort of nice—a little cluttered, cozy, lots of red and leather and there was a piano and a warm, old Persian rug. The smell was wax and lemon and apples, and cacti bloomed in the window and a vase held six tulips.

"Oh look, you have tulips already; I haven't seen any yet."

Steffi ignored me. "Mama?" she cried.

"In the kitchen."

Steffi took my wrist and pulled me to the kitchen. Immediately I saw that this was where Steffi came from—the eyes and the hair and the wiry grip of the handshake. Frau Levy was sitting at the kitchen table spooning something that looked and smelled like plum preserve into a piece of rolled-out dough.

"So you found your way at last?" she said sharply. I hung my head.

Yet it wasn't long before we were laughing. Steffi had spilled the cocoa when she tried to measure it, her mother said that she was surprised that such a thing could happen to an experienced hostess like Steffi Levy. We stayed in the kitchen while the plum roll baked; the heavenly smell made us more and more hungry. We talked of school, comparing Sister Maria Theresa to Herr Scheftelowitz, Steffi's bearded young teacher.

"He's like a lion, fierce and furious; he roars at us. Like a hungry lion."

"She's like a sick angel," I sketched. "Gentle, soft, almost smiling, almost kind, but yet . . . hidden behind glittering glasses, and she has no lips."

Frau Levy told us about a teacher she had had in Warsaw. I saw him distinctly, the anti-Semite, a pale-eyed, sharp-nosed man with a cane in his hand.

Then we laughed about a Christa story. That Christa, the things she told. She thought that the teachers at the Goethe Schule were altogether ridiculous; she had smeared *Harzerkäse*, the worst-smelling cheese there was, under Herr Pichler's chair, and when he tried to open the window, she had protested and said that she had a cold. "He's such a pompous ass," she had shrugged to us. "Who does he think he is, the measly little official!"

"She'll get in trouble, she's so fresh," I said.

Frau Levy shrugged. "Not with a name like von Adelsberg."

Finally the cake was ready. Oh, sweet and crunchy and tart and incredible; I burned my tongue in my greed to eat it quickly. Frau Levy laughed. "Easy, easy, no one will take it away from you." Our eyes met. And a warmth spread through me; she liked me, it was all right. Steffi was watching, beaming like a matchmaker. Steffi directed a smart blow to my arm. "See?" it seemed to say, and I beamed back, "Yes, yes, I see."

I think Renate was relieved that the secret that I asked her to share was, as she put it, "harmless."

It bothered me a little that she did not understand the

specialness; I tried to explain about the warmth, and how close they were to each other.

"Well, of course, if Steffi's mother is a cripple, she has to be home all the time, so she has more time than our mother," Renate replied.

"No, it isn't only that," I argued back.

She didn't comprehend, and anyhow, I resented her calling Steffi's mother a cripple. How surprised I had been that first time! When it was seven o'clock and I had to start for home, Frau Levy had said, "Steff', get my crutches," and I had stood, stiff and awkward. And I had stared. The struggle to get to her feet seemed endless—the fitting of the upholstered end into her armpit, pushing the chair back, and until the rubber end gripped the floor to give the leverage with which, with one hand on the table, she pushed up. And the quick grab for the other crutch. I tried not to, but I stared at the wasted leg which dangled, and the other one in the odd, thick shoe. All the time, Steffi just stood there, not helping her mother, just looking me full in the face. Frau Levy disregarded both of us, swung past, was quickly out of the kitchen and across the foyer and opening the door for me.

"No further than the corner now," she cautioned Steffi, who had asked whether she could walk me part way home. And to me, "You may come again, if you want."

"I do. I will," I said, feeling that I was making a profound declaration.

Steffi had walked me to the corner. She was silent. All of a sudden, I felt angry at her—it was as if, for the umpteenth time that day, she was testing me, daring me to say the wrong thing now, maybe to ask what was the matter with her mother. What did she think I was, a child?

"I think you should help your mother a little more; you left her with all the dishes," I said belligerently.

Steffi ignored that. "She had infantile paralysis when she was eleven," she said.

"Our age."

"Yes."

We were at the corner.

"Auf Wiederseh'n," Steffi said.

We shook hands.

"Auf Wiederseh'n."

Of course, once the novelty wore off, both Steffi and I relaxed, and I spent a great deal of time at her house. Though always, before going to the Levys', I prepared a careful alibi in my mind. However, I was never called upon to use it. Somehow, Mother seemed to see no more reason to inquire into my activities now than she had when I hadn't been able to make a step without Frl. Clara.

One day, after storming up the five floors to Steffi's house, I found her in the doorway when I reached the landing.

"I heard you; you come a-thundering like a herd of elephants, and I didn't want you to ring the bell."

"Someone sleeping?"

"No. It's Shabbath."

"Oh!" I felt embarrassed the way I always did when religion was mentioned between us. I turned to go back down.

"Where are you going now?"

"I better go; I'll disturb your parents."

"Don't be silly. Come on, Papa is teaching me chess, he can teach us together."

Reluctantly I followed her inside. "How come you can play chess if you can't ring the bell?" I asked belligerently.

Herr Levy, who had come out to greet me, had overheard.

"Ah, a very good question," he said and pinched my cheek. "You are in good company with that question, there's a lot of controversy about it."

"I am?" I asked.

"Yes you are, you are in good company. Let me

see . . ." He was searching for a volume among the many in the bookcase. "Where's the Mishna Berura? Ah here—*Omer Chofetz Chaim* . . ."

Before I knew it, I was sitting on a hassock listening to him explain that Chofetz Chaim held the view that chess, being in a category with studying holy books, was permitted as an activity for the Shabbath. The lesson seemed altogether too short. Herr Levy closed the book with a snap. "Too much learning is a weariness," he said with a laugh.

"No, it's so interesting," I protested.

He laughed again. "We'll make a Jewess out of you yet." He pinched my cheek.

Renate thought that had been a hideous remark.

"Who does he think he is?"

"You sound like Mother."

"And he certainly sounds arrogant. These Ost-Juden think they are the Chosen People."

"No, he didn't mean it that way. He was pleased with me, he took pleasure. Listen Renate, they have books and books; there is so much to know about Judaism—not just the Bible."

She was frowning, she looked worried. "All that Jewish business. Listen, Ellen, maybe that's why Mother doesn't want you to go there."

I stared at her. Suddenly I felt sad, no, angry. "You're getting to be like *them!*" I shouted at her.

Renate shook her head.

Father had been gone an awfully long time and both Frl. Clara and Emma were leaving. Mother was in a state.

"There's no living with her," Renate sobbed after Mother had stormed out, slamming the door. That was after she had found the clothes we had stuffed under the beds. Really, I only did that kind of thing because I had to keep up the battle; by nature I was neat, and I liked my drawers to have symmetrically stacked piles of panties, slips, and vests. But Renate was really unable to keep her wardrobe neat. It seemed perfectly ridiculous to her that a skirt she was going to wear tomorrow morning had to be hung up tonight. "What's the difference?" she asked. When we had been younger Mother had told us that our room must always look nice so that we needn't be ashamed if a doctor had to be called in the middle of the night. It was that kind of spurious reasoning that Renate suspected behind the whole conspiracy of orderliness; it was a waste of time, idiotic; Mother's particular torture device. And they had horrendous battles about it, Mother tearing open the doors of Renate's wardrobe, picking up armloads of clothes that lay piled in the bottom, and throwing them into the middle of the room. "How can you be such a pig? So dirty? So unfeminine?" That day, in the heat of the encounter, Mother had even torn open Renate's desk drawer and there found a pair of dirty, inky, crumpled panties—screech—"Ink on your underpants!" Smack.

Mother's smacks hurt; her ring always slipped around on her thin fingers, so that the square, rough setting stung with each slap. Smack, smack—Renate's cheek was marked, there was a tiny red cut, and Mother was wringing her hands.

"Oh God, what have I done to deserve this? This, this . . ."

Her hands in her hair, her eyes wide.

"It's like something out of Ibsen. Oh, how will we manage? The maids leaving and my own daughter, my own grown-up daughter a sloven, a slattern, a pig . . ."

She was going for Renate again, hand raised. Renate cowered.

"Leave her alone!" I screamed, hating Mother.

Renate cried with her fists bored into her eyes.

Mother slammed out of the room.

I started to pick things up. Renate sat on the bed and cried quietly. After a while she said, "Thanks, Ellen." I didn't turn around. I heard her scratch. She had eczema in the inside of her arm; scratching made it worse. "Don't scratch," I said and rolled stockings into flat balls.

"I think she's insane; these rages over nothing."

"Well, your panties in the desk were quite a sight."

"My pen was leaking; I didn't have a rag."

"You could have put them in the dirty laundry."

"I forgot."

I folded sweaters. I didn't know why I was defending Mother, anyhow. "She's upset because of Clara and Emma," I said.

"She's always upset."

"That's true," I agreed.

Emma and Clara were leaving because of a new law that stated that Jews could no longer employ domestic help under forty-five years of age. It was another of the laws that, while already enforced in Nürnberg, was still largely ignored in Berlin. But Emma had heard of it; she wouldn't do anything against the law.

"No, Gnä' Frau, the law's the law."

Which left Frl. Clara no choice either.

It made very little sense to me, though I was aware of some secret connotation that made the adults laugh in their special way. Father had said something about being heartbroken that Emma's charms could no longer entice him into befouling the race, but this kind of statement, I had found, did not bear closer scrutiny. Nor could I comprehend the business of the Nürnberg Laws. The thing about Emma and Clara was said to be a part of it, as was the school situation. And the thing about the Fichtels. That was incredible. The Laws said that Jews could not be lawyers anymore, and that Jews and Christians could not be married.

"But then what will Luz and Rudi do?" I asked.

"I saw Rudi today," Father replied. "He looked terrible."

"But what did he say?" Mother asked.

"He was very bitter. He laughed, he said did I hear the latest? 'About my pure Aryan wife who has left her unemployed, racially inferior mate so that she can continue to practice blond, Germanic law!' I didn't know what to answer."

I looked at Renate. She had stopped eating, she was very pale, which made her eyes look huge. "She left him?" Her voice was hoarse.

"So it seems. Though he mentioned that she had been very generous; he has been allowed to keep his cello and some furniture and half the dishes."

"How can a law force people to get divorced?" I interjected. "It says *until death do us part*."

My father laughed unpleasantly. "These laws can do all kinds of things."

Mother sighed. "Poor boy, we'll have to have him for dinner."

"You keep away from him!" It was almost a scream. Renate had jumped to her feet and stood glaring at Mother. She shook a finger at her. "Just keep away from him," she repeated. "He doesn't need your solicitude." She rushed from the room.

My chest felt tight, I didn't listen to Mother complain about "that child," I asked to be excused. In our room I sat down next to the sobbing Renate on the bed and patted her shoulder. And while I did, I thought—why *did* the Nürnberg Laws affect us? I had known that things were bad for the Jews in Nürnberg. In fact, Tante Gert was going to America soon to "look around."

"What do you mean, she is going to look around?" I had asked. "And what about Uncle Wolf?"

"To see what the conditions are; they are thinking of immigrating to America. Uncle Wolf can't leave his practice."

"Leave home, forever?"

"Well, you see, in Nürnberg . . ."

If Jewish lawyers were not permitted to practice anymore, who knows when it would be doctors? Yes, but . . .

could Onkel Wolf be a pediatrician in America? Well, that's what Tante Gert was going to investigate. "But all that is in Bavaria, we live in Berlin."

"Oh Ellen, don't ask so many questions."

Herr Levy said, "This is only the beginning."

Yet it seemed to me that it would affect the Levys less than us. Frau Levy did her own cooking anyhow, and Steffi knew how to market and make beds and chocolate pudding.

"Maybe it will be nice," I said to Renate. "Maybe Mother will be home a lot now, and we'll do things together like they do at the Levys'!"

"It will be impossible," Renate said darkly. "Mother will drive us out of our minds."

But then Renate was in a dark mood. And she had done a crazy thing, she had gone to see Rudi.

"In his apartment?" I asked aghast.

She wouldn't meet my eyes. "Of course not. I waited for him in front of his house."

"But how did you know when he would come?"

"I didn't. I just tried, and he just came. He was awful."

"What did you say?"

"I pretended to pass by. But he knew. He laughed at me and said that I had come too late for the Shivah, Luz had already been gone two weeks. Then he said I might as well cook him some dinner since I was there."

"So you did go upstairs?"

"What could I do? We couldn't just stand in front of the house, and he was talking so loudly; anyone walking by could hear." She paused and walked around the room. In front of the mirror she lifted up her hair and turned her head this way and that. "The apartment was in an awful mess. Almost bare and with light spots on the wallpaper where the pictures used to hang. And he was all disheveled. Some beautiful Rudi!" Her voice was shrill.

So was mine. "Well, she was your ideal, that Luz." I couldn't understand why I was feeling so angry, nor at whom.

Renate laughed. "I guess he wasn't such a joy to live with. Maybe she was glad to have an excuse." She started to cry. Right in front of the mirror, the tears began to pour out of her eyes; she crumbled to the floor and dug her fists in and howled.

Frl. Clara also cried when she left, even though she was going to marry Karl, the assistant Fish Fritz from the market.

Emma did not cry; she said the new order was good, and the Gnä' Frau had been impossible lately. I felt hurt. Last Christmas I had embroidered a sampler for Emma's hope chest. It said "In God We Trust"; I thought she loved me.

But the good thing was that Frau Bauchenhorn would be our new maid; she would come every day and do the cleaning as well as the laundry.

"Tja," she said as I watched her brush her hair. "Now the likes of me will be in demand; suddenly it's 'Frau Bauchenhorn here, Frau Bauchenhorn there!' "

"But we always liked you," I protested.

"There's some who did and some who didn't," she answered and began to braid her hair.

CHAPTER

7

To everyone's surprise, Mother
turned out to be a marvelous cook. As for Frau Bauchenhorn,
she was worse than no help. "Imagine, she refuses to scrub the
bathroom tiles on her knees! She says she has rheumatism,"
Mother complained.

Renate replied, "Well, Mother, maybe she has; she isn't
as young as Emma was."

"Nonsense, she's strong as a horse; she just doesn't want
to work. Whoever heard of a maid having rheumatism?"

Just the same, it was impossible to deny that Mother was
adjusting well to the new set-up; the complaining didn't count,
she always had complained. As a result we, too, were fairly
gracious about our chores; in fact, we rather liked the new situation, especially because we were on our own so much. Mother
never knew the kind of crazy dishes we concocted when she and
Father were out, nor did she know that we ate lying on the living-
room floor, listening to records, eating with our hands like pigs.
We also read and talked on the telephone and sometimes we got
in the bathtub with our plates. Mother had installed a small lock
device on the telephone to prevent Frau Bauchenhorn from using
it, but we knew where the key was hidden, and Renate still had
her endless conversations with Kate each night. In fact, I was
eager these days to listen to them and had learned about the kiss
that way. When Renate had wanted to leave his apartment on the
day of her visit, Rudi had backed her against the wall. "You don't
want to be kissed?" Renate reported to Kate that he had asked.

"No thank you," she said she had replied. But he had kept her pinned against that wall and had put his lips against hers and after a while he had kissed her eyes and then he had said that she should get the hell out of there and not to dare to come back. Renate had told it all to Kate in a very sophisticated voice. As if she always had such adventures, every Tuesday and Thursday. But after she got off the telephone she had run into our room; I had heard her cry there.

It was crazy, because nothing was changed. Boys still called every night, and I would hear Renate croon, "Oh really? Why, how marvelous!"

I told her it was disgusting; I would never, never talk like this.

"I don't understand," Mother complained. "The telephone bills are still high."

The better I got to know Frau Levy the more did my own mother embarrass me in contrast—her interest in clothes, her make-up, the superficiality. One day when I was walking home with Inge and two boys we knew, I suddenly saw her coming toward us. Oh God, she looked so fancy! The decision not to see her was like an icicle, cold and sharp.

"There's your mother," Inge announced.

What could I do? I introduced the boys. For once Mother did nothing embarrassing. "I'll be home at seven," she declared and went on her way.

"Guess what happened to me today?" Mother asked Father that night. He had just come back from a trip and was having his cognac.

"What, love?"

"I was walking along the street and met one of my daughters, who tried to pretend that she didn't see me."

"That's not true," I yelled.

"Oh yes," Mother continued. "There I was, all prettied up for your return, but our daughter was ashamed of me."

Father laughed. "Maybe you had a run in your stocking?"

"No." She turned to me. "Why didn't you want to say hello to me, Ellen?"

Denial was useless. Attack, I thought, and said brazenly, "Because you are always wearing too much make-up, and because you're so fancy while people are starving all over the world."

Father roared. "Oh ho, the poor children in Africa."

I felt I had won.

I wished Mother were more like Frau Levy, who read a lot and knew about Judaism and talked politics with us; she wasn't so fancy.

"Mother is inconsequential," I said to Renate.

"Their whole crowd is like that."

Steffi, however, liked Mother. "She's so gay," she said. "That's nice."

I couldn't tell her that what she thought was gay was only put on. Especially with Steffi, Mother was always faking. "Hello Steffi, so nice to see you." Who was she fooling? I knew she didn't even like her. Anyhow, since Steffi was kosher, she couldn't eat at our house, and more and more I spent my time at hers. I was happy there.

I hated school now. Enough for nausea and headaches each morning. "I don't feel so good; I think I'll stay in bed."

A hand on my forehead. "No, you're all right, get up."

I despised everything about school. The only criteria was to be *good*. Good, like good little girls, polite, curtsying. And the fact that I was the star in my German class made it worse. I knew my success was fake; the things I would write to please Sister—I even threw God in to get "ones."

"God painted the meadows golden, and little sheep grazed serenely under his gaze."

"Ellen, that is very beautiful," Sister would say, and I

would blush; it was awful, trashy. I was reading Tolstoy at this time. Tolstoy wouldn't say a dumb thing like that in a million years.

But the thing that bothered me even more than always doing what was expected of me were the nuns themselves.

"All that love stuff; you know they don't love us, why do they pretend?"

"They do so, Ellen. Nuns love in the name of Jesus," Renate argued.

"They think we killed Jesus; they hate us."

"Who said that?"

"Liselotte von Bernstein."

"She's just a child. The nuns don't feel that way."

"They do so." I was sure. I had seen the mean look Sister Maria Theresa had directed at Romi's bent head. We had been reading our essays on Christmas. Romi's had started, "We celebrate Chanukah . . ."

Sister interrupted. "The assignment is Christmas, Rosemarie Braun."

"Yes Sister, but we celebrate . . ."

"Never mind. Sit down, we'll hear Lore's essay."

In a way it had been sort of funny, because the Brauns, like us, had only really started to celebrate Chanukah that last year. I had to smile thinking about the tiny tree in a flowerpot which was all we had had. For Frau Bauchenhorn in the kitchen; oh, it had been a strange Christmas.

Renate was shaking her head. "I don't know why you don't like the nuns," she said. "They are so kind."

"They are so—so against nature. Women should marry and have children."

"They are married to Christ."

"A man without children is only half a man," I said.

"What?" Renate stared at me. "What's that got to do with it, and who says so?"

"The Talmud says so."

"The Talmud?"

"A Jewish book; Herr Levy told me. It's full of things God said. Our God, I mean."

"Well, anyhow, they are women."

"I bet God thinks a woman without children is only half a woman, too."

Renate was washing her stockings in the sink; we had to do our own underwear now. I was taking a bath.

"You're getting such crazy ideas suddenly."

"I wish we were in a Jewish school."

For Renate's seventeenth birthday our parents took her to the Opera and out for supper. A long pink dress was made for her, with white swansdown around the sweetheart neck and the sleeves. I couldn't believe it when I saw her—Renate was grown up. Her heavy hair piled high in front and hanging down in back, tied with a big pink bow, her huge eyes, and lipstick.

And that wasn't all! She had declared that she wanted to stay in Berlin that summer and not go along on our vacation trip. She had worked it all out; she would stay with Kate, they would attend Berlitz School for Languages and take typing and stenography. "After all," she had said, "I have only one more year of school, and if I prepare now, I can get a job as soon as I am finished."

There was nothing wrong with her reasoning. Mother agreed. What puzzled me was the question of when she had done all this growing up, all this thinking about the future, and why she had arrived at such sober decisions. And was that all there was to it?

"But do you *want* to be an interpreter?" I asked. "I thought you'd be a lawyer."

"Oh that was just a childish wish. Like being a fireman."

"It's not the same at all. I think you changed your mind because Luz turned out to be a louse."

"Don't be silly, that has nothing to do with it; I just

don't have the time. And anyhow, Jews can't go to the University anymore."

I had forgotten.

"In any case all I want is to make some money and get out of here as soon as possible," Renate concluded.

"Well, of course," I said, angry suddenly, using Mother's look-at-my-poor-hands voice. "You have such an awful life."

She laughed at me, then sobered. "Look Ellen, it's different for me, I can't let Papi support me all my life, and you know that I don't get along with Mother. Also we'll have to leave Germany sooner or later; I have to be prepared."

"How much does Rudi have to do with your decision?" I asked sharply.

"Rudi? Don't be silly. I haven't seen him in ages." Her eyes, very bright, looked straight at me, yet I knew that she was evading.

"Look, I'm not Mother, you don't have to lie."

"What do you mean?"

"I think you are staying in Berlin because of Rudi."

She was neatly rolling the thread back on the spool and fastening it in the little wood slot. At last she glanced up and now her eyes were really looking into mine. "I can't bear to be so far away from him."

"Then why do you run away every time he comes?"

She got up. "Oh Ellen, he doesn't see me for the dust. He loves Luz."

"Luz? You're out of your mind. After what she's done to him?"

"What has that got to do with love?"

Afterwards there was plenty to think about—not just Rudi or the potato salad business, as I called it in my mind, but what she had said about Mother. I mean, we had ranted against her all our lives, but it was a game, wasn't it? What had changed the quality of the game for Renate? And leaving Germany? Renate was crazy; one didn't leave home. All that talk about the

Nazis; it was obviously only half as bad as the grown-ups made it. Except maybe for lawyers.

Father had come back from his last trip full of fantastic stories. He had said that on one hotel in a small town in Silesia it had said "Jews and dogs not allowed."

"Oh Papi, you and your stories," I had protested.

He looked at me quietly. "I'm afraid this isn't a story, Ellen."

Uneasily, I searched his face; one never knew with Father.

The tale I liked better though was about his last visit with Herr Grautner. We had heard about him for years, he was a beer brewer who hated beer and drank only champagne. When Father had seen him last week, Herr Grautner had gotten very excited.

"He stalked around me," Father said, "as if I were a prize ox he was thinking of buying. Then he came up close and put his hands on my cheeks; I thought he wanted to kiss me and got ready to run, but all he did was turn my head this way and that."

"Didn't he say anything?"

"He just mumbled things like 'perfect, marvelous, amazing.' "

"And what did you do?"

"I just waited. You know he is eccentric. Finally he told me that he belongs to a group of race experts at his club, and he thinks that I might be a near-perfect type of Aryan, and could he measure my skull?"

"Did you let him?"

"Sure I did. He measured and jotted down and shook his head. Finally he said, 'Westheimer, you are the absolutely perfect Aryan. Can I present your measurements at my meeting tonight?' I said sure, but not to forget to mention that I'm a Jew. You should have seen his face! 'You're what?' he shouted. 'A Jew,' I said. 'I don't believe it,' he insisted."

"Did he buy his champagne?"

"Yes. But I have a feeling . . ." His voice trailed off.

"What, Papi? What?"

"Maybe it will be better if I don't go back."

"You shouldn't have told him that you are Jewish," Mother cut in.

"I couldn't resist."

So we started off on the summer vacation without Renate. It wasn't the same, of course. To begin with, no one sang. Father was worried about accommodations along the way. "You don't know what it's like in the provinces, Eva," he said. Mother shrugged. "It's just one night; tomorrow we'll be in Cranz."

We were going to the seashore in East Prussia, and we would be staying with a friend of Father's. He was a Würzburger originally, had studied law and settled in Königsberg. Now he wasn't permitted to practice, and he had converted his summer house in Cranz to a little pension. I was looking forward to meeting him and his wife, especially since they were expecting a baby during the time we would be there. Father would work East Prussia while Mother and I would be staying in Cranz; that way he would not have to depend on hotels.

The trip to East Prussia was always divided into two slices. Not only because it was too long a stretch to drive in one sitting, but also because you didn't go through the Polish Corridor except in broad daylight. This Corridor was a narrow passage through Poland. It linked East and West Prussia. As far as we were concerned, it was just another unfair price we Germans were paying to the victors of 1918. All the same, I thought it was exciting; in a vest-pocket way you were traveling through a foreign country, and of course, it was pleasurable to see the contrast between Germany's fat cows and Poland's skinny ones,

Germany's friendly houses with white curtains blowing and flowers in window boxes and Poland's ramshackle, rundown abodes. It was also exciting to go through the frontier proceedings. Papers were filled out, seals were attached, stamps pasted all over documents; it was really being out in the big world!

I had made the crossing before and was looking forward to it. I was also anticipating the night in Stettin; I remembered the pretty town square, Hildeplatz it was called, with its ancient fountain, and the pleasant Kaiserhof. The last time we had been there I had only been seven or eight years old, and the doorman had let me wear his uniform hat and had allowed me to push the revolving door for incoming and outgoing guests. However, when we rolled into town, we saw that the square was renamed Hindenburgplatz and the hotel Adolf Hitler Hof. Also, the sign was there—Father drove by without actually stopping, but we had time to read it. I also recognized my old friend, the doorman.

"All right, the Rabbi for us," Father said.

"Must we?" Mother asked.

"Where else?"

"No one would know."

"No!" Father said it explosively.

Rabbi and wife, both small and round, greeted us before their tiny house; for supper we had chicken. "Don't eat the skin," Mother whispered to me. But I was blissful; I would sleep in one bed with my parents that night, in one giant bed, under one giant feather quilt.

In the morning, Father tried to pay something, but the Rabbi wouldn't hear of it. "If we can't help out our own in times like these . . ." To my surprise, Mother kissed the Rabbi's wife, and everyone got all choked up. "Times like these!" Mother said, and she nodded her head.

Once the formalities of entering the Polish Corridor were passed and we were humming along the road, Father cautioned us to keep our fingers crossed. "I'd sure hate to have a flat tire in Poland; they'd as soon shoot a German here as help one," he said.

Then Mother started to laugh. "Oh God, that house," she gasped, "and those little people." Her laughter sounded funny, but I joined in. "And did you see that the Rabbi's wife wore a wig?"

Father was quiet at first, then he started to guffaw too. "Eva, your face when he said we have to help our own!"

Mother stopped laughing. "But I was touched; truly, I was."

"Yes, I know; that's what I mean."

Suddenly she was crying. She let her shoulders hunch forward and put both hands over her face, and she cried. Father took a tighter grip on the wheel, but he said nothing.

Father's friend, Herr Schönemann, ex-lawyer, now farmer, handyman, innkeeper, and his wife—"Call me Tante Lore"—had the biggest protrusion I had ever seen; it was like a shelf jutting out soon under her chin, bulging forward, hanging low. She waddled and had high red cheeks and very blue eyes.

The house itself could have been anyone's villa. There was the usual winter garden, separated from the living room with a beaded curtain that tinkled when you walked through it, and the usual stone balustraded terrace. Upstairs, we had two nice bedrooms. The garden was half flowers and half vegetable beds.

There was also a wire-fenced duck and chicken yard, and best of all a small neat sty in which a clean little, pale-pink pig lived. His name was Balduine; I grew very attached to him.

Right beyond all this bucolic splendor, separated only by a hedge that was full of almost ripe raspberries, started the dunes. And behind them, as far as the eye could see, white beach and the beloved Baltic Sea. I spread my arms wide to let the wind and sea smell rush at me; I ran down to the water's edge. And suddenly I felt small and lonely. The beach stretched on both sides of me, immense, forever. The sea, though it just slapped the sand gently with a murmuring sound, had a deep look, a drown-

ing look, a dark look lurking under the sparkly sun-rippled sur-
face. Tears stung my eyes. I let them roll out, channel my cheeks,
and I turned my face into the wind to let them dry. I was always
crying these days.

As promised, Frau Schönemann gave birth about a week
after our arrival. I really wanted to stay in the house and listen
to her moan, but Father took me away right after breakfast. That
night, they let me have a glimpse at mother and baby; I hardly
recognized Tante Lore—a pale, beautiful lady with lots of tum-
bled golden hair. The baby had apparently taken her high color
into his face; he wasn't too attractive.

And so to bed. The connecting door between my parents' and my room was not very soundproof. If they talked in
normal voices on the side closest to mine I could understand most
of what was said, but they were wandering around; undressing, I
gathered. So it was only snatches I heard.

". . . very brave girl." Father's voice.

". . . to think, people just like us." Mother's. And after
a while, ". . . don't they leave Germany?"

"She isn't Jewish, you know."

". . . but for a lawyer!"

And later still, Mother, in a kind of wail, "Oh
Ernstl . . ."

I lay and thought. "People just like us"? I shook my
head. I couldn't see how they were like us anymore than I could
see us being the Rabbi's "own." I mean, we were Berliners, Father
didn't wear baggy work pants, and we neither had a pig nor a
tiny house . . .

I was almost asleep when I thought of Rudi and Luz.
Frau Schönemann had not left her Jewish husband. Did that mean
that one did not *have* to? Or only when one was a lawyer? A
Gentile lady lawyer? Yes, of course—if she had stayed with him
they wouldn't have let her practice either. A wave of fury washed
over me; Luz had thrown him over for her practice, for the
"fleshpots" I thought. I clenched my fists. I just hoped that he

would forget her quickly and fall in love with a nice lady. I pictured that lady—as dark as he was and also tall, actually, a sort of dusky version of Luz. Yes, that would be best. Then Renate would stop this nonsense too.

CHAPTER

8

I had met a boy at the beach in Cranz. That day, after the sea had run high the night before and it had stormed, the sand had been flat and a pale, wheat blond, strewn with amber. Normally you found only tiny chips of amber on that coast, but that day the pieces I found were enormous, some as big as the nail of my thumb, and I had hardly taken time for dinner and feeding Balduine before coming back to find some more.

The boy came from the opposite direction; towheaded, in gym shorts and sweat shirt, he was bent over in the posture of the collector. As soon as we met he started to talk.

"Look at the size of this," he said, and held out a larger piece of amber than I had ever seen, beautifully formed like a big teardrop, in a light honey color with darker markings in its depth.

"Oh, it's beautiful," I cried. "It looks like a pendant. Where did you find it?"

"Over yonder."

He talked funny. "Where are you from?" I asked.

"From Saxony."

That explained the twang. We were off. His name was Horst, he was fourteen and was going to be a scientist.

"I am Jewish," I had said right away when he told me that he belonged to the Hitler Youth.

"You are?" He looked at me. We were sitting in the fortress he had just finished shoveling. "Golly, how fast you do that; it would take me forever," I had said. It came out smoothly. In spite of myself, I had learned a thing or two from Renate.

"Listen, Ellen, you are kidding, aren't you?"

"No. Why?"

"I always thought that Jewish people have black hair and big noses."

"Only in the *Stürmer*," I said and laughed.

But suddenly I felt worried. Horst had blushed and was kicking the walls of our castle. The *Stürmer*, I knew, was that anti-Semitic newspaper which always depicted Jews with enormous noses doing terribly criminal things. Maybe I shouldn't have made fun of it? I had heard Herr Schönemann say that the *Stürmer* was the Nazi's Bible.

Horst had finally looked up. "Well, I don't care," he had said. "I like you anyhow."

After that, we met every day. We exchanged songs, parodies, teacher stories, and life histories. We swam and dug ourselves a giant tunnel, and when the raspberries ripened, we picked the whole hedge for Tante Lore. He agreed with me that it would be barbaric to eat Balduine and he signed the petition I addressed to Herr Schönemann to cease and desist from slaughtering my pig.

When he left Cranz a week before we did, he gave me the big piece of amber. He had patiently bored a tiny hole through its upper tip and threaded a ribbon through it. I gave him a photo of myself and Balduine on which I had written "To remember your friend Ellen." After we had exchanged these gifts, we stood awkwardly. "Here, I'll put it on for you," Horst said and took the pendant out of my hand and hung it around my neck. Then he leaned forward and kissed me quickly on the lips, and then he turned and ran.

So I had something to tell those girls when we started back to school.

"How did it feel?" Inge asked about the kiss.

"Oh beautiful," I answered.

I only told Steffi the truth. "It was so fast, I didn't feel a thing; I mean, it was just nothing. I was disappointed."

"You shouldn't have let that Nazi kiss you," she said angrily.

"He isn't a Nazi."

"Is so, if he belongs to the Hitler Youth."

"But he likes me."

"You should have more pride."

My other big story was that I had been painted. Yes, by a real artist. Among the guests the Schönemanns had that summer was a permanent boarder. He had his studio over their garage, and his name was Hans Wildestein. Though he looked more like an athlete than a painter, blond hair wildly tousled, craggy-featured. He always wore high laced shoes. I was used to having people make a fuss over me, but Herr Wildestein didn't even acknowledge that I existed. Which is why I was so astonished when Father told us.

"He wants to paint Ellen—with his dog."

The dog, Siegfried, was a huge German shepherd. I had carefully avoided contact with him so far.

"He does?" Mother's voice was arch. I realized that she was pleased, flattered. That settled it for me. "I don't want to be painted by *him*," I protested. "He's awful."

"I told him we would discuss it," Father said indifferently.

"You could wear your pink voile, Ellen, and your hair is long enough now to wear with a ribbon," Mother coaxed.

"No," Father said. "He wants to paint her in her track suit."

"My track suit?" I wailed.

Father laughed. "That's already a compromise." He turned to Mother. "He wanted to paint her naked on his horse. I said it was out of the question."

Mother burst out laughing, then she remembered me and sobered.

"He must be insane," she said primly.

"He's got some kind of Teutonic vision—Wagnerian, German girl, German dog, German sea!"

"But doesn't he know?"

Father shrugged. "I told him."

"Where does he have a horse?" I asked. I had never even seen that horse, but maybe he would let me ride it, if I let him paint me.

"He keeps it over at Schneider's, the farm up the road."

"And he wants to paint her by the ocean?" Mother was still trying to adjust to the track suit.

"Yes."

Father looked at me. "Would you like to be painted, Ellen?"

"What about the monster?" I hedged.

"Siegfried? Wildestein said that he's gentle as a lamb; he hopes that you won't hurt him."

I snorted. But I was already sold on the idea.

A kitchen table was moved into the garden—Herr Wildestein would paint the ocean in later—and the dog and I were posed on it. It took a little doing until the beast would allow me to put my arm around him, but afterward he was peaceful, would rest his heavy head on my knees, and breathe loudly and smell awfully bad. The whole thing was a big bore. The fantastic thought that this man had wanted to paint me naked could not transform him into a romantic figure, though God knows I tried.

And when the picture was finished at last and I got to look at it, the last romantic bubble burst. The ocean was there, and the dog, and a girl in a navy track suit, but it wasn't me. That girl had my hair blowing in the wind and blue eyes. She had a sullen mouth and brooding, faraway-looking eyes, and well, she wasn't even pretty.

"I hate it," I said to Mother and Father. "It doesn't look like me at all."

"Well, no," Father agreed, "but that's how he sees you. He's going to call it *German Girl by the Sea* and exhibit it in Königsberg, at the Schloss Gallery."

Many mornings now Renate and I walked to school without waiting for the others. The separation had changed our relationship. Not only did I feel more independent, I also felt that I had matured in the solitude of the summer's reading and thinking. In direct ratio to my increased maturity I saw Renate diminished; she was no longer the undisputed dispenser of wisdom nor the unquestionable leader. This new sense of autonomy must have made me arrogant. Renate called me on it pretty soon. "What's the matter with you, Queen of Greatness? Afraid a diamond will break out of your crown?"

Immediately, I felt remorseful; I didn't want her to be mad at me. I threw my arms around her, blotting out, for that moment, that a real ambiguity had entered our relationship.

There was the matter with Rudi. Had she seen him over the summer? "A couple of times," she admitted reluctantly. She was obviously sorry to have told me so much before we had left. And while she never used the outright lies she told Mother, she tried to avoid and evade, not to tell me that Rudi had been moody, sarcastic.

"But how many times did you actually see him?" I insisted.

"Three."

"And for that you missed the summer in Cranz?"

"That's not so. I had a very good time. Kate and I . . ."

"Oh Reni!"

"Oh Ellen!" she mimicked me. Then, furiously, "You are unbearable."

"But what do you want with him?" I said in my exasperated voice. "The man's too old and too sad for you."

Then she nodded agreement, her eyes veiled. I felt uneasy. And that wasn't all. There was also that business with Mother. I thought it was exaggerated, and I simply couldn't understand Renate's love for the nuns. She told me that she had been to see Sister Maria Clothilda during vacation.

"You mean you went to see her when you didn't have to?"

"I wanted to discuss my language program with her; she's very intelligent."

"You ought to have more pride," I said.

But then I was confused, remembering why Steffi had said that to me. Was this the same type of situation? It felt that way to me, yet I didn't know why. That is, I didn't know why until Renate wrote the poem. A poem called "Love," about Jesus. "God's son died for the love of us," it said.

Renate showed it to me shyly. After all Mother's poems that we had laughed at, it was no wonder that she was embarrassed. I mean, to be dealing in Mother's merchandise, rhymes on love. There were, after all, only limited possibilities. However, she felt strongly enough about the poem to brave it. And what was I to say? Here was this poem; I hated it. She watched my face as I read it; finally I had to speak. "But he isn't God's son," I said.

"How do we know?"

"I know."

"How?"

"Because I'm Jewish."

"The Jews could be wrong."

"No," I said angrily. "Don't be silly. After all the suffering and dying they have gone through—they wouldn't have if they weren't pretty sure. Though . . ." I paused, "of course, the Christians did that too."

I had just finished reading *Ben Hur*.

Renate got up from the desk. The sheet of lined school paper on which she had written the poem was lying on the blotter. She reached out and crumpled it with one hand, then she dropped it into the wastebasket. I wanted awfully to say that, otherwise, the poem was very nice, but I kept quiet.

Later, after Renate had gone, I went to find the crumpled poem, but it wasn't in the wastebasket. It had obviously been retrieved while I had been on the telephone with Steffi.

I resumed a systematic nagging about leaving the Catholic school, but made no progress. I don't think Mother really heard me; she was too busy with her running battle with Frau Bauchenhorn. Also, she was looking for a new apartment.

When we had come back from our summer vacation, Herr Feuerhahn had come out to help Father with the bags. After they were stored in the elevator, and Herr Feuerhahn had pocketed his *Trinkgeld*—literally, "drink money"—he said, "Oh, by the way, Gestapo was 'round asking did Jews live in this building."

We all stood very still and looked at Herr Feuerhahn. He strutted a bit and ruffled his neck feathers, and his small eyes looked right into Father's. " 'Course I told them there was you people and the Cohns and the Rappaports on the third floor."

"I see," Father said calmly. "Well, thank you, Herr Feuerhahn."

We filed into the elevator, but couldn't start it because Herr Feuerhahn was still holding the outside gate.

"Ja, they took Herr Cohn and Herr Rappaport in for questioning, but you weren't at home."

"No, that's right, we weren't home," Father replied.

"Well, thought I'd tell you."

"Yes. Thank you again."

Mother took Father's hand as soon as the elevator started to move. Renate, who had come downstairs to greet us, looked as if she might cry, and I suddenly realized what it was that was different about the superintendent. He had grown a little mustache while we had been away. I started to giggle. "Did you see how dumb he looks with that toothbrush under his nose?" I asked.

I nudged Renate, but she didn't answer me, so I just kept on giggling. All the way up to the fifth floor.

Anyhow, Father decided that we could do with a smaller apartment because now that the grandparents lived in Berlin we did not need the two guest rooms we had always kept in readiness for them. So Mother was searching for just the right one.

In early October Father came back from another trip to Königsberg. He brought *German Girl by the Sea* home.

"Three hundred Marks," he fumed.

"But why did you buy it? We don't even like it!" Mother asked angrily.

"There was this item in the Königsberg paper." He pulled a clipping out of his wallet and gave it to Mother.

She read aloud, "What recent painting by Hans Wildestein is not what it represents?"

Father was shaking his head. "How they could know . . ."

"What does it mean? Let me see," I broke in.

"It means that Wildestein shouldn't have called a portrait of you *German Girl*."

"But I am German."

Father nodded.

"Aren't I?"

"It seems that we haven't the right to call ourselves German anymore."

"But you are a front fighter."

He pulled me in his lap and pushed my head under his chin. He hadn't done that for a long time, and I really didn't fit anymore, but I inched lower to make myself fit. "All this will pass," he said over my hair. "It's a kind of madness. Our people won't stand for it."

"Our people? You mean the Jews?"

"No. The Germans."

My neck was cramping; I had to sit up.

"Where will we hang the picture?" I asked.

"We'll see."

Somehow, though, it was never hung. It ended up in the storage room of the new apartment house.

The new apartment was in the Hector Strasse, not far from where the old one had been; really a nicer neighborhood, closer to the Kurfürstendamm and shaded by enormous linden trees. The layout was nice; Renate and I had a lovely room out toward a back yard in which, aside from the rack on which one could beat carpets clean, there were flower beds tended by the superintendent's wife. We would be moving in on the first of November, and Mother was so happy with her find that she gave in to my wish to spend the one-week October vacation in Caputh with Nanny.

Caputh, actually Das Jüdische Landschulheim Caputh, the Jewish Country School Home Caputh, was located about an hour outside of Potsdam, which, in turn, is a suburb of Berlin. Nanny went there because Tante Ruth was getting a divorce from Onkel Kurt and was staying with the grandparents.

Since some of the children who boarded in that school went home for vacations, "vacation children" were accepted; I would be a vacation child.

Father drove me out the day my school closed. By the broad river Havel, so wide at that point that I thought it was a lake, the Landschulheim consisted of a main house as well as several smaller buildings which were scattered throughout the village of Caputh.

I was to share a room with Nanny at Reimerhaus, the residence of the "big girls" and the "small boys." It was a large villa right on the Havel. That Thursday evening, the first meal in the airy, modern dining hall at the main house, was wonderful. Though a counselor sat at the head of each table, there was a babble of voices and an air of great informality. After supper we all helped clear the tables, and then we played handball in the gathering dusk. I was good at it. When it was too dark to play,

Hanns Ehrfurcht, who was Nanny's beau, walked us back to our house. Hanns was already fifteen, his mother was living in Paris, his parents were divorced too. I thought that this must be the bond between him and Nanny.

"When my mother is really settled, my sister and I will go there to live with her," he told us.

"But won't you hate to leave Germany?" I asked.

"Are you kidding? Though I'd rather go to Palestine."

"To Palestine?"

"That's the only real home we have, our Jewish home."

"But aren't you German, like me?"

"I used to think so."

"Oh all that talk about the Nazis! I think it will just pass, and everything will be as before," I said seriously.

He laughed. He had an odd way of laughing—his narrow head would bob up and down quickly, his thin lips flattened and showed sharklike, very white teeth. "You do?" he asked. "Well, you're a dumb bunny."

I felt immensely flattered.

Nanny and I talked for a long time in bed.

"Everyone is so Jewish here," I summed it up.

"Not like our family," Nanny agreed.

Big girls had to help little boys to get ready for Shabbath. It had been a glorious day of doing all the things I liked, but everyone kept saying, "Wait till tonight . . ."

Nanny and I bathed eight of our little charges, aged seven to nine, in preparation for the big event. It added to my feeling of maturity, I forgot that actually, really, they were the first naked boys I had seen up close, ever. But doing so from the Olympian vantage point of my big girl position, I couldn't really let myself be conscious of my interest in the matter. We had a mad hassle to find clean underwear and white shirts and navy shorts for the little fellows, but finally they were spick-and-span, and we turned them over to our counselor. At seven o'clock, bathed and dressed ourselves, we walked to the main house. There was a sense of anticipation; maybe because we were so clean and shining and the small boys kept saying that it was Shabbath; their faces glowed.

The dining room was transformed. White tablecloths instead of checkered oilcloth, flowers on each table, and candles. Hanns, in a deep man's voice, sang the blessing over the dark red wine and uncovered two beautifully plaited holiday loaves. He broke them into many small pieces, and a delegate from each table was dispatched to bring us our share; then we blessed the bread. Between chicken soup and roast chicken we sang. I didn't know any of the tunes, most of them were in Hebrew, but the feeling was unmistakable—a joyfulness and a freedom, and some of them had a sighing melancholy that spoke to me even more. I felt tears sting me, choke me; I was at home at last.

After dinner and prayers we pushed the tables aside and danced. The horah was easy to learn; a few basic steps and hands on my shoulder on the right of me and hands on the left; they tore me along, the rhythm took over, and I stamped my feet and swung my legs, and my body was full of spirit. All over the big room, children danced, making boy circles and girl circles, and boys around girls around boys, all the boys wearing yarmulkahs in embroidered patterns, silver and gold and red and blue.

All too soon our counselor came with cookies and the news that it was time to go home. But that evening some of the boys sat on the steps of our house with us for a long time. A few other big girls also joined us, and our counselor came after she had put the little boys to sleep. I was the novice, and they tried to enlighten me. In two hours, in a strangely still, hazy night, the lessons Herr Phirsigbaum had taught me in Jewish Religion took on completely different outlines—from the Maccabean Revolt to the present, a chain. A chain of events, a chain of generations. I thought it was good; I was a link.

Home was a real shock after the week in Caputh, especially home three days prior to moving day. To begin with, no one would listen to me, and I was bursting to tell. Only Steffi showed a real interest. Immediately, she started yearning with me to get back to Caputh.

"Oh Steffi, if you could come too. Maybe next summer. It would be even better for you, you know all the songs; you would understand everything. I was so dumb, I didn't even know what Zionism is."

"I don't know much about it either. Father has his doubts that they are right. He says we'll return to Palestine when the Messiah comes."

"But we can't wait for that; especially not now."

"No . . ." she pondered. "Anyhow, it would be too expensive."

"What's too expensive?" Herr Levy asked, coming into the room.

"Nothing, Papa."

"Don't nothing me. What's your pleasure, Sarale—you want I should buy you a fur coat?"

We laughed.

"I want her to come to camp with me next summer," I said, and I told him about Caputh. He listened to me carefully, nodding his head, stroking his chin as if he had a beard growing there.

"It would be good for her," he said as if to himself, and to me. "They are kosher?"

"Oh yes!"

"They don't write on the Shabbath, they keep the laws?"

"I think so," I said uneasily. Who could tell? There were so many; I heard of a new one every time I was at the Levys'.

"We'll see," Herr Levy said and got up.

"Don't worry, Papa," Steffi said. "I probably wouldn't like it anyhow."

"We'll see, we'll see!" He stroked her hair and left.

"I think there is a chance," I cried excitedly.

"We'll see," Steffi answered, just like he had said it.

"Why does your father call you Sarale?" I asked.

"It's my Jewish name. What's yours?"

"I don't think I have one."

"Don't be silly, you must. How could your father make a blessing on you in Synagogue?"

"I presume he says, 'Dear God, please bless my beautiful, virtuous daughter Ellen.' "

"He can't do that."

"Why can't he?"

"To start with, he can't talk to God directly. The reader or the Rabbi makes the blessings, and they have to say, like for me: 'Sara bas Yehuda.' "

"What does that mean?"

"Sara, daughter of Yehuda."

"So why can't he say 'Ellen, daughter of Ernst'?"

"He just can't. They aren't Jewish names."

I shrugged; it seemed kind of silly to need an intermediary. Ever since Caputh I had wondered whether there mighn't be another brand of Judaism from the one Herr Levy knew. A younger one, maybe, for children like me.

Moving day with my mother wasn't a hectic, chaotic, screaming day; it was a carefully worked out campaign with beautifully meshing logistics, and Mother was at her best throughout. Bathed and elegant and with her make-up on straight when she greeted the moving men in the morning, and by nightfall, while maybe a dimmer version of her earlier self, she was still essentially the same. And miraculously, we got into clean, fresh beds that night, in an ordered household, and the few cartons and barrels that hadn't been unpacked yet had disappeared discreetly into a big cupboard. Of course I missed some of the fun because I had to go to school, but upon my return, already to the Hectorstrasse, we had macaroni casserole and a salad, and then Mother put us to work. She had lists from which she gave out assignments, and schedules that were followed, and she was serene and smiling.

Around four o'clock I saw Rudi walk into the open front door, wink at me, squeeze between two packing cases, and from behind put his hands over Renate's eyes. "Guess who?" She had been hanging coats in the big hall wardrobe; it had carved hearts and painted angels on its door. I saw her freeze, becoming very still, and then, for just a moment, she leaned back against him. He held her, then let go.

"Oh, it's you," she said in a bored voice.

He laughed. He was wearing a blue shirt with sleeves rolled up and heavy hiking boots and walking shorts.

"My God, where are you going?"

"To work. I promised your mother. Where are the big things that need a man's strength?"

Mother came along the corridor. "Oh, there you are, Rudi; I was beginning to despair. I need you so." He followed her into the back of the apartment.

Renate and I looked at each other. "I need you so!" I intoned passionately, and we burst out laughing. Renate's skin was brightly flushed.

Later Rudi put the extra blankets on the top shelf of the linen closet and Renate reached them up to him. He took them from her by reaching down, grasping her wrists, running his hands over hers and so onto the blankets. I stood and stared. Renate, her hair slipping out of its loose bun, her eyes earnest though she was constantly chattering, seemed not to notice. With my mouth already opened to make a remark, I closed it again. There was a strange feeling in my stomach. When I handed Rudi the glasses for the top shelf in the kitchen, I wished that he would stroke my hands too. But he did not.

I was in bed already when I heard Mother's angry voice. Renate came slamming into our room.

"What happened?" I asked.

Renate began to get undressed. Her movements clumsy, she bumped into the dresser, she muttered.

"What happened?" I asked again.

"Just more of Mother's sweetness," she snapped.

"But she was so cheerful! I never saw her laugh like she did at supper. Papi said it was her moving-day cheer."

"Are you kidding? That was for Rudi's benefit!" She threw her dress in the bottom of the wardrobe.

"Hang it up," I said automatically.

Turning to me, her eyes blazing, "Didn't you see how she carried on with him? And then she dares tell me that I'm making a fool of myself. 'You're just a child to him,' she said." Renate bent down and picked up her dress.

"But what brought all this on?"

"Papi said that Rudi had told him that Luz is getting married again."

"Oh!" I exclaimed.

"Yes, that's what I said too, so she jumped at me. 'Don't get any ideas and make a fool of yourself,' she said."

"What did Papi say?"

"He just made soothing noises, you know him! I told her though."

"What?"

"That there was nothing as foolish as an older woman fawning over a young man."

"Oh Reni, you didn't!"

"Yes, I did."

Suddenly it hit me. "Poor Rudi," I exclaimed. "Did Paps say he was upset?" Then I added, "He didn't seem upset."

"Luz is marrying an old guy—Professor von Heidemann; he was their professor in law school."

I shook my head. Renate had put the dress on a hanger. Not only that, she had buttoned it up neatly and had closed the belt buckle. Now she hung it in the wardrobe and closed the door—smack on her finger.

"*Verdammte Scheisse!*" she yelled.

I burst into laughter; it was rare for Renate to curse.

9

Aman Father knew had opened the first automat in Berlin. Our parents and all their friends had gone there one evening after the theater. Apparently they had felt that they were roughing it, but in a madly modern way, and since anything different tickled their jaded taste they raved about the sandwiches.

"It sounds so American," I said. "I bet they have one in New York."

Mother didn't know. But the next time we were in town, she took us to the automat. It was quite a day.

We each received one Mark, and we first went to the lady who sat in a cage making change. She punched some buttons in a thing that looked like a cash register with a snout, and the five- and ten-Pfennig pieces came sliding down the curved ramp. Then we took our time making our selections. But finally the moment came: clink, clink the money dropping, click the window opening—my roll with liverwurst, Renate's roast beef on rye; a miracle! We carried our tray to the table where Mother was sitting with the owner of the place. After we were introduced, he went to get us free lemonade from the back, which disappointed us greatly; we had looked forward to getting drinks with our coins. As I ate my sandwich I gazed at the dessert windows. I could see a napoleon next to the slot where a cream puff reposed. How would I ever be able to decide? I hardly listened to the conversation until the word *Caputh* struck at my ears.

"I have heard of it," Herr Grünbaum was saying with a shrug, "but they are too radical for me."

"Radical?" Mother asked.

"Zionist!" He spat the word out.

Mother looked at me accusingly. "You didn't tell me, Ellen!"

"I didn't think that you knew what Zionism is."

She tinkled her Oh-you-silly-child laugh, but the look she gave me was sharp. I gathered that Herr Grünbaum was looking for a school for his Johann.

"It's great in Caputh," I said. "All the children are happy; the teachers and counselors understand them!" There, let her chew on that.

Herr Grünbaum had ruddy cheeks and a high pot. "Happiness?" he asked and guffawed the male version of Mother's laugh. "What about discipline? Good German discipline?"

I shrugged. "Can I get my dessert now?"

"Go ahead," Mother said.

But when I came back—I had taken the petit fours since I couldn't make up my mind between the cream puff and the napoleon—Mother was annoyed. "That was very impudent," she said.

Herr Grünbaum had been called away.

"What?" I asked.

"You know what."

"Well, do you know what Zionism is?"

"Ellen, I'm going to speak to your father about you. Of course I know! All those Ost-Juden who want to live in Palestine and make the desert bloom."

I hated the sneer in her voice. "What's wrong with that? I'd like to go too."

"Ridiculous! Germany is your Vaterland."

"Then why don't the Germans want me?"

The conversation seemed familiar; I realized that I was taking Nanny's role while Mother played me. I had had that very talk with Nanny.

"That's silly; it's only a few Nazis who don't like Jews."

"But they are in power."

"Oh Ellen, what do you know about politics?"

She was departing from the script. She made me furious; I knew a lot more about politics than she.

I was telling Frau Bauchenhorn all about the automat.

"Imagine that!" she kept saying. "Imagine that!"

"You should go; it's so neat."

"It's not for the likes of me."

"Why not?"

"I haven't the money for such nonsense; we're not rich like the Jews."

I looked at her curiously. She was brushing her hair with long, hard strokes. She too? I almost asked whether she didn't like me anymore, but I was getting too old for such questions. Instead, I touched the heavy gold stuff that was her hair.

"Did you ever cut it?" I asked. "It's so thick, so gorgeous; you look like the Lorelei."

Her face was usually angry these days, but just then it softened. She fanned her hair over her shoulders and laughed coquettishly, trying to keep her lips together so the gap on the side where a tooth was missing wouldn't show.

"You really do," I said.

She forgot the tooth and laughed out loud.

"You have pretty hair too," she said in her booming voice.

I felt better.

The Kränzchen met for the first time in the new apartment. I wore the housecoat Tante Gert had sent to me from America. It was long, down to the floor, red roses printed all over the cotton fabric; it had a zipper down the front. The girls all agreed, it was gorgeous, like a formal dress, so glamorous. I looked at least eighteen in it; easily, maybe more! How they must live in New York! I mean, everyone knew that there were all these millionaires and gold in the streets and Eleanor Parker dancing up Broadway, and of course the housecoat proved it! Imagine dressing like that just for breakfast! Which made Tante Gert's letters from America even more difficult to understand. They were full of how hard it was to get affidavits, and that the relatives in New York were rather poor. The relatives were a branch of family I had never previously heard of—Father's mother's sister had gone to the new country as a girl. Now there were all these new cousins—Elyce and Werner and Bill and Herta. They were awfully nice to Tante Gert, but they didn't have much themselves.

"Werner is somewhat better off than the others," she wrote. "He manages something in an office."

He was going to try to give an affidavit to Tante Gert and Onkel Wolf, and she was going to stay right there in New York until she had it in her hand. Onkel Wolf would have to take a language examination, but he would not have to repeat his medical studies in order to practice in America. "That is, this is the law right now!" Tante Gert wrote, "But there is talk that changes will be made and that foreign doctors will have to take another degree, or, anyhow, that they will have to repeat their internships. Of course, all this is due to pressure from the members of the various medical societies who see a threat in all the immigrant doctors swelling their numbers."

She continued to say that she felt it was of the utmost importance that she and Wolf get to America as quickly as possible. "The sooner Wolf can start to work, the sooner we can furnish affidavits to you, my dear ones, because I am sure that you, too, will see that you will have to make the move."

I had read the letter twice; it still didn't make sense. The housecoat was more convincing. Anyhow, Tante Gert would be back soon to "pack up," she had written. Pack up! As if she was going on a picnic. It was strange. The girls agreed with me on that. And they just adored the housecoat too.

During the summer Christa had cut her hair and that day she wore the uniform of the BDM, Bund Deutscher Mädchen, the Club of German Girls. She told us all about the meetings.

"They make us march like soldiers, and we sing, and we have lectures."

"What kind of lectures?"

"Yesterday we had a speaker whose subject was 'The German Woman, Her Responsibilities.'"

"And what are our responsibilities?"

"As far as I could make out, to have lots of children who can fight for the Vaterland." She spoke caustically.

"What's wrong with that?" Inge asked.

"My father says that he hopes that I'll achieve more than breeding cannon fodder."

"Christa!" Katrine was shocked.

"If you don't like it, why do you belong?" Steffi asked sharply.

"Everyone in my class at the Goethe Schule belongs."

"Like sheep," said Steffi.

Christa looked at her curiously. "That's what my father said," she replied, then she laughed. "Don't worry, Steffi, I won't turn into a Nazi. Papa says he'll go back to Africa before he becomes part of the rabble."

"I don't think you should talk like that," Inge said doggedly. "The Nazis are the party of the Führer. After all, he is the leader of our country."

"My country right or wrong!" I said. I wasn't sure whether I meant it sarcastically or whether I was serious. It was confusing. If Inge expressed respect for Hitler, who could blame Luz, for instance? Was Luz bad? Was she bad now because she wanted to remain a lawyer even under the Nazis or had she always been bad? I thought about the conversation I had heard about Professor von Heidemann; he was a Nazi and yet he wasn't. ". . . good to have a decent voice to interpret these crazy laws," Grandfather had said; the professor would be made a judge now that he had joined the Party. Right or wrong? I knit on, my eyes busy with the fancy pattern Christa had talked me into using. Steffi was being awful again too. So aggressive; she was a completely different girl when we were with the others than when we were alone. But the strangest thing was how Christa liked her. I felt a wave of jealousy. Christa had been at Steffi's for Shabbath. "I loved it when her father sang the blessing and when her mother lit the candles, and how she put her hands near the flame and blessed it. We don't have lovely customs like that," Christa had said.

"Do your parents know that you went?"

"Sure."

"Don't they mind?"

"Why should they?"

"I'm not allowed to go."

"But I thought that Steffi is your friend."

"She is, but my mother won't let me go."

"But why not?"

I felt ashamed to say.

"Why not?" Christa insisted.

"Because they aren't German."

She laughed. "My father says that's one of the reasons why he likes me to see Steffi. 'There's an oversufficiency of Germanicness in our land today,' he says. I think he's regretting that we came back."

"And your mother?"

Christa blushed. "Oh Mother!"

Suddenly remembering that I had heard that Frau von Adelsberg drank too much, I was sorry that I had asked. Christa was following my thoughts. "A lot of white women in Africa drink. The climate. They get depressed."

"My mother does too," I said quickly.

Late that winter Mother and Father left one morning very early before we went to school. Father was carrying

Mother's little suitcase. She had kissed us, and she had cried.

"My beloved girls," she had said. "If I never see you again . . ."

"What's the matter? Where did they go?" I asked Renate.

"I don't know."

"But she must have said something to you."

"Just that she has to go to the doctor for a small operation."

"An operation? What kind?"

"I don't know." Renate was frowning.

"What did she mean, if she never sees us again?" I insisted.

"Oh, you know Mother; she dramatizes."

I didn't feel reassured. What's more, Renate didn't either. We rushed home after school.

They only came back in the evening. Mother walked carefully, and Father herded her to bed.

"God be thanked," she said to us when we went to kiss her good night. She was very emotional; I was afraid she would cry; I got out of there quickly.

In bed, we heard their voices from next door. They went on for a long time.

"I heard Papi say that what with these times, it's no time to have babies," Renate said.

"What does that mean?"

"I don't know." I knew that wasn't true; Renate knew all right, maybe even I did.

Mother stayed in bed for three days. We brought her trays.

And then in the spring, Grandmother died.

It seemed incredible. Just a couple of weeks earlier Mother and I had met her by chance at the market. We stood and chatted for a while, but then Grandmother said, "I have to go home; I feel terribly tired." Mother had shrugged, annoyed. And after Oma had left, I said, "Maybe I should have gone with her; she looked awfully white."

"That's the white powder she uses. She likes the dramatic effect."

I kept thinking of that when they took Grandmother to the hospital.

"She is dead," Father said the night he came home late. His face was gray, angry. I didn't hear the details until later— that it had been cancer of the liver, and that the last days had been hell, and that it had been my father she had called for. To hold her in her agony. They had hated each other cordially all through the years. Oma had talked of Father as "The Wine Salesman," Father spoke of the "*shiksa*" or "She." Yet, it was he who shared the dying with her.

"Oh how she fought," he said admiringly.

"The peasant stock in her!" Mother replied.

Even in death, Grandmother was not forgiven.

Which made it hard to know how to behave at the funeral. Seeing Mother and Tante Ruth in tears and Grandfather walk behind the coffin, a broken man with bent shoulders. And all the snatches of talk to remember. Mother saying, "She threw the keys at Vati's head; he was bleeding." And, "How she beat me, with her fists." And Father saying, "The crazy slyness!" And my own cache of memories—bringing Chanukah into the house and the little umbrella, and her face at the market. Also a very secret memory of recent vintage. I had come to the grandparents' apartment one morning to bring Oma something, and she had opened the door hastily, saying, "Sssh!" and rushed back to the living room, where the radio was blaring. By the time I had shut the door behind me and followed her, the program was over. Turning off the machine, she turned around to me. Her eyes were shining with a strange, blue light. "That was our Führer talking to us German women," she said.

I remembered the chill it sent into my stomach, but right

afterward the blue light dimmed and she was Oma again; her cheeks smelled of carnation.

Nanny and I walked behind our mothers in the funeral cortege, and when we looked at each other, we giggled. Because it was so strange. I didn't know another person who was dead.

Later in the afternoon, everyone was at our house, and Nanny and I asked to go for a walk. It was nice out, balmy with the sweetness of falling linden blossoms, which made a yellow carpet under the trees; it was like walking on crushed velvet. Our mothers were furious with us because we had giggled during the funeral. "Haven't you any feeling for my grief?" Mother had asked. Tante Ruth just treated us to icy silence. Her fiancé was there, a large fat man with very little hair on a big head. His name was Herr Heinrich Schrubber; we called him The Scrubber without Bristles.

"Do you like him?" I asked Nanny curiously.

Nanny handled a lot of things with giggles—so that's what we did that Sunday afternoon, we giggled; we felt pretty rotten.

Grandmother's jewelry was divided in an atmosphere that I found peculiar. I thought of Ali Baba and his forty thieves in their cave before the mountain of gold coins. The little heap of jewelry on our dining-room table didn't much resemble Ali Baba's loot, but there was avarice in Tante Ruth's voice and exaggerated politeness in Mother's. While the negotiations went on, the bell rang and a tall, thin man was shown in. He was a very distant cousin of Father's. His story was one that was getting to be awfully familiar—a lost judgeship and no money to get out of Germany. Father pulled out his wallet and extracted a ten-Mark note, then he shook hands with Ludwig, asked to be remembered to Uschie and Berta—whoever they may have been—and then the man left. The family went back to determine what should be done with the heavy gold watch chain that had belonged to Oma's grandfather. And there was no doubt that both Mother and Tante Ruth wanted the blue sapphire earrings in the diamond setting.

They each wanted them badly. I thought about how they had matched Grandmother's eyes.

I was standing behind Father's chair, looking on, feeling detached, thinking ironic thoughts. And then I saw the thin chain with the tiny Mogen David. "I never saw grandmother wear that," I interrupted and leaned forward to touch it with my finger.

"It's nothing; it has no value." Mother shrugged.

"But it's gold, isn't it?" I asked.

"Yes, but it hardly weighs anything. Mother bought it in a moment of religious exultation once."

They all laughed.

"Can I have it?" I asked as casually as I could manage; I wanted it desperately. It made me feel a little sick; suddenly I was one of the forty thieves.

"Sure," Mother said carelessly. Tante Ruth nodded.

I wore my Star of David always. There was only one thing wrong with it; it was too small. I wished that it were much more conspicuous, especially after Steffi was hurt one day when a bunch of kids pushed her down and called her a "Jewish pig." Looking at her poor knees, all crusted with scabs, I felt awful. No one ever said anything like that to me. Looking like any other German child was a camouflage I was beginning to feel guilty about. Yet, it was Steffi who said, "Put the Mogen David into your sweater; there's no sense provoking an incident."

I told her hotly that I wouldn't; I was proud to be Jewish, I didn't care who knew it.

But Sister Maria Theresa agreed with Steffi. She told me to wait for her after class.

"Look Ellen, that star you are wearing, what is it?"

"It's a Jewish star, Sister."

"Yes, I thought so." She looked at me out of her milk-white face, eyes obscured by the angle of the light that fell on her glasses. "I wish you wouldn't wear it to school," she said then.

"Why not?"

"You know we do not permit wearing jewelry."

"But the other girls wear their crosses."

"That's different. This is a Catholic school, after all."

She paused. I waited silently.

"I mean," she continued, "it is you who is the guest in our school; you mustn't flout that into the faces of the other girls."

"Why not?" Oh, I was furious.

"Because it will provoke incidents; we don't want that in this school."

I knew I had already argued way beyond what was permissible, yet I still thought I might win. "It was my grandmother's," I whispered, "the one who just died."

"I'm sorry, Ellen, but I am just thinking of your own best interest."

"But I made a vow!" This was a lie, but the nuns set great store by vows.

"You did? What kind?"

"That I would always wear the Star of David." I let my voice ring. The light had moved enough to clear Sister's glasses; I could see her cool gray eyes and her level glance. "All right," she said. "I certainly won't interfere with your vow. Just wear it inside of your clothes."

Our eyes locked, we were sworn enemies. Outside, in the corridor, I felt that my legs were trembling. I leaned against the wall until I was better.

10

It was a spring of strange discontents. Mother was waspish, and while we were told to attribute it to her grief, Renate shocked me by summing up my secret thoughts. "Grief, my foot, she hated Oma."

We were more indulgent with our own concerns. I was fairly obsessed with my nausea and headaches.

"Look, Ellen," Renate said, "I know that you want to change schools, and I don't blame you for faking with Mother and Father, but why carry on with me?"

"But I do feel awful every morning when I wake up and think that I have to face the old crows again; I'm not faking."

Renate shook her head. I don't think that she believed me. But then, she was not too interested anymore in these matters. It was as if she were already living in a different world, her physical presence in school only a small inconvenience—of no real concern. For Mother's benefit we still started on "walks" together, but the routine was fairly well established; at the next corner we headed in opposite directions.

"Meet you here at seven."

"Where are you going?" I would ask.

"I don't know yet."

"Well, with whom?" I knew she wouldn't lie to me outright.

"Will you stop that? Who do you think you are? Mother? The Gestapo?"

One day I said outright, "What's Rudi doing now that he can't practice law?"

"Something hush-hush for the Jewish community."

"What does that mean?"

"Oh Ellen! If I knew that, it wouldn't be hush-hush, would it?"

They were all so ridiculous with their secrets, like little children!

One night, after an unusually balmy day, Renate and I were lying in bed. The windows were wide open, music drifted from across the courtyard, sounds perceived as part of the woolly feeling of being almost asleep. And then, pushing me back from the brink of softness, I heard voices singing "Deutschland, Deutschland über alles," and suddenly I was wide awake, open to a terrible sadness. I listened and the familiar words sank deeply into my mind. It was as if I had never heard them before, and tears welled up in me, and I let them spill from my eyes.

Then the tune changed. The "Horst Wessel Lied," the Nazi anthem, triumphantly shouted from a thousand throats. In a flash, I was out of bed and banged the window shut. And stood and listened to the silence before I crawled back into bed. Then I started to cry again, but louder this time, angrily. I wanted to waken Renate; how could she sleep through this?

It was close in the room now, each tick of my clock a small reverberation. I let the sobs die down and lay and listened— like a hammer beating upon my mind the clock ticked; life was too sad.

When we had been small, Renate and I had had a system of communicating that was a natural end to our nighttime ritual.

We had called it "Hmmm saying" and it meant that if one of us either wanted to say something else, or just wanted to know whether the other was still awake, she could say "Hmmm." In case the other was still in a condition to reply, she said "Hmmm" back.

We hadn't used this system in a long time. Somehow, it had just fallen by the wayside of getting older, like Renate's need to have me go ahead of her to turn on lights when she wanted a late snack from the kitchen. But that night I tried it.

"Hmmm," I said loudly.

There was no answer.

"Hmmm." I practically shouted it.

"Oh shut up, Ellen," Renate said crossly in a wide-awake voice.

The Lesler Schule or, as it was officially called, Die Jüdische Waldschule Grunewald, the Jewish Forest School in the Grunewald, sounded like the ideal place for me; its direction did not have the onus of being either Zionist or religious, and I thought that its location—smack in the fresh air, classes were held outdoors and the children tended their own vegetable gardens—would appeal to Mother. Then luck had it that Mother met Frau Lesler, the school's founder and owner, at a party. She was impressed by her—"A very cultured lady; she knows Grandfather."

For the first time there seemed to be real hope.

Not really expecting anything from him, I still tried to enlist Father on my side. To my surprise, he listened to me thoughtfully; he nodded. Blue eyes gazing out of the window, "Yes," he said, "yes . . . maybe it is time."

Mother took me for the interview in the middle of a flower-bursting May.

Oh large Frau Lesler with hanging chins, in a tentlike dress, fat feet overflowing vain shoes. Her sister, Frl. Heine, gay voice shrilling, was also present. I liked Frl. Heine's shriveled monkey face with the bright, black button eyes, thin legs and tiny feet, the tinny laugh. I was accepted to enter the Quarta in the fall.

"Don't talk about it yet at the Liebfrauen," Mother cautioned.

I don't know how I managed to keep such a big secret; I was bursting with it, overflowing with feeling good, right, in step again. I even wrote beautiful essays for Sister; what did I care? Not for long.

Renate cried when she said good-by to the nuns. Old Mother Superior kissed her on the forehead. "God bless you, my child," she said to her. To me she only gave her fingertips in that disgustingly limp, fishtail way. Maybe it was because I was bursting with glee; I could hardly restrain myself from dancing up and down and shouting, "Yea, yea, I don't have to look at your old nun faces again!" But I acted perfectly respectably. I curtsied and said, "Thank you for everything," and yes, I would be a good girl in the new school.

Inge, Katrine, and Romi were miffed at my desertion.

"Why don't you change with me?" I urged; I felt I had a foolproof "Wear Mother Down" recipe they might as well benefit from.

"Why should we?" Romi announced her spokesmanship.

"But you hate it, too."

"No more than we hate any school."

"But don't you want to go to a Jewish school where you won't be a 'guest'?" I mimicked Sister's voice. "Where you belong and can feel at home?"

"Oh Ellen, you're exaggerating. You're showing off, as usual. We are perfectly at home at the Liebfrauen."

"Yes, as long as we act like . . ." I hesitated, then I shouted, "As long as we act like a depressed minority!" I had just read the phrase in an article in a Jewish magazine that had lain on the kitchen table at the Levys'.

Romi stared at me. I felt triumphant, I had really told her. But she shrugged. "You're crazy," she said.

Inge mixed in. "Anyhow, Oma says that the discipline is good for us."

"It isn't discipline, it's deception to always act holy," I argued.

"That is so discipline."

"Anyhow, my parents wouldn't hear of it!" Katrine summed it up.

When we got home, I saw that we had pork chops for dinner. I stared at the golden brown chops, the crispy fat at the edges, I smelled their aroma; suddenly I felt sick.

"What's the matter, why don't you eat, Ellen?"

"Why do we eat pork chops? It's forbidden."

"Are you out of your mind? You love pork."

"Not anymore."

"Since when?"

I sat with my mouth closed. I couldn't tell her. Herr Levy's face when he said "pork" and "unclean" and how God had forbidden it.

"Ellen, what is this nonsense?"

"Jews shouldn't eat pork."

She laughed. "Are you going to be kosher next?"

Father spoke up. "She doesn't have to eat the chops if she doesn't want them."

Mother's face got red. "Ernst Westheimer, what is this new insanity?"

Father closed his mouth. He looked stubborn. I thought that he was remembering how his father had died after they stopped being kosher.

"I'll never eat pork again!" I said, encouraged by Father's demeanor. Let her beat me, let her starve me, let her put me on bread and water under house arrest, I would not! But Mother only shrugged.

Renate found a job almost immediately. Now she was really in the other world. She would work for a patent attorney who had a lot of correspondence with French, English, and American inventors.

"Are you scared?" I asked.

"Strangely enough, no!"

We both knew what she meant. She had been fearful

about the dark, about spiders and everything that crawled, about the dentist—most of all, I suddenly realized, fearful of Mother. And the patent attorney held no terror to compare? I felt a terrible sense of leave-taking. It was much more than the job or the summer separation; it was even more than the sudden understanding.

And so I started off on the summer vacation with my parents again. At four A.M. this time—we would drive through, have no stopover in Silesia. "Avoid the whole business with the Rabbi!"

Father drove straight through Prussia, Silesia, the Polish Corridor into East Prussia. We would go via the Masurian Lakes.

"You have never seen a hotel like this," he told us. "It consists of small villas strung out along the shore of the lake. They are super modern, all glass and steel, but beautiful, letting the landscape in."

"And when did you discover this marvel?" Mother's voice had the edge that went with questions about his trips.

"Did you hear that, Ellen? Now we'll have a Grand Jury investigation."

"Well, you never mentioned it before."

"I drove all around trying to find a damned hotel for you without the sign, so you wouldn't have to stay over at the Rabbi's, and you act as if I kept a harem there."

I was staring out of the window, letting the telephone poles stripe my eyeballs. I was listening, though more to the sounds of their voices than to what they said. And instinctively I knew that Mother was right. Right about what? I wondered then—these sudden bits of wisdom I was constantly getting these days were confounding. Half the time I didn't understand how I knew, or even what; yet, I knew!

As Father had promised, the hotel didn't have the sign; we had come to call it The Sign. It was dark when we arrived and we were tired. I fell into bed quickly without even closing the striped draperies. Which is why, when I awoke in the morning, the panorama was a complete surprise. One whole side of the room was a huge window, a window behind which milk-white fog moved restlessly like a great theater curtain about to rise. Vaguely, I noticed the gay scatter rugs, the white stucco walls, the strong blues and greens of the upholstery in the room, but really, I waited. And then the curtain began to lift with infinite slowness—higher and higher, revealing the silver-smooth lake, the dark pines, the lighter firs. Halfway up, the fog seemed to pause for dramatic effect, and then it tore apart and scattered, and a blue sky shone upon the lake, which had lost its mirrored look. It was a moving palette now, a palette of blues and purples and pinks, crusted in aqua, sparkling—it was beautiful. I grabbed for my diary. What an essay for Sister this would have made!

Outside, I stepped with bare feet on the soft pine needle carpet and walked the hundred steps down to the lake. A narrow strip of gray sand and then the clear water, silver gray up close like this. It was utterly still except for wakening bird chirps, and the almost nothing sounds of the quiet lake. Dragon-flies skimmed across a bed of water lilies over to the right, and translucent circles widened where a fish had poked a round snout up. My eye rested on the flat distance. Suddenly, reality was peace. Not The Times, not The Nazis, not The Jews. Not even Renate and Rudi.

We stayed there for three days, very lazy, very calm. Mother and Father were happy with each other, which allowed me to relax and give up my watchful listening to the tones of their voices.

On the last afternoon Mother and I were to take a sight-seeing tour by boat to view the interlocking chain of lakes for which the region was famous. Mother, whose swimming looked like a turtle's heavy wake, head erect and sticking upward, legs snapping regularly like pincers, and with the most frightened, grim expression on her lips, Mother naturally did not relish the idea of a boat trip. But Father had to visit customers, and I begged and begged, so in the end we went.

The boat, just a large fishing cruiser with benches screwed to its deck, did not inspire Mother's confidence, and she watched anxiously as quite a few people boarded the craft. It was a gray afternoon, a sharp, gusty wind blew. I loved it and stood by the helm, feeling like a Viking. The captain regaled us with history, geography, and, of course, the location of battles, and all the time it got a little cooler and a little darker, and Mother got a little more panicky.

"We shouldn't have come; it's going to storm," she wailed.

"Of course it won't, see, over there, it's getting lighter already."

"No, no, it will storm, and we are overloaded."

She forced me to share her bench in the most sheltered corner. Pretty soon the captain handed out slickers.

"We'll have a little rain," he said jovially.

Now Mother was totally frightened, the skin around her nostrils gray.

"It's nothing, Mutti, we are perfectly safe, you heard him, just a little rain."

She didn't hear a word I said. And then, just as the first heavy drops beat down, we heard between the far-off rumble of thunder the faint scream of a car horn.

"There's my husband; it's my husband's horn," Mother yelled.

Embarrassed, in her wake I, too, saw across the lake at the shore a car right by the water's edge, and next to it a waving man.

Somehow, Mother prevailed upon the captain to put us on shore. I suppose he felt the detour worth his while to avoid the company of hysteria. And Mother stood by the railing, waves and gusts of wind and rain and thunder not daunting her now, while she yearned toward Father, who grew bigger as we approached the shore. Nor did she mind climbing into water up to her knees when the captain said he would not go in any closer. She just held her shoes and skirt up with one hand,

and with the other she reached toward Father, who, also shoe-less, was coming to lead her ashore.

I waded behind them, feeling foolish as the boat turned back on its course, but also feeling funny and all choked up, and suddenly glad to be in the dry, little car.

"I saw the weather come up," Father said simply, "and I knew how scared you'd be; so I drove along the shore road until I saw the boat."

I rubbed my hair with my sweater and fought tears as I listened to Mother's sobs. "Oh Ernstl, thank you, thank you!"

Marriages were funny, I thought. That morning I had seen Father hush a bellboy who was saying that it was good to see him again, and did he have his nice wife along again? Father had hushed him with a five-Mark note.

Renate was not much of a letter writer, but that summer she wrote to me privately. Not that she said much; a bit of gossip about Kate, or that she had seen Katrine with a boy. Then, at the end, she might add, "We went swimming at Scharmützelsee," or that they had seen a Merle Oberon movie. The *we* was never explained. I took it to mean Rudi and she. I also felt the message lay in the letters per se rather than in what she said. And I wrote back, long chatty pages, saying nothing much either, just trying to hold on.

When we came home though, there was a strangeness; I felt shy, she was suddenly beautiful, a grown-up lady with an interesting mouth.

"How come you wear so much lipstick?" I said, staring.

"Here, I bought you one too. Just don't let Mother catch you with it."

"Thanks."

I opened the small tube, screwed the scarlet pomade up and was sickened by its sweet odor. "Thanks," I said again.

CHAPTER

II

I had expected to be a star in sports at the new school, and when, on the first day, I was put into the third squad in gym, I protested indignantly, "But I am good . . ."

I was told not to worry, that everyone started in third and worked up from there. To my surprise though, I found that I couldn't do some of the things they did in that third squad. Not throw the shotput, nor jump high enough or far enough, nor even do the 100 meters in good enough time.

It was that way in every class. I suppose, without realizing it, I had accepted the propaganda line that a Jewish school would be inferior to the Liebfrauen Lyceum, but, far from my being ahead, I was constantly on unfamiliar ground at the Lesler Schule. They did projects in geography and reports for history, and in German class I saw very quickly that sunset essays would be laughed out of the room. Then, of course, there was Hebrew of which I knew only the merest rudiments; in short, I realized that this move implied more work and adjustment that I had thought. Whether that was what I found so challenging, or having boys right in the same classroom, or whether it was really the atmosphere I had yearned for—whichever it was, or all of it together, I was blissfully happy.

And an immediate success with the boys.

"They called me Bleach Blonde and Peroxide Baby," I told Mother at dinner the first day.

I saw little of Renate. She loved her job, and often she would call in the evenings, "Mutti, I have to work late!" I knew she was lying, that she was seeing Rudi.

Sunday mornings Renate wanted to sleep late now. I would lie in bed waiting for her to wake up. I would cough a little, and she would pull the covers over her head. Finally, I'd give up and tiptoe from the room. Often I met Father on these quiet Sunday mornings. He was home a lot now; there were so many places where he couldn't go anymore, and his stomach was bad again in spite of the herb tea; he took little white pills. I would ask him what was the matter with him, and sometimes he confided in me—about staying in that hotel in Mainz and being awakened by a telephone call. "Get out of town, we don't want Jews here!" About coming to an old customer—"I thought he was my friend," Father said—who had asked whether it was true that he was a Jew. "And then he said, 'I can't buy from you, Westheimer, you people tried to ruin our country.' "

And then, of course, there was Krause.

Krause had been a name—a name that was woven through the stories of my childhood like a red thread. Krause, the competitor, Krause, traveling for Wine, GmbH, and trying to steal Father's accounts away. To me he had always been a funny figure; Father told with glee how he outwitted him, reached the customer first, had a better price on the Hochheimer Spätlese 1924, was the only one who carried Remy Martin. Krause was fat and had a handlebar mustache; he was a joke. But now Krause had the jump on Father. Father was a Jew; Krause was gaining ground.

Father looked the same on those Sunday mornings, his old slim, erect, elegant self in the blue silk robe with the ascot, but there was a sadness about him. I studied him. Was his hair thinning? There were lines around his eyes now, the blue was more intense, too intense. It made me feel guilty to see him sad when I was so very happy.

"Let's go to a soccer game today," I wheedled. "Berlin is playing Frankfurt this afternoon."

Or: "Let's go to the Avus and give the Opel its head."

The Avus was the racetrack nearest Berlin.

Or: "Would you like me to cook you some hot farina?"

The hot farina cooked in water with salt and dotted with butter soothed his stomach. And he would cheer up. "All right, we'll go to the soccer game if Mutti lets us."

How he would yell! "With the head, you idiot!" "Kick it, you dumb ox!" "The goal, the goal, are you blind?" "Right front, pass, pass!"

His cheeks would redden, and he looked like the picture of him that stood in my room—a boy of fourteen in knickers, holding his cap, his head covered by golden ringlets.

"What happened to your curls?"

"I lost them in the war."

"How? I mean, I know you had to cut your hair short, but why didn't they grow again?"

"The weight of the steel helmet."

Fact and fiction, and I, now a cynical and questioning audience. "Did you really crawl through the cross fire to bring water to your patrol?"

"The bullets covered every millimeter of ground; it was impossible to get through, there wasn't a centimeter . . ."

I interrupted: "I know, they shot you dead!"

"Ellen, what's the matter with you?"

"Oh, Papi, these old stories, and what difference does it make now that you were a front fighter?"

He drew himself up. "I served my country."

One Friday afternoon, inspired, I said, "Let's go to Synagogue."

"Why, what's . . . is it a holiday?" Father asked.

"No, just Shabbath."

He looked at me thoughtfully; he was seeing me. "You are getting awfully interested in religion; is it the new school?"

"No, the Levys." Suddenly I knew that I could tell him about the Levys.

"You have been at their house?"

"For years."

He listened to me for a long time, then he shrugged. "These people . . ." he started, but I wasn't finished yet.

"Don't you see, they have strength, they belong!"

"We have always belonged. This is our country."

"Isn't Judaism a kind of country?"

Father got up. "My father thought so, but I don't know. . . ." He looked down at me. "Don't tell Mother!"

"I won't."

We went to Synagogue that evening; Father and I, hand in hand. At the door we parted. I went upstairs to sit in the first row of the women's section, he stood downstairs among the men. I could see him plainly, how he opened his siddur, and after a while, moved slightly with the rhythm of the prayers. I watched from my perch and felt happy. The lofty height of the beautiful room, the dark red stained windows, the velvet of the curtains before the Oren Hakodesh, and the Rabbi and Cantor in their black robes. The sermon was about Abraham binding Isaac to the altar. The Rabbi explained the parable—binding Isaac to duty, to Jewish observance, to obedience—father leading son.

It became our ritual. I found that going regularly to Synagogue every Friday night, aside from giving me a chance to get to know Father better, had other advantages. I no longer sat upstairs in the women's section but discovered that children, boys and girls together, could sit downstairs in a section of benches at the far right of the synagogue. There I met a lot of friends, and we managed to have a good time in spite of the stern glances that came our way from the patrolling Herr

Bildhaus. Herr Bildhaus was the Shammes, a small man with hands apparently permanently folded behind his back.

Father kidded me that it wasn't religion that had made me initiate this new Friday routine, but I said that I couldn't help it if boys went to Synagogue too. Father and I were wonderfully companionable on those Friday nights, and when we came home there would be lit candles and braided challas now. This was the concession Mother made to our new religiosity. Nevertheless, she still could not manage to control her expressive eyebrows while Father sang the blessings. In the euphoria of those lovely evenings, I said once, "Ach, this is so great; I wish we could have Pesach again too!"

"Oh no you don't!" Mother screamed at that. "That's where I draw the line."

A few years earlier while observing a Seder, Mother had vowed that Pesach would never be celebrated in our house again. There is a place in the ritual where a cup of wine is poured for the Prophet Elijahu and where the door is opened for his invisible appearance. On that evening, just as Father poured the wine, the door to our dining room had sprung open by itself. It had swung open slowly with a peculiar little moan. After Mother came out of her screaming hysterics she made the vow.

Father and I shrugged—one couldn't have everything!

Tante Gert stopped off at our house on her return, but first she deposited their affidavits with the American Consulate.

Before she had left for New York, Father had been amused about her American Adventure. "Ach, you know my sister Gertrude, she likes drama, a little excitement."

What marked the passage of time now was to see the change in Father's attitude toward the American Adventure. They sat for hours and hours and talked. I was so glad to see Tante Gert that I squeezed in close to her on the couch. She looked beautiful; she was wearing a tailored suit with long jacket, and her platform shoes had a strap around the ankle. Her long, long nails were lacquered red; she was already a bona fide American. Snuggling close, feeling happy, I listened to the talk though much of it was boring. Affidavits and visas and exit permits and passports. Visitors' visas and the American quota. But there were interesting stories too. Like the night Tante Gert arrived in America.

"They wouldn't hear of my going to a hotel. Elyce insisted that I stay with her and her mother."

So Tante Gert had traveled to the Bronx with the strange cousins, had met her mother's sister, old Tante Gretl, had talked to Elyce and Werner, whose German was funny, had communicated in sign language with Herta and Fred and Andy and Martha, who spoke no German at all. She had never really sorted out who was who, or how she was related to them all, but she had eaten dinner with them that first night in the foyer of Tante Gretl's and Elyce's apartment at a big, pulled-out table. She had wondered why she wasn't shown to her room; there were four doors off the foyer; surely there was a lot of space. And she had still wondered what was behind those doors when, late at night, she had not been able to sleep lying next to Elyce in the big double bed; Elyce snored. Finally she had tiptoed out to investigate. The doors led into closets; only then did Tante Gert realize that there were no wardrobes in the apartment. Clothes were hung in closets in America.

"It was all so strange and cramped . . ."

My eyes had grown heavy; and they had started to talk about visas again. Onkel Wolf would go ahead on a visitor's visa, Tante Gert would pack up and await the regular visas. It was high time to get Wolf off to safety, she said; he was getting threatening phone calls; Nürnberg was impossible! I roused when she said, "And it's overdue for you to start, Ernst!"

"What would I do in America?" Father asked. "They don't drink wine there; they're hardly civilized—just firewater." He laughed. "Firewater, whiskey, that's all they drink. I know,

I read it. In Texas even the cows drink whiskey, and in Ohio," he pronounced it O-hee-oh, making a kind of yodel out of it, "they drink corn liquor."

"That's not the point; you can't stay here."

"Ach, I don't know. This nonsense can't last much longer."

"Stop sticking your head in the sand; ostrich politics," she insisted.

"A handsome bird, the ostrich."

"A stupid bird. You have no right to be so blind, you have a family, two girls . . ."

"Which reminds me," Father changed the subject, "isn't it time already for you to have some children?"

Tante Gert glanced at me, shook her head. "Just before I left, Wolf and I just decided it was impossible now, these times . . ." Her voice trailed off.

"Yes," Mother said, "we, too . . ."

In Germany a girl was considered no longer a child when she became fourteen years old. "*Vierzehn Jahr' und sieben Wochen, ist der Backfisch ausgekrochen*," or, literally translated, "Fourteen years and seven weeks, the baked fish crawls from its cocoon." So a Backfisch is equal in concept to a teen-ager. Yet, when my period set in, though I was only thirteen, I felt that I was past the stage where I should be considered a child. Mother had hugged me and said, "You're a woman now," and she had given me a small gold locket. Why then, did she immediately forget her own pronouncement and keep treating me like a child? I tried to negotiate a new bedtime, a greater allowance, and lipstick on the grounds of my new status, but Mother tipped an expressive finger against her brow. However, I did feel grown up the next day because Renate and Rudi invited me for tea at Leon's. "To celebrate," Renate said.

Aghast, I asked, "You didn't tell him?"

"Don't be silly."

"But what did you tell him about why you wanted to take me someplace?"

Ignoring my question, she asked instead, "Do you think girls tell men everything? Not much! The more mysterious, the better."

"That's silly."

"You'll see."

He was wearing a navy tie with white polka dots, we had napoleons, and we were very polite. He dipped a sugar cube into his coffee and held it to Renate's lips. She took delicate little licks, even though she had her own coffee. "Hm, hmmm," she murmured.

"What does it taste like?" I asked.

Rudi laughed and dipped one for me. I sucked at it, careful not to let my lips touch his fingers, then said rudely, "Bah, it's just sugar." At that they both laughed inordinately. They were acting pretty silly, so I went to the powder room. And when I came back Renate was leaning her forehead against Rudi's, her eyes were closed. The waiter stood nearby, trying not to look at them. I wished I could just walk out and go home.

A few nights afterward, from under the green layers of sleep like green water, I heard Mother yell.

"You have been to the man's apartment?" she screamed.

I smiled; such a dream, so real.

Only later did I really wake up. Renate was sitting on her bed, boring her fists into her eyes, crying. She always cried ugly, red-nosed, wet. And her eczema would flare up, and she would scratch. I watched her a minute, detached and still swaddled in the peace of sleep. Renate had been born with a streak of white in her dark hair, running from the crown down the back of her head. Mother's friends had various theories about it—that it was an omen of sorrow, that it was an omen of the coming of a small blond sister, that Mother had clutched her head in fright while she was pregnant with Renate. When Renate was younger she had hidden the coarse streak under a large hairbow; now that she wore her hair simply drawn back, she tried to comb the top hair over it to conceal it. But that night, disheveled, the white streak glowed dully in the light of the bed lamp. It tore me out of my detachment. Achingly. I wanted to comfort her. "Come in my bed," I whispered, and Renate turned off the light. In the dark I heard her strip off her dress and kick her shoes aside; then she was under the cover with me. We didn't cuddle like we had when we were small; instead I took Renate in my arms, and she cried into my shoulder, my neck. I didn't mind the wet face, the sniffling. I wanted her to feel better, to stroke her poor hair, to help. And after a while she calmed a little.

"The things she called me," she said and started to sob again. "She called me a whore!"

I waited until the new storm subsided. "But why did you tell her that you were with Rudi, and at his apartment?"

"She met me at the door like the damn Gestapo. 'Where were you? It's two o'clock.' In her awful screech. I got so mad I screamed back that I had been at Rudi's house. So there!"

"Oh Reni!"

"I don't care. I don't care what she thinks. Or anyone. It's my life."

"You know she doesn't mean it."

"She means it all right. She's jealous; she'd like to carry on with Rudi herself. But he looks right through her, he's had enough of deceitful women."

"Oh come on, Reni."

"No, it's true. She can't stand that I have him, it's like her worst fears come true, it's what she was always afraid would happen with Papi . . ."

"Reni!" I said it sternly. I should slap her face. We had learned in First Aid that a slap was the best antidote to hysteria. But Renate was crying again, so I stroked her hair instead. At last she calmed, and then she slept. I eased my arm out from under her head and lay apart from her. I was very awake now. Damn Mother, anyhow. Even though Renate was all wrong—all this wasted emotion; we had bigger problems, didn't we?

In a way, it was the same with my feeling about the maids. Ever since I had been small I had sided with the maids against my mother; it had seemed the natural thing to do. Though they were adults, they, like I, were subject to Mother's authority, subject of her whims, of the tyranny of her moods, of lost keys and suspicions. Mother called their endless search for loopholes in the fabric of obedience to her their "servant psychology." The little shrug that went with this phrase was more contemptuous than angry; it had always annoyed me exceedingly. Whether that was because it had touched me with guilt—in my secret heart I knew that I shared the maids' attitude —or whether the snobbism of it revolted me, in any case, when-ever Mother started in against the help, I used to be automatically on their side.

Now, however, and almost imperceptibly, this had started to change. And it was not only because of my growing maturity, it was mainly because Mother's relationship with Frau Bauchenhorn was really too bizarre. It was Frau Bauchenhorn who cracked the whip and Mother, who, more and more meekly, bowed to the lash; I realized that I was detesting the Bauchen-horn. And not because I minded that the apartment had assumed an air of gray neglect, nor that the meals were slung at us; no, I resented the mutters, the slamming of doors, and the whole gamut of angry contempt that she exhibited toward us.

The last straw was meeting her late one afternoon just as she was leaving our house. In front of our apartment building stood a fat SA man, legs apart, hands locked on his back, sending a shiver through me. He stood in the "at ease" pose which was used for waiting and guarding; I scurried past him quickly. That's when Frau Bauchenhorn came out, and I saw a grin spread the coarse face, making it a red beer-drinker leer, brown teeth winking; he scurried to her and took her arm, then they walked off together.

"Muuuuuttiiiiiiii!" I came into our apartment bawling for her the way I used to when I was small. "Muuuuuttiiiiii!"

"I'm in my room, Ellen," she called out.

She was. Sitting before her dressing table, putting on mascara. She would spit lightly, in a ladylike way, into the little pot before she rubbed the black dye with the small brush. Then, holding her face stiff, wide-eyed, a Dresden doll, she brushed upward, stroking blond lashes black. It was a reassuring sight. I threw my books into the small boudoir chair and myself on the bed. Immediately she yelled, "Get off the bed!" That was reassuring too. The coverlet on my parents' bed was lilac velvet, the throw pillows genuine Brussels lace; Mother was a dragon about keeping us off this magnificence.

"Let's fire Frau Bauchenhorn," I said, rolling off the bed onto the floor.

Mother held the little brush suspended before her face. She had a slightly rakish air, one eye blond-lashed, the other dark. In the mirror, she sought my expression. "We may not get anyone else," she said tentatively.

"Even though," I insisted.

For once, we understood each other. "You are right," she said. "Enough is enough!"

I jumped up to hug her. "I'll help a lot," I promised.

"Let me finish my face; then we'll see what's in the icebox for supper." She went back to her wide-eyed grimace, stroking upward.

There were Jewish maids available now, and the choice was between them and the "over forty-five" Gentile ones. We went through quite a roster of the old ones before Mother was ready to try a Jewish one. The objection to a Jewish maid was, of course, that she wouldn't know her place. And in the end, Mother hired Rosemarie simply because she fell in love with her. Rosemarie was twenty-two years old, small and delicate with a soft, pouty underlip and bright, brown eyes. The daughter of a lawyer, herself halfway through law school, she was waiting for her exit permit; she was going to England.

Rosemarie handled Mother with soft-voiced firmness, she got the house back to its old shine, and when she served cold cuts, the platter would be decorated with blooming radish roses, with carrot curls, and the roast beef would be rolled into cornucopias from which little mustard pickles peeked. Mother talked about it a lot, about how a *Gute Kinderstube*—literally "a fine nursery," meaning a good upbringing—always showed, and that I could take Rosemarie as an example that work does not degrade, that a lady is a lady whatever she does. But all this was said to me in a whisper—in spite of Mother's very words, she could not bring herself to treat Rosemarie as an equal; Mother's Employer Psychology was too strong for that.

"Why can't Rosemarie eat with us?" I asked.

"Oh Ellen, don't create problems!"

12

As soon as it was warm enough, Steffi, Christa, and I started to go swimming at the Hallensee Schwimmbad. An artificial lake, only a ten-minute streetcar ride from where we lived, it had a warren of beginners' pens achieved by a network of plank walks built over the side of the lake. Along these walks stalked gleaming-muscled Adonises, holding aloft their fishing rods from which little children dangled.

"One and two, breathe and breathe!"

The tots in the water, held afloat by broad leather belts to which the anglers' lines were attached, thrashed mightily.

Of course Christa, Steffi, and I were far above these little fish. In fact, Christa was an expert swimmer; she did everything well, and Steffi was excellent too. It was the one sport her father thought highly of. Once, when Herr Levy had been a little boy, he had been chased by a gang of his neighbors. From what Steffi said, they had always been after him. Steffi reported that the Poles had been anti-Semites long before the Germans ever thought of it. That time, Herr Levy, about ten or twelve years old, had escaped from his tormentors by running into the small river that flowed through his village. In his fright, he had forgotten that he couldn't swim, had floated downriver and away from the voices that taunted him before he could realize that he was in deep water. As soon as this knowledge sank in, Avram Levy sank too. The story was every bit as exciting as my father's best, ending in rescue and his determination to learn to swim. Which he did, all by himself, in that little river. And since Herr Levy thought that swimming was a synonym for lifesaving, he found the money to let Steffi take swimming lessons. She had been put on the fishing line at four years of age and had in the meantime learned every different style. Steffi could crawl and do the butterfly, backstroke, and side-kick as well as the conservative breast stroke, which was all I could master. In fact, I was a poor swimmer. Unfortunately, an instructor had once told my mother that I was a natural in the water, which had led us to believe that lessons were superfluous for me. However, I could stay afloat, and it didn't really matter —there were millions of boys at the Hallensee Schwimmbad, that was the attraction.

Beyond the beginner pens, broad planked walks stuck out into the lake. Along these walks were rows of long wooden chaise longues which could be rented for a few Pfennige. That was where we headquartered—in our blue or green or red trunksuits, with our striped terry towels and the bottles of sun lotion. I had talked Mother into the sophistication of a black suit that year, and I felt absolutely ravishing.

Under Christa's tutelage, Steffi had learned to relax and at the Schwimmbad we compared lifestyles as represented by boys. Steffi's, whom she had mostly met at her Synagogue (she did not attend ours, which Herr Levy said was too "goyish"), seemed to be earnest and dark. "Typical," we said. "Just like Christa's boyfriends are typical, blond and tall, every one of them!" Only the boys I knew straddled the extremes. We talked about it often, how different they all were, and how they would never have talked to each other but for us. In fact, we got malicious fun out of mixing them up together and watching their discomfort with each other. Steffi could laugh at these things now, her sharp tongue honeyed with humor; she wasn't constantly hitting out anymore. Through Christa's eyes we also began to regard some aspects of the times with irreverent laughter, aspects which might otherwise have scared and depressed us. When one of her swains refused to shake hands with one of ours, overlooking the outstretched hand of the Jewish boy,

Christa did not wait for him to be out of earshot before she said icily that here was an obvious case of retarded mentality. Another game she played was her imitation of Hitler, Göring, and Goebbels. Her theatrics required a black Ace (imported) pocket comb as a prop for the mustache and a pillow for Göring's belly. As to Goebbels—the cruel limp, the sucked-in cheeks, the rhetoric—Christa said, "You should hear my father, he can do it much better than I." But we thought that she was pretty good too.

"Not so funny!" Herr Levy said when he overheard us, but Steffi said, "Ah, Papa, sometimes you have to laugh."

Herr Levy patted her hair and nodded his head. "So laugh, Sarale, laugh." Then he smiled at Christa and me, did a little dance step, and said in his soft singsong, "Yes, yes, *Kinderle*, laugh."

One of the boys I had met at the Hallensee Schwimm-bad was Mossi Fürstenbach. He was of gangling height in his blue swim trunks, red-cheeked, and shining-eyed. I barely reognized him when I saw him at Synagogue the next Friday in his dark suit. I noticed the strong eyebrows, the black hair, and the seriousness of his nice eyes. I introduced him to Father.

"Fine boy, good manners," Father said. "Where is he from?"

"What do you mean, where is he from? Where should he be from?"

"He doesn't seem like a German boy."

"Maybe that's why I think he's nice," I said crossly.

Yet, when I saw Mossi again, I asked.

"I'm from Kiev," he answered.

"That's in Russia, isn't it?" I hadn't been Steffi's friend all these years without learning something. "Was your family driven out by a pogrom?" I asked.

"No, my parents left when the Bolsheviks took over in Russia."

"You mean they were rich?"

"Well, my family had a paper factory and a sugar mill and a bank."

"That sounds rich all right."

"Don't be vulgar." He grinned. He had nice white teeth.

But I was surprised; I guess I had still thought that all Ost-Juden were poor, though I knew definitely that they weren't all dirty. I brought it up at dinner that night.

"Oh, there were very wealthy Jews in Russia," Mother said. "The Sokolovskis came from Moscow. You should have seen my mother-in-law's diamonds. And marvelous emeralds."

I looked at Father. I was afraid that he would be hurt by mention of her first husband, but he seemed unperturbed.

"How come Renate doesn't go to see him anymore?" I asked.

"Didn't you know? He emigrated to Holland last fall."

"Oh." I thought a while, then. "Could I go to Mossi's house if he asked me?"

"Why not?"

"Then why can't I go to Steffi's?"

"Don't start that again." Mother sounded cross.

Father threw me a warning glance, but I avoided his eyes. No, I wouldn't let it pass again.

"Isn't it time for your cake? I can smell it." Father was trying to head me off.

He was right, the cake did smell done. Walking to the kitchen, I thought bitterly that he was an avoider of issues. Ostrich politics, as Tante Gert had said. Why did he always ignore problems? That wouldn't make them go away. You had to do something about them. Gently I stuck the long aluminum needle into the middle of the cake, withdrew it, noted that it was clean; my cake was done. Yes, and it was high time that I stopped the nonsense of going to the Levys' secretly; Mother could be made to see.

Aggressively, I returned to the dining room; now was

the time. "Mother," I said loudly.

"Ellen!"

We had said it almost simultaneously. We laughed.

"Ellen!" This time she had been faster than I. "Ellen, we have decided about this summer."

"You have!" All thoughts of issues fled—the summer! Would they let me go to Caputh this year? I sat down carefully, passing my hands along the back of my legs to straighten my skirt; if I didn't wrinkle it, it would be good luck. "Yes?"

"Papi and I have decided to go to Hungary, to Budapest. Our passports will run out in October; God knows when they will be renewed."

I listened impatiently—get on, get on, what about me?

"Anyhow, Renate, of course, can't leave her job, but we think that you would love Budapest."

Only the tentative note in her voice kept me from despair.

"On the other hand, if you really insist, I suppose this would be a good summer for Caputh."

I was out of my chair, my arms around her neck, yelling, "I insist, I insist, really!" And then at the phone.

"Steffi? Listen Steffi, guess what?"

The marvelous thing was that just two weeks earlier on a rainy afternoon Herr Levy had come into Steffi's room, where we had lain on the floor pasting pictures of movie stars into her scrapbook. He had waved a tiny black book at us.

"What's that, Papa?" Steffi asked.

"That, Sarale, is riding in a canoe."

"What do you mean?"

"That's dancing the horah."

"Papa?"

"That's singing 'Simche B' Jerushalajim!!'"

"He means Caputh," I shouted, jumping up, but Steffi remained on the floor; she was crying. Herr Levy sat down on the floor next to her.

"Here," he said and opened the little book. He pointed to some tiny figures. "See? It is enough!"

Steffi cried into his shoulder. Frau Levy was leaning against the door jamb, one crutch under her armpit, the other limp by her side. Tears were streaming out of her eyes too.

Which explains why we had been so afraid that I couldn't go. Herr Levy had saved for nineteen months; it didn't bear thinking about what would have happened if my parents had said no again.

Our parents finally met each other at the bus stop.

Father was decent. He shook hands with Herr Levy and bowed over Frau Levy's fingers. Mother was dreadful; gracious, yes! Oh damned gracious. And while the honey smile stayed plastered to her teeth, I saw her sharp eyes listen, saw them hear that Herr Levy called me *Kätzele*, and saw them observe that I knew how to help Frau Levy with her crutches; suddenly I felt a spiteful satisfaction that Mother was finding out in this manner. I kissed Frau Levy first before I kissed Mother good-by, which earned me a cool, stiff cheek. But when we were inside the bus, when I saw the Levys standing next to my parents, all in frozen attitudes of the wave, and the forced smile, I felt bad. Not spiteful anymore, just bad. Frau Levy with overbright eyes and Herr Levy, shrunken next to the straightness of Father. And Father, all unconcern, only a friendly, have-a-good-time in his eyes, and Mother completely preoccupied with coping with my duplicity.

"She couldn't care less that she won't see me for the next four weeks," I thought.

In fact, she was glad that I wasn't coming along to Budapest, she had never intended for me to go. The reason that I was going to Caputh was because it was convenient for Mother.

Steffi and I were assigned to a room at Reimanhaus, right next door to Nanny, and we sailed right into a full summer program. The water sports, bicycle tours, games. Steffi took to it like the proverbial duck. Her short black curls bouncing, the flashing eyes full of happiness. Her long legs were brown in the short canvas shorts from Palestine which we were all wearing.

"See, it's as I told you; this is even better for you than for me," I said, and she agreed that it was great, *knorke!* Within a week she was a Zionist—her father was wrong about passively waiting for the Messiah; she would convince him of that.

So I didn't really know what it was that bothered me one night. I just couldn't get any rest. Everyone else slept. The moon was right in the room with us. Like dusty sunshine, it lay in a broad stripe on the floor; what was I feeling so uneasy about? Wide awake and as a tongue moves gingerly over the smoothness of a tooth, I searched for the source of my pain. Mutti and Papi? The scene at the bus terminal? No, not really. Renate? Yes. But why? Then I remembered. The day before leaving for Caputh I had seen Luz Fichtel. No, Luz Heidemann. She had been waiting at the bus stop at the corner of Wilhelmsdorferstrasse and Kurfürstendamm. Quickly, I had looked away, but she had seen me. "Ellen," she called and I had to stop.

We shook hands. I felt awkward; embarrassed and angry. I wanted to say something cutting, letting her know what I thought of her but as I met her eyes, saw her clear blue look and tendrils of wheat-colored hair and her soft pink lips, the anger evaporated. Instead I was suddenly sad. In fact, it was eerie, but I knew that she understood just what I felt, and I was not surprised when she asked, "How is he?" and that I answered, "All right, I think." Her bus had come quicky, and I had walked on and not thought of it again until now.

And what did it have to do with now? Because I was thinking about pain? But whose? The pain I had sensed in Luz? The pain I feared Rudi would give Renate? Or just pain— grown-up sorrow? Oceans of it, waving wheat fields; my stomach hurt. I threw myself on my other side, face to the wall, away from the moon and the fragrance of the night. The whole thing was ridiculous, simply ridiculous. First of all, who cared about Luz and secondly, if she still loved Rudi that didn't mean that he loved her, and even if he did, he need not hurt Renate because Renate was old enough to take care of herself; she wouldn't let herself be hurt. And anyhow, I was probably imagining the whole thing. After all, what was so remarkable about Luz asking how Rudi was? Probably all divorced women inquired about their ex-husbands like that—"How is he?"

On the last day of camp when our parents would come to pick us up, we were going to perform *Twelfth Night* for them. I wanted desperately to play Olivia.

"If music be the food of love, play on!" to have that said about me, and for me, cold and haughty, to be "the owner of the heart which now abhors to like his love."

I would smile; I would be irresistible.

However, I was picked to be Maria, the ribald maid. But since Nanny's friend Hanns played Toby, I didn't really suffer too much; he was very funny.

And so the day of the play came and it was bittersweet; the summer was over. Our counselor had burned my hair into a thousand ringlets to make me look like Maria. I teetered on her high, high heels and shouted raucously, "Why appear you in this ridiculous boldness before my lady?"

In the audience Father laughed so loudly that it was quite a scandal. He laughed even at the spots where he was not supposed to laugh.

Renate said that it had been the happiest summer of her life. She was wearing her hair differently, piled softly on top with only one long strand hanging over her shoulder and a deep wave over one cheek.

"Look at my neck," she said to me as she brushed it up.

"Yes, oh swan."

"Seriously, I never noticed before that I have a good neck."

"And God knows what other hidden charms." Oh my tongue had sharpened during a summer of living on repartee!

Renate blushed. "The job is fantastic. Herr Dr. Klain says that I'm the best secretary he ever had. Do you know that we just wrote a patent for a snake charmer in India?" She was babbling.

I knew it, and I knew why. But the snake charmer caught me just the same. "Seriously?"

She launched into the story. This Indian gentleman had invented a better reed flute, he was employing eighteen women to carve these flutes, and his brother-in-law who was a sailor from Hamburg had advised him to have it patented. Only later that night, alone in our room, I thought again of the blush and the neck, the glow and the new laugh. "Where are you going?" I had asked as she stuffed the little silver bag Mother had passed on to her.

"Oh . . . out . . ." vaguely.

"Do they know?" With a motion of my head I indicated the direction of our parents' bedroom next door.

"I'll be back before them."

They were having a reunion party with some people they had met in Budapest. "Half the Jews of Berlin were there," they had told us. "Everyone is trying to travel before we lose our passports."

It was only the second night I was back home; no one seemed to feel it necessary to celebrate reunion with me. I called Steffi, and we talked until her mother chased her off the telephone, but I told her absolutely nothing about Renate.

13

The famous Sign finally made its appearance in Berlin too. The Olympic games were over, the foreigners were gone. Now movie houses, restaurants, and beaches proclaimed that Jews and dogs were verboten. As it happened, I witnessed the posting of the Sign at the bath-house on the swimming beach at the Stölpchensee.

It was a beautiful, warm Sunday during the first week-end in September. Though it was a long ride to the Stölpchensee —on the train and the bus—Steffi had argued that it would pay. "One more breath of good air before we go back to school," she had begged; she missed Caputh.

Mossi Fürstenbach and a friend of his came along with us. And Steffi had been right, it was worth it. The lake was a shimmering expanse of blue, dotted generously with sailboats, and the crescent-shaped beach had unusually light sand, which was still warm and soft to the touch. Dark green pine woods abutted the beach from above. And a feeling of the last of summer made us exuberant.

We had all been swimming but had found the water too icy to stay in for long, and now only Mossi remained in the lake; the rest of us were playing rummy.

"He must have snake blood," Steffi proclaimed. "It adapts to any temperature."

"No," his friend argued. "It's his age. When you get to be sixteen your blood cools."

I laughed but picked up Mossi's towel and walked down to the water's edge. I worried; he had just gotten over a bad cold, he shouldn't stay in so long. I motioned to him to come out. Mossi had a funny way of swimming, a combination of many styles, which he called the Fürstenbach Stroke. It took a while for him to reach the shore. And when he finally stood up in the shallow part and waded toward me, I felt very affectionate—he was such a nice boy. Making windmills of his long arms, shivering exaggeratedly, he clowned, tried to hug me with ice-cold arms.

"Stop it," I scolded. "Here, put this around you; you'll be sick again tomorrow."

"Yes, little mother." But he let me drape the towel around his shoulders.

We turned to look out over the lake once more before rejoining the others, and that's when we saw it.

Where the water had been calm just these few moments ago, it now churned with the approach of ten or twelve black motorboats—in fan-shaped formation, they were zeroed in on the beach. From the largest boat came the bullhorn sound; a sort of moaning siren, chilling me.

Quickly, we walked back to the others.

"Put the cards away," Mossi commanded. He was shivering badly.

"You stayed in the water too long," I scolded. I rubbed his back, making the rough towel scrub hard over his skin.

"*Achtung! Achtung! You are surrounded!*"

Indeed the sound seemed to come from all around us. Our eyes traveled the slow circuit, saw the motorboats now idling just off shore, they were really dark gray I noticed, the black-clad SS men by the boathouse where a huge truck was parked, and up above us, along the edge of the woods, more SS; every few feet, machine pistols pointed into the crowd. And the crowd of maybe two hundred people who moments earlier had been sunning themselves, had been eating sandwiches out of waxpaper and drinking beer from green bottles, the crowd who had been throwing brilliant beach balls at each other—that crowd stood now, mesmerized, transfixed. And the round booming voice of the megaphone was as a fence all around.

"Do not be alarmed! Everyone will be released! This is a search for Undesirables!"

At the end the bullhorn coughed a hoarse echo—*Undesirables!* Booomm—ending in a little screech.

"That's us!" Mossi's friend cracked and we hushed him quickly.

The bullhorn directed us. Somehow, we had gotten dressed, were herded into lines, stood waiting—a men's line, a women's line. It was hot and strange; I noticed how tangled Steffi's curls were and gave her my comb, and we inched slowly toward the big SS man who was examining identification cards.

Ahead of us was an enormous woman. I craned around her fat back to see the SS man look at the student bus pass of a tall girl with fat pigtails. He was joking with her, it slowed up the line.

"Na, Gretchen, na, not even a drop of Jewish blood?" And motioning her on, to the fat lady, "How about you, Frau Müller?"

Frau Müller's layers shook, her giggle was obscene, silver tinkly as from a table bell, too small for her bulk.

Then it was my turn. He glanced carelessly at my bus pass, then at me; blackheads twinkling like facets of mica points in his craggy face, he laughed "Ellen Westheimer? Eh?" Suddenly he bellowed out, scaring me. "Hey Klaus," he yelled across to the other line, "hey, look at this one!"

He had picked up a strand of my hair, held it aloft. The other SS man looked over. "That one?" he shouted back.

I yanked my hair free. "Can I go?" If only my voice hadn't shook.

"Ja, ja, go, little one."

Then Steffi was through too, and we walked toward the exit. And that's when we saw them nail up the Sign—Jews and dogs verboten.

"Well, that's clear enough," I said, trying to avoid Steffi's eyes.

"Where are the boys?" she asked.

We saw Mossi's friend first. "They are taking all the Jewish men over sixteen!" he was chattering. "I am telling you, I heard him, they are taking all the men over sixteen."

"Heard whom?"

"Heard the officer."

We looked into each face that passed, we waited.

"But where is Mossi?" I blurted to his friend at last.

"I don't know. He was ahead of me in the line. I told you but you won't believe me—they are taking them over sixteen. I heard him . . ." His voice went on and on, grating.

Just the same, we kept on waiting for Mossi.

Later a truck roared off. We scanned it carefully. Was Mossi among the men in back? We couldn't see. So we stood there some more.

At last Steffi said it. "Let's go," she said. Then we ran for the bus.

At the train station we said good-by to Mossi's friend, who was going in a different direction. "Don't forget tomorrow," he yelled after us.

"Tomorrow?" Steffi asked after we were settled in facing seats. "What's tomorrow?"

"Remember? He asked us before. He is having a birthday party."

"Oh ja. I remember now." Steffi looked stricken. "It's his sixteenth birthday, isn't it?" She took my hand. "Oh Ellen . . ."

I nodded, then stared out of the window. But it didn't help; I started to cry.

The Jewish Kultur Bund had been created as an answer to the edict that banned all Jewish actors from performing for the German public. The same law also prohibited Jews from attending any German performance. It was really a laugh; *they* thought that they were penalizing us, but we had all the finest talent now and the best performances just for ourselves. Even Mother admitted that *Norma* sung at the Kultur Bund topped anything she had ever heard at the Staats Oper.

Mother was more doubtful about the excellence of the forthcoming play in which I would appear. Our *Twelfth Night* at Caputh had been such a success that arrangements had been made to have us present it in Berlin at the Kultur Bund. However, since some of the vacation children had come from the far corners of Germany and couldn't return, we had to recast.

"And thus the whirligig of time brings in his revenges"; I became Olivia at last. All through that fall I was allowed to go to Caputh every Friday afternoon to attend rehearsals over the weekend. So was Steffi, who played Viola; perfectly! She was the real star of the play.

And then, two days before the performance was scheduled in Berlin, "permission to assemble" was withdrawn.

"They can't do that!" I stormed over the phone when Hanns called with the news.

"Yes they can."

"Some grubby little official, feeling mean."

"Don't be a baby, Ellen. It came right from the Reich's Ministerium für Kultur."

"Does that mean that they are closing the Kultur Bund for good?"

"Who knows?"

I could practically see Hanns, standing there in Caputh, shrugging his shoulders. Damn him. No, damn them. Don't be a baby, he had said. He sounded like my parents with that scared awe of officialdom. The Nazis, the Nazis, I was getting sick of it all.

Christa was terribly disappointed that the performance was called off. She had taken a great interest; Steffi and I had to render an exact account of our doings in Caputh after each weekend; she said that it sounded like a wonderful place. "How I envy you," she said.

"That's crazy, be glad that you're a fine, blond Aryan," Steffi teased.

"You think that's so great? I tell you, it's not! My father is half out of his mind; the things he says. Every day when I come home from school I'm scared.

"Scared of what?"

"That they have arrested him."

"But Christa, they only arrest Jews."

"That's what you think—the Nazis make it worse for Aryans who oppose them."

Steffi and I shook our heads; Christa was almost worse than our parents with her talk about the Nazis. Her father didn't want her to go to the BDM meetings anymore. "His face turns turkey red; he becomes furious when he hears what they tell us."

"So don't go; you don't care, do you?" I said.

"Ellen, you're so stupid; I have to go. If I stay away they'll investigate us. I have to go for Father's sake, but he just refuses to understand. Every Wednesday we have the same scene—'*Himmel, Herrgott, Sakrament,* I will not have you . . .'" In spite of herself, Christa started to laugh, her father's cursing was famous.

Just the same, I asked Steffi whether she didn't think that Christa was overdramatizing the whole thing. "I mean, they can't possibly investigate every child who doesn't come to meetings."

Steffi shrugged; her father thought that nothing was beyond the Nazis.

"Yes, but you know that your father is an awful pessimist."

"Who knows? Sometimes I wonder; maybe he's right."

"It couldn't be that bad," I said vigorously.

"No, I guess not," Steffi agreed.

Renate and I discussed it too. She said that Rudi had told her that it was true, that the Nazis did keep a sharp eye on nonsympathizers.

"How does he know?"

"Oh he knows a lot."

"Because he used to be a lawyer? Anyhow, what does he do there? At the Jewish Community Office?"

She looked at me seriously. I had been at the desk doing my homework, but had turned around to face her in the little slipper chair before the window. It was Sunday afternoon and the first nasty autumn weather of the year.

"I really don't know," she said. The rain was drumming on our panes.

I felt suddenly happy, it was, at last, a good conversation we were having. As in the old days. "Or can't you tell me?" I asked.

"I couldn't if I knew. But I really don't. I think he is protecting me by not telling."

A shiver rippled along my spine. "You mean he does something dangerous?"

She nodded. "Not officially, of course. Officially he pushes papers around." She laughed. "His phrase."

"Have you any idea?" I was whispering.

So was she. "Most of all, I keep wondering—who helps him?"

"You mean?" We had both seen Willy Frisch in *Poppies*. Willy, chief heroin smuggler, link in a chain. "You mean he might be smuggling something? Jewels?"

She shrugged. "I don't know. He keeps disappearing for three, four days; then he is back."

We stared at each other. The windows rattled in a gust of wind. Again I shivered. Then, in my normal voice, which sounded loud, "He probably sees his other girl in those days."

Renate rose, she was pale. "Very funny! And don't ever talk about it, with anyone. Do you hear?"

Insulted, I replied, "I'm writing to the Gestapo now."

But after Renate left, back in the middle of biology, I wondered—jewels? Yes, people smuggled jewelry and money out of Germany. Money for poor American relatives to deposit in their bank accounts in order to be able to give affidavits. And people smuggled people too—one heard such stories.

It was already cold, a windy day, when I saw that Mossi had come back. He was standing before the Synagogue with his father. I started running toward them, but as I came closer, I slowed down; there was something forbidding in the way they stood there. At last we faced each other. "Hello, Mossi," I said lamely.

"Hello, Ellen." He didn't introduce me.

I didn't know what to say. I wanted to ask a million questions, I wanted to touch his hand, to cry how happy I was, but the sick shock had dried my mouth. "I'm so glad to see you," I managed at last.

"Yes," he answered.

He was looking at me and yet I felt that he was not seeing anything. And what was it that was so different about him? Not just the stubbly-haired head. Of course he was awfully thin, and the pallor instead of the red cheeks . . .

I opened my mouth to say something else, anything. But he spoke first. "Well good-by," he said. His voice was raspy.

"Have you got a cold again?" I blurted, but they walked into the sanctuary without answering me.

From then on I saw Mossi in Synagogue every Friday night. Except that he didn't sit in the children's section anymore. If I ran into him face to face, I would say, "Good Shabbos, Mossi," and I would smile, but he just looked at me blankly, as if he didn't even see me.

"I mean, I think it's crazy. It's not my fault that he was arrested," I said to Steffi.

"My father says that they all act like that when they come back."

"Who?" I asked loudly. Everyone always got that funny, hushed tone into their voices when they talked about such things.

"Everyone who comes back from concentration camp. From K.Z.," Steffi added.

"Well, I just don't understand. We were such good friends. I thought he would ask me to be his girl pretty soon. I mean—before . . ."

Steffi shrugged.

"You'd think he would feel better if he talked it out, if he confided in me. He can't brood about it forever."

Steffi shrugged again.

And now our ice-skating rink, a converted tennis court called Das Wintermärchen, the winter fairy tale, also sprouted the sign. We had skated there since we were little when, in long snakes, we had raced around and around, annoying the grown-ups who, with cross-linked hands, were gliding about sedately. And Mr. Grieg's masterpiece had blared over the loudspeaker, again and again. We had drunk countless cups of scalding Maggi bouillon purchased from Herr Bautner, who also sold coils of licorice, hot cocoa, and jelly apples in his wooden hut. Finished. Jews and dogs verboten!

"I hope they go out of business; most of the children who skated there were Jewish," I told Father. Then I laughed, "Though I never saw any dogs skating at the Wintermärchen."

"It isn't their fault," he replied. "They have no choice; such orders come from above."

"Sure, sure. Why don't you weep for them?"

"Ellen!"

Of course, I didn't care! What with school and my friends, Synagogue, and the youth performances at the Kultur Bund, I was too busy to skate that winter anyhow. I really was. Also too busy to worry about Renate. Anyhow, she said that she was happy, so why was she crying at night when she thought that I was sleeping?

No, they hadn't closed the Kultur Bund, just forbidden that one performance, ours. It certainly didn't make sense.

"Since when do you expect them to make sense?" Steffi asked.

"That's true. And I bet no Christian children get to see Shakespeare and Ibsen all in one month," I answered; I was scanning the youth program.

We agreed on that too and therefore managed to talk ourselves into a third ticket to *Hamlet*. Christa was wild to go.

"We've got it!" I shouted over the phone when we had obtained the extra ticket.

"Oh, great!" Christa shouted back.

"Don't wear your BDM uniform by mistake, wear something Jewish."

"Donkey! Like what?"

"Like a sad face."

"That's easy with my *tzuris*." Christa used all the Jewish expressions she had picked up at Steffi's house. I did too; that is, I did away from home. At our house they were considered dirty language. Mother said she would not have me talk that way.

CHAPTER

14

Christa met Carlheinz Breiten-
bach at the Jewish Kultur Bund, at the *Hamlet* performance. It
was the first time in our lives that any of us had witnessed
"love at first sight."

"First of all, they are too young, and secondly, he's
Jewish," Steffi stated.

"He's nineteen already," I protested. I didn't want
anything to be less than perfect with this romance.

"So Carlheinz has found himself a little *shiksa*." My
mother laughed.

"Are you serious?" I asked. I stared at her with all the
contempt I could muster. "Even you can't be that blind! Christa
a little *shiksa!*"

"I was only kidding." Mother pulled back.

When a Jewish boy found himself a little *shiksa*—always
little, like little dressmakers—it meant that he was up to no
good, that he was sowing his wild oats. "He wouldn't do that
with a nice Jewish girl!"

It made me furious. It was just one more thing in a
long row of grievances. I felt that Mother had an uncanny
talent to miss the point of anything that concerned me. We
might as well live in a different world, in another century.
Only her nerves were suffering under the Nazis. I spoke about
it to Steffi. "It's as if she thinks that she's the only sensitive
creature in the world, and it's their friends who drink too much
because of their worries and their friends whose marriages are

breaking up because they are under emotional pressure," I said. "But she never once considers that there might be pressures on us too. I don't want to die a virgin!"

"Ellen!"

"Well, I don't!" But I started to laugh. "Actually, that phrase isn't original with me; Katrine used it the other day."

"She didn't!"

"Yes she did. She said that rules were for the good old times when a girl could expect normal things to happen to her, like graduating from school, getting engaged, working on your trousseau, and getting married."

"I still expect to do all that," Steffi said.

"Yes. But you know what Katrine means."

"Oh, Katrine!"

We sat and thought of Katrine—of Katrine, waving her fingers to dry the daring nail polish she sported away from home. "It's wild, isn't it? Gerhardt loves it."

We were hearing a lot about Gerhardt. He was eighteen. Between ourselves, Steffi and I had speculated how far Katrine was going, whether she let him kiss her . . .

In any case, Katrine had real dates; Gerhardt had a car and money. As for her parents, they didn't know that he existed. "They'd kill me," she had assured us.

As a result, Katrine went through quite a routine every day when she left her house. First the long braids had to be undone, brushed, fluffed, and twisted into an upsweep. This hairdo made her look very old, at least seventeen we thought. Then she had to put on the nail polish and rouge and mascara. She often used my house for this ritual and also arranged for her alibi with me. "I'm going to Ellen's," she told her parents truthfully; sometimes she would stay for fifteen minutes.

"Dear God in heaven," I had once said to Steffi, "she looks like a courtesan."

Romi was wearing lipstick too, but she didn't have to do it secretly. "My mother thinks if she is broadminded I won't do things behind her back," Romi had remarked, laughing her new laugh, very high. It was like the cigarettes. She was permitted to smoke one a day, which she did officially. "Mother beams 'Look how clever I am, how modern'; she even lights it for me. She should know how many I really smoke; Packs and packs; I am addicted!"

Now Steffi expressed what we had been thinking. "Some great moral influence those nuns are having on Romi and Katrine."

I nodded, but then I insisted, "Just the same, Katrine has a point. Life is just not normal anymore. I mean, we may have to leave Germany, or *they* may close all the Jewish schools, and anyhow, with no one allowed to go to university, how can the boys become doctors and lawyers? How can they marry and support us?"

"My parents didn't have much education, but they believed in keeping the rules."

"That was because of their religion!" I said it positively; I was sure.

Steffi nodded thoughtfully. She and I were always discussing religion these days; Steffi was wondering about some of the things her parents took for granted. Was religion outmoded? But now she said, "I guess it's good to have rules!" Her face lit up; she hated to be in conflict with her parents, she was always glad to be able to argue their point of view. "How else could they have survived the hardships, the persecution in Poland? Why, without religion . . ."

"Of course," I interrupted excitedly; things were crystal clear suddenly; I had never thought of it like this before. "And that's what the 'enlightened' "—I said the word angrily and with irony—"German Jews don't understand and don't have—moral standards. Instead they drink and mess up their marriages. And break the rules, like Katrine."

"You don't think she really does?" Steffi asked. Her eyes were very big.

"I don't know," I answered. "The way she talks, as though there were no tomorrows . . ." I stopped short. What an awful thing to say. The cold hand was around my stomach. I stared at Steffi, whose eyes had gotten even bigger.

"What would you do?" she asked in a whisper. "I mean, if you really knew that you would die tomorrow, would you . . ." She couldn't finish the question.

I thought about it deeply. And as I did, I realized that it was not really a new thought. I had already scrutinized it when I had come to terms with Renate's decision. Or had I? Come to terms with it? Of course not. I didn't even know anything about it.

I burst out laughing. So did Steffi. We laughed and laughed. When we could talk again, I answered her question. "If I knew positively, I mean absolutely positively, I guess I would, but . . ." And we burst into giggles again. "The question would be: With whom?"

Steffi, Christa, and I often had these conversations now. It was Christa who was most realistic about The Times. "We have to be prepared for anything; there might be a war."

"Oh Christa, no."

But all three of us felt that there had to be a way to stay decent, as we called it. Decent was more than moral, decent was also being a good sport, a good friend, having a sense of humor, being tough. After we had worked Katrine over thoroughly, we decided that what was wrong with her was that she wasn't decent anymore. We did not file this charge against her on moral grounds; we felt that she was soft, succumbing to the pressures of The Times.

It was different for Renate, of course, because she was older, and it was different with Carlheinz and Christa. In spite of Christa's cool realism, she regarded her falling in love with Carlheinz as an outright miracle, right out of the fairy tales. As for their difference of religion, she thought that was too bad, and of course she would have to become Jewish when she married him. But it was only too bad in the way that she thought it had been too bad that Romeo's and Juliet's people hadn't gotten along. Unlike them, she and Carlheinz would be smart; they would triumph.

"Just the same, you're too young," Steffi persisted right to Christa's face.

"You're right," Christa agreed. "We are too young." She shrugged. "But it happened." There was no arguing with miracles; they were a kind of reality as well. And because Christa accepted them, we did too. All together, who could tell about love? Steffi said that some people were fated.

"How do you know? You've never even been in love." I challenged.

"I just know!"

An edict was passed by the government which decreed that all Jewish women would henceforth carry the name Sarah in addition to and before their first names. All Jewish men would be known as Israel. The official who issued my new identification papers laughed loudly when he looked at me.

"Ho, Sarah Ellen; you sure are some example of a non-Aryan." He pinched my cheek, but I jerked away; I wouldn't joke with any of *them*.

Mother was very upset. "I might as well have kept the name Selma; Sarah is just as bad, another cow's name."

"It is not! Sarah is a proud name, don't you know any Jewish history?" I argued.

Herr Levy had read us from the commentaries of the sages, all about Sarah. The wife of the patriarch was considered a heroine; Herr Levy had said that as usual the Nazis were making donkeys of themselves. Any Jewess would be proud to carry a name of such fame; that's why he had chosen it for his Sarale. . . . I left the Levys' house feeling peaceful; if *they* had intended humiliation, they were wrong. But I could convey none of this to Mother. "This Sarah business is terrible," she insisted. "And my poor Ernstl—Israel!"

Father laughed. "They picked a good one for me," he said. "It so happens it's my Jewish name anyhow."

"I didn't know you had a Jewish name," I said, surprised.

"Sure. Israel ben Moshe. My father's name was Moses." Mother snorted but we ignored her.

"But why didn't you ever tell me?" I asked. "And why don't I have a Jewish name?"

He shrugged. "Well, you know, we had gotten away from all that."

"It's a good thing that the Nazis corrected your oversight."

"Don't be fresh, Ellen," Mother broke in. Father said nothing.

Tante Gert had been as good as her word. Our affidavits arrived six months after she had emigrated. Onkel Wolf was working at a hospital, he had passed his language examination. Tante Gert wrote, "Though God knows how; he speaks English with the thickest Bavarian accent; but the children at the hospital love him. Do you remember how he would come into the room with his hat on upside down and say, *'Ich bin der Dokter Lutsch-Bonbon?'* Well, now he says, 'I'm Dr. Lollipop.' It works just as well in English." Soon he would go into private practice.

Father opened a bottle of champagne and we drank to America; Mother cried.

"Oh Mother, really! I can't wait to get out of here," I said, but then I went to my room and cried a little bit too. It would be so strange.

When Father came home from the American Consulate the next day, he waved a blue card. "We have a number!"

"What is it, what kind of a number?"

"A quota number. 5683."

"Is that good?"

"About two years, the man said."

Mother brightened.

As I said to the girls, two years was a lifetime; I couldn't hold my breath that long.

Grandfather was also, and visibly, relieved. But he insisted that it was terrible; that the criminal Roosevelt was to blame for everything, that the stingy emigration quotas were a disgrace. Then he shrugged. "No one cares what happens to the Jews.

"Including you!" I replied.

"Ellen!" Mother exclaimed, but Grandfather laughed. "She's got a point."

Grandfather and I had lately become friends and roommates. He had had a bout of pneumonia, and Frau Hegelsheimer, his housekeeper, had not taken proper care of him. So Mother said. As a result, he moved in with us for his convalescence, and since we didn't have guest rooms anymore, he slept in Renate's bed, while Renate camped at Kate's. I had dreaded both the invasion, the embarrassment, and the need to accommodate myself to him, but it worked out surprisingly well. Evenings he sat in the living room drinking cognac; I had my room to myself. And when he came to bed in his long nightgown he turned the light off discreetly before I heard the click of his teeth dropping into his toothglass. Sometimes we talked in the dark—he told me about his childhood, about how he had helped in his parents' bakery, until it burned to the ground. "Then they sent me to be an apprentice in Leipzig." And he told me how he had sold a pair of shoes to the Grossfürstin von Würtenberg, and how he had saved my mother when she was eight years old and had been caught in a burning house.

"That's probably why she is so afraid of fire," I said. "Such an experience can make you hysterical."

"To be sure," Grandfather agreed earnestly. Then he snorted. "That, and being hysterical by nature!" We giggled in the dark. Then he slept, snoring mightily. I liked him.

Though I was glad to have Renate back, I was sorry when he was well enough to go home; I felt that he had to be lonesome now that Jews couldn't go to the zoo anymore and he had no place to meet his retired gentlemen friends. I visited him often.

"What's the matter, Ellen? Short of money again?" he asked when I came the third day in a row.

"No, I just thought you might like company."

"Well, that's very nice of you."

Frau Hegelsheimer called him for dinner.

"Would you like to join me?"

"No, thank you. I have to go home; I just looked in."

He was sticking the big white napkin between the two top buttons of his vest, then he uncorked the half-bottle of wine which he drank with each meal, poured the first quarter glass, tasted it loudly on his tongue, and said, "Ah!" I felt he was all right and left satisfied.

Mother said that he had his skat and his poker and the newspaper; he was fine. Father agreed with her. "Of course he is all right. As long as he can hate Roosevelt and make fun of Ruth, he is fine."

Tante Ruth had long since married The Scrubber without Bristles. She now pushed him around in the same manner in which she had ordered Onkel Kurt about; I couldn't see where the change of husbands was any improvement, though Nanny said that the difference was that Heinrich never got mad. He just said, "Yes, sweetness," and "Of course, love," and "Naturally, *Liebling*" to everything.

"It drives Mother wild!" Nanny laughed.

Nanny was going to England with a children's transport soon.

"But what about your parents? I mean, won't you miss them?"

"Come on, Ellen! I have been away from home for a long time, and anyhow, until your parents go to America and send papers for Mother and Heinrich, they have no way to get out."

Listening to her, I thought about the fact that suddenly

it was completely taken for granted that we must leave. I said it out loud, "It's not *if* anymore, it's *when* and *where*."

"Yes. And what about the people who have no place to go? What will happen to them? Like Hanns and his family."

"Maybe they'll be the last to laugh," I suggested. "Maybe all this will blow over, and there we will be, scattered all over the world, and they'll sit nicely and snug at home."

"Maybe." Nanny shrugged. Then she laughed. "Anyhow, if you can't get my mother and The Scrubber out, they'll go to Shanghai."

"Shanghai, China?"

"Yes, he has a cousin there who owns a fleet of rickshaws. Can you imagine Heinrich pulling a rickshaw?"

The image was marvelous; we could see it clearly. Heinrich between the shafts, Tante Ruth on the little seat inside the rickshaw. His round, oily face with the grin and dark spots of sweat on his blue pajamas. Tante Ruth would wield the whip—faster, faster. "Yes, my treasure, yes, I'm running already!"

"Not too funny," I said remorsefully after we had laughed sufficiently.

Grandfather once reacted to a remark I had made about them by shrugging and saying that Tante Ruth wasn't the best judge of men, but then, neither were the men she had married connoisseurs of women.

Frau Levy was not doing well. She was finding it harder and harder to get around. She had developed phlebitis in the bad leg. Because of poor circulation, Steffi said. Steffi was doing most of the housework now. More and more that spring Christa and I were at the Levy's helping Steffi. Herr Levy was busy at the store. "More Jews come in for alterations now because they have less money to buy new things," he explained. This brought along a modest prosperity for the Levys, and Herr Levy had bought a phonograph for his wife and Steffi. To our surprise,

Frau Levy loved Sara Leander and Marlene Dietrich as much as we did. She had a lovely alto voice and sang along with us. Her face was very, very thin now and the eyes and the tangled curls made her look more like Steffi than ever before. She talked fast in a light voice and she laughed a lot. One day when we were there, Christa and I decided to leave early because Frau Levy was running a fever; we felt we were in the way. I kissed her, felt her hot, dry cheek, and smelled the apple and cinnamon scent that was all hers.

"I love the way she smells," I said to Christa on the way home.

"All mothers do—mine smells of *Schnaps*," Christa replied bitterly.

Another time, when I picked up Steffi to go marketing, it burst out of her—"Oh Ellen, she is awfully sick!"

I kept on studying the shopping list, my throat felt tight. Carefully, from stall to stall at the market, we selected fish and cheese and the broad noodles which lay on a large, coarse linen cloth that was only a shade lighter than the noodles. We called the fat farmer's wife who made them the Nudel Liese. They were the best noodles to be had.

"What does the doctor say?" I managed at last.

Steffi shrugged. That shrug told everything.

"Isn't there anything he can do?" I insisted.

"He's trying a new medicine."

"It will work!" I said it positively.

"Your words in God's ear," Steffi answered.

Back at her house, we washed the lettuce, the carrots, and the *Kohlrabi*. Frau Levy told us what to do and under her direction we prepared dinner. Herr Levy closed the store at one o'clock and came home. He walked straight to his wife and kissed her. With his lips pursed on her forehead, I fancied that he took her temperature while he kissed her. He would turn from her and he and Steffi would exchange worried glances. Frau Levy was running a continuous fever.

Once at the table, neither Frau Levy nor Steffi would eat much.

"Why don't you eat?" I whispered angrily to Steffi while we were doing the dishes.

"What do you mean? I did eat."

"You won't be much help to them if you get sick too."

She stopped pretending. "I just can't! It won't go down."

Walking out into the late afternoon sunshine, I felt like a freak. All my worries were petty. At home, Mother was making supper, Rosemarie was off. I went to help her. Suddenly I thought that I didn't appreciate her enough; what if she got sick like Frau Levy? But it was unthinkable; Mother wasn't the type.

All that spring I was mad for tennis. I played every day at the J.S.K., the Jüdische Sports Klub, to which I belonged somewhat reluctantly because it was where Renate played and the only club my parents allowed me to join. Most of my friends belonged to the Bar Kochba, which was off limits for me because it was Zionist in philosophy and direction. The J.S.K.'s courts were near the Bayrischenplatz, and the only one of my friends who joined with me was Katrine. In fact, she was a kind of star there. Her tennis was excellent and her torrid romance with Gerhardt was our main topic of conversation. She lorded it over me in a very regal fashion. The six months which she was older than I, she said, made all the difference in the world. Accordingly, Gerhardt treated me kindly and like a dear little sister; sometimes they would give me a ride home in his car.

When Father heard about these rides he was furious.

"You won't enter that boy's car again. I forbid it categorically!"

"Oh Papi, Gerhardt drives as if his grandmother was lying in back with a ruptured appendix." This was, of course, not strictly true, but I considered that the situation called for strong measures.

"I don't care," said Father. "They are constantly arresting Jews for minor traffic offenses; I won't have you drive around with that boy."

"You drive."

"I've been driving for twenty years; and anyhow, I'm thinking about giving up the car too."

"You are?" Father without a car? That meant that he wouldn't be able to travel anymore. Had things become that bad? I shrugged off the thought. "What will I tell Gerhardt and Katrine? They'll think I'm a baby."

"Tell them anything you want, just don't enter that boy's car again."

Steffi said that he was right, and so did Christa.

"Listen," I argued with them, "I think you're both crazy. My father is being hysterical, that's all. I mean, what do you think they'd do to Katrine and me, even if they picked up Gerhardt? Shoot us?"

"You don't know," Steffi answered. "You may not always be able to ride on your blond hair."

Steffi's remark about the hair rankled. It reminded me of Mother's preoccupation with it. I had always thought that her pride in my blondness was ridiculous. Now I considered it carefully. Obviously, to Mother my light hair was the essence of my German looks, my passport to belonging. Steffi's remark indicated that I accepted Mother's premise. I decided that I must have a talk with Steffi, I would tell her that she was completely wrong.

In any case, I started to take my bike to the tennis courts.

A week later, riding there in the heat of midday, I thought resentfully how much more comfortable I might have been in Gerhardt's car. It was dry and still and I was early for my lesson, the only moving thing on the dinner-hour street; even the leaves on the trees that lined the avenue were motionless, dusty and limp. At the Wernerstrasse I began looking for the sign which should have been visible from there—it must have fallen off the rickety clubhouse, I thought. That clubhouse! A shack of wide, rough boards, and inside, the men's locker to the right and the women's to the left, and the smell of stale sweat and feet. The shower on the women's side didn't work and the toilet gurgled loudly, and since it was adjacent to the bar, it was embarrassing to use it. In the bar, which consisted of five tables and assorted chairs, but with flowers on each table, Frau Hildebrandt reigned supreme. She brought the flowers fresh from her garden every morning, she sold beer to the grownups and lemonade to us, and she also sold what she called *Amerikanische Sand Vitsches*, two slices of bread with limp lettuce, runny butter, and either Wurst or cheese. She was big and round, her huge bosom jutted forward, her face was red and beaming; I liked her. And for some reason, I was her favorite; she poured my lemonade glass extra full, she called me *Kleines*, little one, and she told me all about Hermann, her red-haired spitz who had a delicate constitution. She had to chew every bite of food for him and then feed him from her mouth. "That's the only way he'll eat," she said.

Riding along, pedaling as fast as I could, racing to victory in the seven-day race at Dresden, my ears pulsed with speed, I slid around the last corner and saw the club. Immediately I backpedaled to slow myself down. The club sign was stuck on the fence post, the courts were deserted, red clay baking in the stillness of the afternoon sun; something was terribly wrong. And in front, parked by the curb, was Gerhardt's car. I dismounted, pushed my bike along, and tried to breathe deeply; my chest felt tight. As I came abreast the club gate and the car, there was the curious choice of where to look. At the gate an official looking notice was posted. "By Order of . . . ," I read. And the car—slashed tires, the door hanging half off the hinge. I chose to look at neither. I walked slowly, carefully, I fastened my eyes to my bicycle, turned the loose rubber grip on the right handlebar around and around, feeling ridged rubber with tingling fingers. It took a long time to pass the scene, to walk as through a tunnel. And then the empty street was ahead of me, and I felt easier, and there came the familiar figure of Frau Hildebrandt. My face broke apart in a relieved grin; I hurried toward her. But when I was almost upon her, I saw that she looked past me, her face set in rigid redness, her eyes steely, determined not to see me. Quickly I averted my eyes from her and walked even faster. At the corner I stopped. I looked after her. Frau Hildebrandt's straight back was retreating steadily, getting smaller; otherwise, the street was empty, baking somnolently, dappled in sun and shade under the still trees. I scuffed my feet, making white marks on the cement squares, and I thought ruefully that Father would say, "I told you so."

But then I shrugged and swung back into the saddle. Around the corner I zoomed, stirring the air to life, thinking, "I am the wind."

The club remained closed and Gerhardt had disappeared.

All we knew was that his father was notified to remove the car and was charged a heavy fine for "Leaving a wreck littering the street." There had been blood all over the front seat, but not a trace of Gerhardt.

CHAPTER

15

The legend Move In, Move Out with Walter Trout was still painted in big white letters on moving vans though the firm did not belong to Herr Trout anymore. The trucks and their slogan were a familiar sight around Berlin.

The Trouts were distant acquaintances of my parents'. They had, so I heard, a castle by the Scharmützelsee.

"What do you mean, a castle?" I asked Mother.

"That's what they say; the Rotkorns were there for a weekend once, they say it is absolutely a castle."

It seemed that after Herr Trout had been forced to sell his moving business he had converted his summer house into a hotel.

Father shrugged. "It's the only place we can still go to, now that our passports have expired."

He was right. No Jewish passports were renewed except for the express purpose of emigration. In fact, in our family, Renate was the only one in possession of this valuable document. It had been issued to her as a result of an earlier plan Father had pursued. About a year ago it had become known that young girls could obtain one-year permits for England if they were requested as domestics. The requests were obtainable for a fee through a certain source. Father had followed it up, gotten all the papers for both Renate and me only to find that I was under the age limit. So it was decided that Renate, too, would stay together with the family, and that we would all await the American visas together. But, in any case, Renate had a passport and the joke around the house was that she should be sent to London, that there she would quickly meet and marry an American millionaire who would expedite our papers. The only one who did not care for the joke was Renate!

"Don't think that this isn't exactly what they'd like me to do," she said.

"Oh come on!" I laughed at her. "After Mother's experience with being married off, she'd hardly do it to us."

"That's what you think." Renate went back to her book.

The windows were wide open. I stared at her; she was sitting on our one comfortable chair. She was in some mood these days! Suddenly I said what had been on my mind. "Is Rudi *that* important to you?"

Renate put down her book and got up. She walked to the window, touched the curtains that were fluttering in a soft wind, stared out. She spoke in a low voice. "You just can't imagine how it is—I wake up tasting it, hurting . . ."

"But I thought that love makes you happy. They say it's like flying."

"Maybe that's the way it used to be—before. Now it seems to only be snatches—in between . . ."

I couldn't take my eyes off her, her expression. She was tucking in her blouse, stuffing it into the waistband of her skirt. I shook my head as if to clear it. I had seen her like this before. *Déjà vu?* No, this was real—two weeks ago, when Rudi had the grippe. We had taken some food to him. In his kitchen I had rummaged around. "Where could he be keeping his orange juice squeezer?" I asked Renate.

"Here it is, stupid." She had known exactly where to look.

"Thanks. For everything! Go sit with him."

Later I brought the glass in. I knocked and listened with hot ears to the shuffling. Renate had opened the door, tucking her blouse into the band of her skirt, her eyes huge and dark, pushing at her hair, saying crossly, "Since when can't you press down a door latch?"

"My hands are full."

Rudi had laughed. His cheeks had been a bright pink. From the fever, I thought. His bed was rumpled.

"Don't go near him; he's catching." She had taken the glass from me.

Now, remembering, I blushed. "It's almost summer," I said quickly. "You should get away. Papi said so too. He said you should come to the Scharmützelsee with us, that your boss has to give you a vacation.

"I can't get away just now; we're too busy."

But I persisted. "Listen Renate, I think you should. And Rudi too. Let them get used to the thought."

She flared. "I don't want Mother mixing in."

"But Renate. There is nothing she could do."

"Oh you know her, and Papi will make his dumb jokes."

"So what? Rudi knows him, he wouldn't care."

She calmed down. "All right, maybe. I'll talk to Rudi."

"Do it now. Come along this weekend."

"He isn't in town. No, not this weekend."

My first sight of the "castle" was, of course, disappointing. It neither looked like Schloss Charlottenburg nor like the Jagtschloss Grunewald, nor like Sans Souci. Those were the only castles I had ever seen. However, the house was certainly big and there were wonderful gardens around it; it was really a park. The lush lawn ran all the way down to the lake. And at the lake, a boathouse with a sundeck on top and there was a narrow, light gray sand beach. Gay umbrellas, slatted wooden cots, a white float bobbing off shore. "Say, this is great," I crowed.

The other guests were of my parents' crowd, very gay,

very attractive. There was only one thing wrong, Mother said. "There are no children for Ellen." But since it was in no way obvious when I wore a bathing suit that I was only fourteen, I passed as one of the "younger set." In any case, I passed during the days. At night, however, come ten o'clock, like Cinderella at midnight, I disappeared. Mother saw to that.

In a way, I was glad. Somehow the place scared me a little and it was hard to always act sophisticated.

But the thing I hated most was watching Mother and Father. Champagne for breakfast and the high-pitched laughter down at the beach. Once, when I ran into them and a group of their friends, Father grabbed my shoulders and pushed them back. "There, show what you have," he shouted and all of them thought it was funny. And at dinner it was more wine and naps were taken under the trees, in back of the gazebo. "The garden of Eden," Father said, "where the lamb lies with the lion." I avoided looking at Mother, I didn't want to see her response to that one; I also kept away from the proximity of their particular paradise.

Right after naptime the cocktail parties started; they never really stopped from then on. "Our" party and "their" party melting into the "regular" party which took place on the terrace just before supper in the dining room. I would sit with my parents while we had the evening meal, I would try to be on an island all by myself, buffeted, though, by waves of laughter. Why was everyone always shrieking? Some evenings I could hardly wait until it was time to say good night; I was reading Dostoevski.

Lying there, windows open wide, music and voices softened by distance, I could hear the isolated high laugh of a drunken woman, the occasional shout of a male voice. Also sometimes, the aching melodies of the special songs of that summer. Among the guests were two friends who wrote lyrics and music of haunting tunes; one especially—about a stranger in a foreign land, coming into a small kosher restaurant and finding candles on the tables and familiar food and people who know someone you once knew. Some of the older people cried when they heard that one. I, too, felt funny; lonesome already.

One of Father's friends, a jolly man, nicknamed me The Mezuzah. He said that it was difficult to pass without kissing me. "Can I take your lovely daughter rowing?" he asked Father one afternoon. With it went a deep bow, a funny face—may-I-have-this-dance-my-dear? Father laughed and so did I. I took his proffered arm. "I'll show you a special place," he promised.

I loved rowing; no, being rowed. It was nice of him to take me.

Off into the shimmering lake. All was blue, the sky, the lake, his eyes; he had a little mustache. I lay in the bottom of the boat on a pile of canvas pillows, my hands locked behind my head, feeling fine, suddenly quite grown-up. He was humming one of the songs that I liked so well. But when the little boat crunched to a wobbly stop and I sat up and looked into the dark pine woods that ringed the shore, I shook my head. "I'm not going in there," I said flatly.

"Afraid?"

"Careful."

"Little Mezuzahs shouldn't be so careful."

Listening to myself, surprised at the sophisticated dialogue I was producing, I answered, "That's how I stay pure."

"All right," he said, "but can a tired man rest after rowing a lady about?" He inched off his seat and was on his knees next to me.

"You'll upset the ship!"

He reached over the side and pushed the boat back into deeper water; it floated smoothly. I closed my eyes, felt the sun on my eyelids, saw colored circles all in golds go around and around in my head. And then Father's friend kissed me. Like in the movies, a long, slow kiss, warm and dry, and then his mouth moved, and he nibbled on my lip, and it was moist; I felt my chest tighten. All the time I was watching the scene behind my closed eyes—I was being kissed, really kissed, by a grown-up man, a dangerous man. But when he put his lips, suddenly burning, on my neck and cupped a breast in his hand, I sat up, startled.

"Careful," he shouted, but it was too late. Back and forth swung the little craft, and I slid over the side, he after me. It wasn't very deep, we were able to stand. We rightened the row boat and then from opposite sides of it, we looked at each other. He burst into shouts of laughter. I joined in, but I really felt like crying.

It was embarrassing to land in my wet shorts and sweater, but luckily Mother wasn't around the dock. Only Father was right there. He watched us tie up. "What happened?" he called.

"I took Ellen for a swim," his friend replied earnestly.
Father made comical eyebrows.
I climbed out and started walking away.
"Bad little Mezuzah," Father's friend called after me, but I pretended not to hear.

The costume ball had been planned as the climax of the summer. Without much discussion, it was perfectly clear that this party of parties was more than farewell to the season. By next year some of us would probably be at the "Small Kosher Restaurant in a Foreign Land" which we had been singing about. And maybe we would meet there and maybe not, but, as Father put it, "In any case, let's have another!" He raised the champagne bottle to his mouth, he stuck the whole neck between his lips; he drank deeply.

He also insisted that he and Mother would go to the ball as Adam and Eve. "Oh Papi," I said impatiently.

"Don't 'Oh Papi' me! Why do you think that I married a woman named Eva? She *is* the primary woman. And it's an inexpensive costume—I mean, how much can two fig leaves cost?"

"Very funny!" I was stitching away on Mother's skirt,

sewing playing cards all over the black cotton. I thought angrily that, in spite of the fact that Mother would be a gypsy rather than Eve, she would be naked enough. Her peasant blouse was cut plenty low and when she had just tried it on in front of the mirror, she had pulled it down even further. At her age!

She interrupted my thoughts. "Did Renate tell you what she will be wearing?"

"No. It's a secret."

"Well, at least she came along," Father interjected.

"At last! Her highness has consented to honor us at last!" Mother said.

"You know that she couldn't before. She had to work every single Saturday." I defended Renate. Though, actually, I had been somewhat annoyed too. The whole fuss—and Rudi would join us later. I had asked why he couldn't just come with us and she had almost bitten my head off. "That's the way we want it," she had yelled. However, she had been nice about helping me with my costume; I'd be an Apache. And it was fun to have her here. We had swum in the lake and Renate had put the V.F. in his place—V.F. for *Vater's Freund;* he had tried to flirt with her too and she had said sweetly, "Oh, you must be the gentleman Ellen has told me about." He had blushed, yes, the V.F. had really turned pink; we had almost died laughing.

"Here, all fixed." I handed the finished skirt to Mother.

"Thank you, Ellen. Where are you going?"

"I'll be on the terrace."

"Oh, the tea dance."

"Yes, Renate is waiting for me."

Really, she wasn't exactly waiting. In fact, she was the belle of the party, whirling from arm to arm. I sank into a wicker chair to watch. And then I saw Rudi. He must have just arrived, he looked hot and dusty. I had never noticed how thick his eyebrows were. He beetled them. "Drinking again?" he asked me in a surly voice.

"Sure." I waved my lemonade.

Renate dropped, laughing, into the chair next to me. She was flushed, shining. Someone handed her a drink, another young man squatted next to her, trying to hold her eyes, continuing a story, and she nodded and smiled, but she had seen Rudi, and reaching up and behind her, she knew that he was there and he took her hand and put it to his cheek. Her color deepened and his brow cleared. My throat felt tight.

"Can't I stay up tonight?" I pleaded when we picked our parents up for dinner.

"No, only tomorrow for the party." Mother was firm.

"But I'd be with Renate, you wouldn't have to worry." I looked at Renate for confirmation, but she avoided my eyes.

And so in bed, the same old music floating up again through the open windows, together with a tang of fish and earth and farm, together with jasmine and roses and perfume. And remembering Renate's breath when she kissed me good night, hot and sweet, gin and excitement. "'Be careful," I had said inexplicitly, and she had laughed and tossed her hair, which she had worn long. I tried to wait for her but fell asleep. Later I started up, the little clock said two in shimmering numerals. Renate's bed, bright in the moonbath, was still empty. Also at four o'clock in the gray light. Next it was day and Renate slept, curled into a ball, frowning earnestly. I tiptoed into my tennis dress, I didn't want to wake her, to talk to her.

Rudi was at the courts, we played a hard set. In fact, I played better than ever before in my life, and when we finally stopped, he said, "You're quite a killer, you almost beat me."

"Maybe you'd do better with some sleep."

He put his hand on my nape and walked next to me.

"Listen, maybe you shouldn't be so angry."

"Me? Angry? You must be kidding!" I pulled away from his touch.

"Or jealous?"

I gave him a look of what I hoped was withering scorn and ran down to the beach.

That night Renate locked me out of our room; there had been no way to find out what she would wear. So I dressed with my parents, hurrying, trying to get out of there. But I kept being pressed into service—painting Mother's beauty spot, fastening the red carnation in her hair. I also attached the loop earring to Father's left lobe. It was a difficult operation since the loop was designed for pierced ears; *Leukoplast* finally did the trick. He was an unconvincing pirate; even the torn, wide open shirt which showed his smooth, tanned torso was not quite in character.

"I think pirates need a mat of black hair on their chests," I said. "Maybe you'd better button up."

He laughed and continued to paint a mighty mustache to his upper lip. He was singing, "*Ja, wir sind die Herren des Meers . . .*"—yes, we are the rulers of the sea—the only pirate song any of us knew.

"Ernstl, maybe you'd better lie down a little before we go. You are pretty high," Mother suggested.

"Don't worry about me. Just see to it that you don't drink enough to get mixed up about which room you sleep in."

"It isn't I who have trouble distinguishing between a lion and a lamb," she answered tartly. I wasn't sure whether her response was friendly, but I didn't stay to find out; it was time to escape.

"Remember now, two glasses of punch, no more," Mother called after me.

"I won't." Ha, I intended to drink as much as I pleased tonight; later, she would be in no condition to watch me.

I went down to the ballroom. It was dark except for candles on each of the little tables around the dance floor, and it was hot. An odor of wine, of strawberries. And flowers. I joined the other young people at the long table that had been reserved for us. Someone hugged me. "Ah, The Mezuzah!" The nickname had stuck. "The French Apache Mezuzah! Are you drinking tonight?"

"Of course. And no disappearing act either."

And so to dance; it was marvelous to be at a grown-up party.

A drum solo was keeping us spellbound when Renate and Rudi appeared. The drummer was doing fantastic things with the brushes, wind and rain; he finished with a flourish. Then there was a gasp—Renate and Rudi were Jane and Tarzan, clad in leopard skins, looking terribly naked. Both were barefoot and Renate had large white flowers in her hair; Rudi led her by the hand. Of course, things were rather going around and around for me by then—the punch was potent—it was such a dream, so it did not seem too odd. Everyone at our table rose to toast them and I wondered only what it was that kept Renate's animal hide in place; it was slung so precariously over one of her shoulders and covered her minimally in all the right places.

And the music started again and it went faster and faster. A rainbow spot swept the dancers and after that, it all was unreal: glimpses into a kaleidoscope; Mother being dipped wildly in a tango; Renate and Rudi, glued together, sliding languorously; and my own laughter, strange in my ears.

"What time did you get to bed?" Renate asked.

"Two, I think. A bunch of us went swimming." I squinted my eyes against the glare of the sun on the lake, dipped the paddle carefully to keep the canoe on an even course; my head ached. I remembered how cold the water had been and how tired I had suddenly felt. "Enough for French Mezuzahs," someone had said and brought me to my door. I had not heard Renate come in.

I splashed water and watched the spray glide back into the lake, I wondered when she had come to bed, but, of course, I could not ask.

"Don't tip us," Renate warned. She was sitting with her eyes closed.

"Do you have a headache too?"

"Who wouldn't . . . the way she yelled!"

I concentrated on my strokes and we glided smoothly ahead, "What's so bad about dressing up like Tarzan and Jane?" I asked. "It was a costume party, after all."

"You mean: 'Exposing yourself and making a fool of yourself and flying in the face of convention and mortifying your mother and father.'"

"I wish I had a Pfennig for every time they mortified us."

Renate was still mimicking. "'And as for you, Ellen, you are obviously too young to be allowed out. You made an exhibition of yourself too—the way you danced!'"

It had been a very bad idea to visit our parents this morning.

16

About a year earlier, before the Sign adorned the movie houses, Steffi and I had smuggled ourselves into an "over eighteen" performance of *Camille* with Robert Taylor and Greta Garbo. We had prepared ourselves carefully by wearing my mother's clothes and lots of make-up, especially mascara. It was marvelous, the saddest picture. We sobbed uncontrollably. Afterward we had stood in front of Schwartz's Jewelry Store and waited for the streetcar. We were still numb with grief, the bright afternoon sunshine hurt our eyes; it was an incongruity. And then I looked at Steffi and, horrified, turned to the mirror in the display window and saw myself. What a mess we were! Streaked mascara making black rivulets on our cheeks, smeared lipstick—even Steffi's beauty spot had rubbed off. We began to laugh.

Strangely enough, and it terrified me, that's what I thought of during Frau Levy's funeral. Steffi was again a little girl dressed up to look like someone older. In a black dress, her hair so neat under a hat, her face so tear-stained. I was sitting next to Christa; we were crying too. The Rabbi spoke about Frau Levy's gentleness, her goodness, her gaiety. "A woman of valor, though she walketh through the valley of the shadows, she knoweth no fear." But I kept thinking about the time we had seen *Camille;* there was something wrong with me.

Mother and Father made a Shivah visit. I had asked them to come, had instructed them how to behave. "Don't shake hands, just sit down."

"Ellen, really, your father comes from a religious

home, you don't have to tell him how to act," Mother said. "And anyhow, this Shivah business is barbaric—that poor child, to have to see all these people at a time like this."

"You don't understand. It's a comfort to have people come and show that they care." It had just been explained to me by a neighbor of the Levys'; I'm afraid I had looked upon it like Mother did before that. But now I flared at her, "Anyhow, if you think it's so awful, don't go! You probably wouldn't fit in anyway."

But they went. I had been there all day, it was the third day of the Shivah. I was making tea and helping the women who had brought the food. They spoke so warmly and lovingly of Lilly Levy. And then my parents came, and I had been right; they didn't fit in. Sitting straight and uncomfortable among all the warm friends. They were too beautiful. No one knew what to say to them. Steffi started to cry when she saw them and huddled down even smaller on her mourning stool, but later she got up and went over to them and thanked them for coming. Mother kissed her, and then, suddenly, I was proud of my mother after all. When the time came for the afternoon prayers, Father stood with all the other men, and he knew all the prayers; I was proud of him too. I left with them afterward, feeling very warm and loving until Mother said, "Still, it's barbaric, sitting on those wooden stools, chastening the flesh!"

Father smiled at me, his let-it-go smile. He took Mother's arm. "Oh shut up," he said lovingly. "You don't understand these things."

"I suppose it's my Gentile blood?" she bristled.

"Right," he intoned, "your *shiksa* blood."

Mother chose to take it good-naturedly. I took a relieved breath. It seemed to me that this was no time for fighting.

A few days later I faced another leave-taking. Only this one hit me so unexpectedly. The telephone ringing—"Ellen? It's Mossi."

And my heart beating fast—"Oh Mossi . . ."

"I want to say good-by." His voice was raspy.

A long pause; hollow, yet vibrating with a strange anxiety. Yes, I knew the etiquette; one was supposed to say something happy—"You lucky dog!" or like the English, "Well, cheerio!" or even a plain *"Hals und Beinbruch,* Mossi!"; but I said nothing.

"Ellen?"

"Yes. Yes, I heard you."

"I know I've been so . . ."

I cut him short. "No, no, don't. I understand."

He laughed. "You do?" Not pleasant. Then, "I am sorry. Ellen?"

"Yes Mossi."

"Will you come to see me off?"

I swallowed. "Yes," I said. "Of course."

The ride to the station was endless. I sat quietly between Mossi and his father, whose hands moved constantly, who smoked cigarettes with quick, deep puffs, and who broke into bursts of loud talk only to fall silent again. Then Mossi would try to talk, but he, too, would stop, sometimes in mid-sentence. And after that they each stared out of their windows and I regarded the back of the neck of the taxi driver; he had a big pimple.

In the station it was gray: a drizzly sky over the glass roof and the long gray train which stood with open compartment doors like hungry mouths waiting to devour—and people huddled in groups, gray also. Mossi was with his father, their hands locked; no, my presence had not been any help. I turned away, but it was everywhere. Then Mossi came and took my arm and we walked up and down. We did not talk, we just watched. A sense of unreality invaded me, making me feel almost impersonal; so many people were weeping. Apparently it was the young people who were leaving, the older ones who would remain behind. Such an atmosphere of sorrow, of heaviness. "I wonder how many of them will ever see each other again?" Mossi asked. His voice was very calm. Yes, he was feeling it too—this detachment, as if we were not a part of the scene.

All Aboard!—a chilling sound. We were back with Mossi's father. They were hugging and kissing; I had never seen a boy kiss his father on the lips. Or a man cry like that. When Mossi hugged me I felt long tremors shake him and I tried to make my body soft, comforting—no, hard, comforting—he tore himself loose. When he stood by the window of his compartment, the train began to move. For a moment our eyes locked, but the train gathered speed quickly, in seconds Mossi's face was gone, only a blur as windows rushed by, strange, distorted features, and then the gray snake cleared the station roof, dipped into the deeper gray of distance, and was gone. I looked around; everything was a haze, only my ears were super sharp and in them was a keening. I had to get out of there! I turned, I ran. Through the long station, out through the turnstile, and into the busy street. It was raining harder now, the wet asphalt shone, there was a streetcar. I jumped aboard when it was already moving, found a window seat, and pressed my nose against the glass. But there were no tears in me.

After that I began writing Mossi almost every day; maybe some of my letters would be in New York before him. He had gone via London where his sister was working as a maid. Their family in America had only been able to give one affidavit.

"I think you are dramatizing the whole thing," Christa said. "Before his arrest you could take him or leave him."

"Yes, but now we have a bond."

"Nonsense. You were only buddies."

"That's why. The bond is that farewell at the station; it's a symbol of our time."

"You lost me there."

"No, I didn't, Christa! You know what I mean."

She blushed. "I guess so," she said finally. "I just can't stand to think about it anymore."

I touched her wrist. I only wanted it to be a light tap, but she grasped my hand. Awkwardly, our fingers scrambled to adjust their hold; at last we were clasped, interlocked. I felt a faintness as I watched the tears flood her eyes. It was just everything! Frau Levy and Mossi and having to grow up so quickly now.

We were going to Steffi almost every day. Sometimes Carlheinz came too; he and Christa could not meet in public anymore. Christa had been censored at a BDM meeting for having Jewish friends and she had plenty of trouble at home too; there was talk about her mother being sent to a sanatorium.

Steffi was keeping house for her father. Herr Levy had shrunk some more; he had become even more humped and insignificant-looking. He talked about getting Steffi on a children's transport, but Steffi laughed at him. "You know I wouldn't leave you, Papa," she would say.

"But I have no place to go, what's to become of us?"

He spoke to us as if we were adults, and we felt that we were. We had to take care of Herr Levy; he was so helpless. For Chanukah he made matching navy-blue jumpers for the three of us and we wore them when we lit the eighth candle with him. Then we sang the "Moaus Tzur" and had potato pancakes—he called them *latkes*—and applesauce. We played dreidel with walnuts and tried to be gay; it was a sad evening, wonderful but sad.

Suddenly I saw death differently. It wasn't the way it had been when Grandmother died; death wasn't a void. Nor was it an embarrassment, a subject to be avoided. At the Levys' we talked about Frau Levy all the time.

"Do you remember how she sang along with the Marlene Dietrich records?" Steffi asked and we nodded and smiled.

"Oi, the time with the horseradish," Herr Levy reminded us. He had come into the kitchen to find us all dissolved in tears from grating it. Then we couldn't stop laughing at his expression of concern; he had thought that a disaster had befallen us.

Herr Levy told us about their courtship. "She was so pert and pretty in spite of the bad leg. And she was forward in those days; the Rabbi thought she would come to no good." He sighed and shook his head; he smiled.

New Year's Eve 1937/38. My parents gave a very big party. Father lay on the floor with Frau Rotkorn and made like a bicycle; so did she. I mean, it was all right for him, he was wearing pants. And Mother stood behind the velvet draperies with Herr Beck; they kissed. There was slow dancing and an incredible number of bottles.

Just before midnight I locked myself into my room. I put "O Sole Mio" on my phonograph though I had thought that I had outgrown it. I cried a little. What would the new year bring? I couldn't wait to see, but I was scared.

Father banged on the door." "Hey, come on out and kiss us Happy New Year!" but I ignored him; I didn't feel like them.

After a while he went away.

The next morning at breakfast Father turned green when Rosemarie brought in the scrambled eggs. "Ugh, take it away!"

"What's the matter?"

"Oooh . . ." His mouth hung open, slack; he put both hands on his chest.

I was scared but Mother remained unconcerned. "It's not your heart," she said. "You have a hangover."

"Nonsense. I never get hangovers."

But a bit of herring seemed to settle his stomach.

The trouble was, of course, that he would have to give

up his car now. The sale was effective as of January third. "I will feel like an amputee," he said.

"God forbid," I said à la Herr Levy.

"Yes, really."

"Ach Ernstl, stop dramatizing. You don't need a car now that you can't travel anymore."

So Father visited customers around Berlin. And sometimes he took the train to towns where he knew people with whom he could stay overnight. But his business had shrunk considerably and I knew that he was worried. I was never told the details, but I think that Grandfather helped us out financially. There were ominous phrases, like "touching capital," and there was real concern now about how long it would take until our American quota number would come up. If I asked, I was told not to worry, that we wouldn't starve, but I noticed economies that had never been practiced before. When Rosemarie left for England, Mother made no attempt to get a new maid. Somehow, we managed rather easily. For me it was also nice to have Father home so much. I liked looking up from my writing to see him sitting in the comfortable chair by my window. He seemed to like sitting with me. "The salon is for the evening," he said. "A man can't sit in a salon during the day."

I did a lot of writing that winter. For the school paper, in my diary, to Mossi, to the relatives in America, and to Renate—folded, sealed pieces of stationery I would leave on her pillow; I wasn't willing to give up communications with her. I wrote away. Putting things down lent them a sense of permanence, it seemed to stem the feeling of rushing time which was suddenly so compelling that I fancied hearing its sound. Even my handwriting was beginning to look adult; I took delight in round letters, in green ink, in beautiful paper with my name printed on top, but most of all in words; I loved words. I felt sorry for Christa, who told me about all the restrictions that were placed on her use of the language. In her school the children were forced to use only "truly Germanic" expressions to strengthen the "national pride," as they said. This eliminated a great many words that were commonly used, and Christa and I took malicious pleasure in translating these offensive foreign expressions in as literal and as ridiculous a manner as possible.

"I have a 'return-you' with Carlheinz," Christa said, avoiding the French *rendezvous*.

"You do? A 'head-to-head'?" I responded; *tête-à-tête* was also on the forbidden list.

Yes, time was important now; we had a peculiar attitude toward it. It was measured by how long it was until your papers were due, also by how long since someone had left. "It was way back when Onkel Wolf went to America!" and "Next year, when we are going to England, to Cuba, to Chile . . ."

Then there was time in relation to how long letters took to reach Amsterdam, Paris, New York, and there was the time during which people disappeared. Gerhardt, how long? Three months during which Romi's Onkel Karl had been away. He had come back, shaven-headed and empty-eyed, and a few nights later he had simply walked across an unpatrolled section of the border somewhere in Alsace-Lorraine. Such escapes were called "black," a term which spoke of moonless nights, dark clothing, and intrigue. Onkel Karl had made it, it was whispered, and best of all, he had carried Romi's mother's diamond ring with him; now the Brauns had *capital* waiting for them in Paris.

"Did you give Tante Gert your jewelry to take out?" I asked Mother.

"Of course not."

"But they say that you can't take jewelry out anymore."

"Well, we didn't know that then, and anyhow, I need my rings."

I had the distinct impression that Mother wasn't about to trust her jewelry to anyone. She bore out my suspicion when she added, "And Gert has always been crazy about my solitaire."

Rudi had given Renate a ring. In a simple setting, a large aquamarine. "Is it an engagement ring?"

She was holding out her hand, turning it this way and that, making the stone glint; she was frowning. "No, just a present."

"Well, it's gorgeous."

"Yes. Don't tell Mother."

"You aren't going to show it to her?"

"No."

In any case, Renate said she wouldn't trust Tante Gert with her ring either.

If Herr Levy's beard had not been the symbol of his mourning, we would have enjoyed it a lot. How a man who was so small and slight and had such thin, sparse hair on his head could have such a luxurious black, curly beard was beyond us. In spite of himself, he was proud of it too. "Ach, oi," he sighed, but smiling, when Christa said, "You are beautiful, Herr Levy; all men should wear beards."

"Nu, your Carlheinz would look fine in one," he said. "Maybe some day he will grow one—when it isn't so dangerous anymore."

Dangerous it was! Now Herr Levy was more marked. Little boys shouted "Dirty Jew!" after him on the street. He never went farther from his house than to the shop or the Synagogue.

Christa was studying Judaism with him. He had explained to her that conversion just for the sake of marriage was not acceptable to the Orthodox, that you had to want to share the Jewish fate, the Jewish experience in order to be allowed to convert.

"Well, then I have to know more about it," she had said. "Will you teach me?"

Herr Levy had checked with his Rabbi, who saw no

harm in it. So Christa sat with Steffi's father over the books. History and Bible and the Commentaries. Christa's cheeks would glow red with excitement and Herr Levy got excited too. "This child has a Talmudic mind," he shouted one day. Steffi and I grinned, we were already thinking of Christa as one of us. Though it peeved me a little that suddenly Christa knew more about Judaism than I did.

Father and I continued to go to the Friedens Temple every Friday night. Sometimes we saw Romi there too. She said that she was in love with the young Rabbi. "Last Friday, while he was preaching, he kept smiling at me," she assured me.

"Oh come on!"

"I tell you he likes me. If he weren't a Rabbi, I bet he would flirt with me."

I could believe that; Romi had become really beautiful. Her smooth black hair, her creamy oval face, she looked serene, almost saintly. But she and Katrine went to the cafés, even the ones with the Sign, and they let themselves be asked to dance. I was shocked.

"But aren't you scared? I mean, if anyone knew that you're Jewish, you could be arrested."

"How could they know? We never let them take us home, and we give them false names, and we don't go back to the same cafés too often.

"But don't you mind dancing with those Nazis?"

"What's the difference? We have to have some fun; it's so dull."

"I wouldn't enjoy dancing with someone who doesn't want me, who hates Jews," I said righteously.

"Oh Ellen, all those fellows think of is dancing with a girl, they don't care."

"They would, if they knew."

When Frau von Adelsberg was sent to a sanatorium, I thought that it was really Herr von Adelsberg who could use the rest. He was stark, raving mad. Mad at the Nazis, at what was happening, at his cousin Fritz, who was a *grosses Tier*, literally "a large animal," meaning a VIP, in the Nazi Party.

"He never was any good, that Fritz," Herr von Adelsberg told us. "When we were boys he used to tie the cats together by their tails. Even the horses knew enough to buck him off." Herr von Adelsberg laughed, then shook his head. "He was the worst rider in Silesia." They had grown up together on the family estate.

In the end though, and inadvertently, Cousin Fritz saved Herr Levy's life. Herr von Adelsberg had been to see him about some family business and gathered certain information. Late that night, he went to see Herr Levy, and later still, after waking Steffi out of her sleep, Steffi and her papa moved in with the von Adelsbergs. The next morning the deportation of the Polish Jews started. When the truck stopped in front of Herr Levy's store, the SS men found it locked. Smashing in the door and of the apartment too did not turn up the Polish Jew Levy; he had disappeared.

I was a little jealous when I heard about it. Herr von Adelsberg had let the housekeeper go. Steffi and Christa took care of their papas—kosher style. I myself helped to carry in small packages of new dishes for milchik and flayshig. What a ménage they were! The two men immediately started on an endless chess game which continued for months. Tactfully, I said nothing about Herr Levy's clean-shaven face. In spite of the fact that he never went out, they had considered it safer for him to shave.

"That's the thing he minds most," Steffi told me. "Having to take off the beard before the mourning year is over. And of course not being able to go to Shul."

Steffi wasn't going to school, either. "How can I? We have disappeared!"

Personally, I thought it was great. Steffi and Christa were living together like sisters; they would have a marvelous time.

"But what will happen to them? I mean, they can't stay hidden in your house forever," I asked Christa. "When your mother comes back . . ."

"Father is trying to arrange something."

In the meantime, I tried to be there as much as possible.

"Since when are you always running to Christa?" Mother asked.

"Well, you know, Steffi is away." I had told my parents that Steffi and her father had gone to visit relatives.

"Thank God, just in time," Father said. "They are arresting all the Polish Jews in Berlin. I hope they are safe."

I felt guilty. It wasn't that I didn't trust my parents; it was just as Herr von Adelsberg had said—"Don't spread the risk." And Mother was a talker!

Renate agreed. "There isn't even any question; of course, you can't tell them; it isn't your secret to keep or not," she said.

Father had asked her whether she had heard from Rudi lately; he politely pretended to believe Renate's fiction that they were just casual friends. At least I supposed that Father pretended. How could he miss seeing the truth? Mother, yes; she never saw anything except herself. Though she had said, "Rudi is a Pole too, isn't he?"

"Yes," Renate said casually, and to Father, "I believe he said something about being out of town this month."

But she was worried. She had gone to the apartment, there was no answer, and the superintendent had said that he was holding Herr Fichtel's mail as he always did when Der Herr was on a business trip. Nothing seemed unusual; it was the same pattern Renate had become accustomed to during the last year. Still . . .

"You have no reason to worry," I told her. "His door wasn't smashed or anything the way it was at the Levys'."

"I know. But it's just that I don't have any idea where

he is, and it's a week already. As a rule he is only gone for four days."

"Maybe you should call his office."

"I thought of that, but I don't know who can be trusted there."

"Wait a while longer."

"Yes." She looked tired. I noticed that she was thin, the navy skirt kept slipping around her waist; she was getting ready to go to her office.

"Your figure is really great now," I said, trying.

"Well, I can't eat. It's an ill wind, etc."

I tried not to understand. "Just don't overdo," I said, "or you'll waste away."

She smiled lopsidedly and left. I felt bad. But what could I do? I wanted to get back to the girls, to the balcony. I was on fall vacation. Where had most of this year gone? So fast, so fast. Yet, so slow.

17

That hazy fall vacation, what did we do? The weather had turned warm once more, belated Indian summer; and a feeling of unreality over our world.

At home, Mother was packing, very purposeful, very busy.

But we, Steffi, Christa, and I? Our world was three by six feet, cement-floored, bricked; the balcony in front of Christa's room. The brick went up chest-high on us, then came the green flower boxes with the pink and white petunias. And in order to be better concealed, Christa had planted string beans which she had trained up on twine to the cement ceiling which was the floor of the upstairs balcony. Thus we had a lush retreat. We put Frau von Adelsberg's best Persian runners on the floor and all the pillows we could find in the house. Every morning, on the way over, I bought fresh rolls and fruit. The three of us would be through with the housework by eleven-thirty when the sun hit the balcony for two hours. All that time Herr Levy would be working. He was making complete wardrobes for Christa and Steffi. At two o'clock we had dinner with him, and then we went back to the balcony.

And what did we talk about all those hours, all that vacation?

I remember only snatches and the dappled shade of the string-bean screen, and all of us grown girls now, yet so subdued. Always, the sounds floating to the neighbors must be as if they came from two girls only, not three—and as to Herr Levy, pale and bent with the glory of the beard gone, he didn't even exist at all.

I think we mostly talked about the future, dreaming ourselves complete lives with husbands and children whose names we knew. Of course Steffi and her family would live in Palestine, and Christa and Carlheinz would both be architects in America. They wouldn't have children for a long time, because Christa wanted to have a career first. One whole afternoon we argued heatedly, interjected only with frequent "Psst, the neighbors!", was it good or bad to have children young?

My own future was the most nebulous, though we were somewhat guided by the fact that my grandfather always said that I would marry a millionaire in America. That is, I would if that gangster Roosevelt hadn't ruined the economy of the United States by then. For all Grandfather knew, millionaires might become extinct if someone didn't stop Roosevelt. I found it hard to imagine. The only rich man I knew was Grandfather, and he didn't live so richly, he couldn't as long as he didn't touch "capital." I explained that to the girls, but they thought it was different in America; there they had swimming pools and butlers and furs and diamonds. Christa brought out her mother's fox boa, and we draped it around my neck to see how I looked in furs. But it was hard to tell over my blue two-piece bathing suit. In any case, I was going to have three children too, Daniel and Jonathan and Michelle, and they would be blond and good at sports and the boys would be doctors and the girl a dancer, or maybe an archaeologist, or a famous writer.

And we would always stay friends, and once a year we would meet in Jerusalem, and all our children would be friends too. Some of them might even marry each other, but of course that would be up to them.

"I just hope, coming from different countries like that, that they'll all speak the same language so that they can understand each other," I worried.

"Oh they'll all speak Hebrew; that's really our language," Steffi decreed.

"But maybe our children won't want to. Maybe mine will say that they are Americans, why should they be Zionists?" I objected.

"Like the German Jews?" Steffi laughed. "Don't be silly, Jews will never make that mistake again."

I nodded. Yes, she was right. I certainly would bring up my children to understand that. I sighed.

"What's the matter?"

"I hope my children will learn languages easier than I do."

Under the cover of their laughter I knew that the sigh had also concerned Renate, who had been on my mind all through our conversation. Whom would she marry? Rudi? I felt uneasy, and I felt guilty. Last night I had heard her cry again, and this morning I had pretended that I was still asleep when she got ready to go to the office.

The reason why we were packing at home was because Father had been told at the American consulate that our number might come up within the year now. It was decided that we should be ready, that a lift would be packed and shipped to the harbor in Hamburg for the day of departure. We would go and live in a pension in the meantime.

A lift was like a big packing case; big like a van. Mother was gloriously happy, she was packing. And shopping. Grandfather had given RM 20,000 to both Mother and Tante Ruth for a virtual emigration trousseau; Mother was getting new furniture. Herr Heinz Beck, he of the New Year's Eve kisses behind the curtain, was consulted; he was an *Innen Architekt*. He presented endless sketches for chairs and couches, desks, breakfronts, and dining tables. Tante Gert had written that the apartments in America were much smaller, that her furniture looked huge and crowded in the low-ceilinged rooms. It was this intelligence that gave Mother her chance to make a clean sweep of it. And as time went by, pieces of furniture disappeared from our house.

"I sold the wardrobes in the girls' room!" Everyone knew that you had closets in New York.

Apparently Mother felt no sentimental attachment to her possessions; she weeded ruthlessly among them and enjoyed ordering new ones. The design she finally chose was good. Small scale, airy and graceful. "Modern and informal, the way they live in America," Mother said.

Mother went to see these pieces of furniture while they were being built, but they never came to our apartment when they were finished; they went straight into the lift. So did barrels of china and glassware—the good Meissen dinner service, the Nymphenburg tea things, the Limoges dessert set. And crates of linen—the Irish damasks and the hand-embroidered breakfast cloths—cross-stitched roses blooming abundantly—and the bed linens with the eyelet embroidery and the button-down quilts. They were new too, covered in lemon-yellow silk. The old ones were sold. "What will we do if we are here another winter?" I asked, but Mother didn't care. The old must go; buy, buy, buy!

The regulations said that you were only permitted to take out one set of silver flatware for your own personal use; all other silver was being confiscated. Mother said that our flatware was shabby; she had seen a magnificent new set of sterling. "I need more money," she told Father.

"Use some of the money you made selling the old things," Father advised, but of course he didn't understand—that wasn't fair. *That* money was Mother's. She had merely sold some of her old things, some of them still from her trousseau. "I mean, my first trousseau," she said. "Why should I use that money for the few measly things we can put into the lift? Vati said he would pay for those."

Coming home to our apartment, emptier and emptier all the time, to Mother madly gay, to Father quiet and subdued in his idleness, and to the knowledge—growing surely and darkly —that soon I would have to stand still and listen to Renate, I wanted to escape. I felt squeezed, angry . . .

"Do you mind not selling the beds out from under us yet?" I snapped at Mother.

"Don't worry, we are taking your beds to America; they are not too big. When we move to the pension, the mattresses will be reupholstered and the frames refinished; it's all arranged. Then they go into the lift."

"I am glad to hear that we'll have something familiar left."

"Oh Ellen, don't be such a spoilsport." She was glowing.

Angrily I wondered whether it had anything to do with her association with Herr Beck. But Father said that women were stimulated by acquisitions. "Women like to buy, men like to hunt," he said.

I, however, was much annoyed by the buying of my wardrobe, which went on simultaneously. I suppose I was really jealous not to have Herr Levy make my things the way he made Christa's and Steffi's. So I suffered through fittings with Herr Phillips and conferences with the underwear lady.

"But how do you know what the girls in America will be wearing? Maybe this will look dumb."

"We won't be able to afford new clothes there for quite a while. It's a good thing you have stopped growing."

"You are lucky that you can shop for your own clothes," I said to Renate. "If I have to go on one more shopping trip with *her* I'll scream."

We were in bed already, Renate was wearing lotion on the eczema, which had suddenly flared up again. Looking at her, my heart sank—this was the time, we would have to talk.

"All right," I said. "He isn't back yet, is he?"

She burst into tears.

"Have you been to his house?"

"Every day," between sobs.

I got up and went to sit on her bed. She clutched my hand. "Oh Ellen, what shall I do?"

"Did you call his office?"

"There's no answer."

"Maybe they changed the number."

"Why should they?"

"Did Rudi ever tell you what to do . . ." I hesitated, ". . . in such a case?"

Renate stopped crying and stared at me, her eyes became even larger.

"What is it?" I asked.

"I don't know." She was scratching, I took her hand down. "I don't know, I just remembered . . . when you said that."

"What?"

" 'In such a case.' Rudi once said something, but I thought he was kidding. You know he always says these crazy things about Luz."

"About Luz?"

"Yes. He said, '*Im schlimmsten Falle*, in the worst case, my Aryan-ex might still come in handy.' That's what he said. But I'm sure he was just being funny."

We stared at each other.

"No," I said then. "He could have meant it. She is married to that *grosse Tier*, remember! They could help if they wanted to."

"But they wouldn't."

"Luz might." I jumped up. Suddenly I felt sure. Of course—I remembered her at the bus stop—"How is he?" Oh, she would help him; I said it out loud, though differently. "She wouldn't hurt him."

"Oh no? I suppose that's why she left him, to be good to him."

I had no answer for that, yet I felt convinced.

"Did you know that Luz is short for Lucrezia?" Renate was saying.

"Like Lucrezia Borgia?"

"Exactly. I just couldn't go to that woman. And it might call attention to whatever he is doing."

"You don't have to say anything except that he is missing."

"I just can't." Renate had gotten up too; she was pacing.

"Yes you can. You must. It's two weeks; he's never done anything like that, he would have told you if he had known that he would be gone this long. With the arrests of the Polish Jews—maybe he was picked up at a railroad station like the story Papi told about Lazlo Blau." I stopped. When had I thought all this out?

We stared at each other again. Then suddenly Renate went into action. In a second she was out of her nightgown, at her wardrobe. "Come on, get dressed," she said over her shoulder.

"Me? I don't think I should . . ."

She turned back to me, her eyes were commanding. "Get dressed!"

The night was still mild, there was a drizzle, and the streets had a shining look with puddles of light under the lanterns. At the corner taxi stand we found a cab without any trouble. We got in and Renate gave the address; it all had an air of unreality for me. Renate turning into a general, efficient, cool, finding Luz in the telephone book, ringing her number, and when she answered, hanging up, telling me to wear a raincoat.

The superintendent came out of his lodge to unlock the door. He grumbled that it was late, that the Herr Richter Dr. Heidemann was supposed to open the door for his guests himself after eleven o'clock. But he let us in and even pushed "8" for us in the elevator.

"I guess we look respectable. He didn't even check whether we are expected." I talked quickly, trying to talk past the dryness in my mouth, the lump in my throat. Renate did not answer, her face looked stern with the hair pulled back like that; the white streak showed.

The elevator stopped, rattled open . . . a foyer, four doors, which? "This one," Renate said, peering at a small brass plate. She gave a short, quick push to the buttonbell.

We stood and waited. I hadn't heard the bell ring inside, the pounding in my ears was all the noise I perceived until, right in front of my nose, on the other side of the door, I heard Luz's voice. "Who is it?"

I looked at Renate. She was very white, sweat pearls lay on her nose, her forehead, she closed her eyes and leaned against the wall.

"Us," I croaked and took Renate's hand.

The click of the peephole, the door opening, Luz.

"I think Renate is feeling ill." Still leaning against the wall, green now, breathing noisily. Her hand was ice cold.

Luz helped me to lead her inside—red velvet shades on gold sconces, soft lights and through the hall into a dark red room, books and chairs, Renate's white belted trenchcoat and Luz in something light blue, silky, a robe. And then Renate in a deep leather chair with a glass in her hand and color returning to her face, a crooked smile. "I'm sorry."

Luz and I stood in front of her. Then Luz turned to me. "Rudi?" she asked.

I nodded.

Calling "Werner, Werner . . . ," Luz walked rapidly from the room.

"Are you all right?" I asked Renate, and she nodded.

A moment later Luz was back with the judge. He shook hands with us; he was dark, his face craggy. I thought of a picture of Moses in my *Israelitische Geschichte*—curly hair streaked with gray, horn-rimmed glasses at which he kept stabbing with a long finger. He sat down behind his desk. "Since when is he gone?"

"I don't know," Renate said cautiously. She was all right now, sitting up straight.

"My dear child, what do you mean—you don't know. You must . . ."

"It's two weeks," I said quickly. He did look like Moses, not like a Nazi.

"Two weeks!" he yelled. *"Verflucht nochmal,* why didn't you come sooner?"

Renate and I looked at each other.

"Oh God, and how often I told Rudi to make sure Renate would know." From Luz.

"I guess he told me," Renate put in. "Only I didn't understand."

"Verdammt!" He combed his hair back with two thin hands.

"Don't, Werner! You know Rudi, it probably sounded like one of his jokes. The child couldn't know whether to trust us."

He got up and started pacing. We watched him anxiously.

"Two weeks." He shook his head. "Two weeks and we don't even know whether they know anything, or whether we are just dealing with the Polish sweep-up." He stopped in front of Renate.

"The superintendent is holding his mail. He doesn't know anything. I mean, he didn't say . . . about the police or . . ."

"Ach Schaefer! *Der Kerl,*" contemptuously. "He wouldn't tell you if he had unlocked the door personally for the Gestapo and delivered Rudi to them wrapped in a bow. In fact, that's probably what he did." He nodded, started pacing again. "Ja, that's what might have happened. In which case it was the Polish raid." He strode quickly to the telephone, picked it up, dialed.

"Be careful," Luz said.

The judge smiled bitterly, then "Klaus? Werner. Heil Hitler. Do you have any of the Polish ham left?" He listened, his brow cleared. "Splendid!" A laugh. "Luz is dying for some; you know how pregnant women are—*verrückt!* I'll see you tomorrow, Heil Hitler."

Our eyes had swiveled to Luz, to her middle. Oh yes, definitely!

The judge had put down the telephone. He sat a moment, nodding his head, then he said, "We have an avenue to the Polish internees—if that's where he is." Soberly, "If that's all it is, we might be able to get to him." And darkening, "If not . . ." He began pacing again.

When we left it was after midnight, but we decided to walk. The rain had stopped, the air sharpened, suddenly it was really autumn. We walked quickly, keeping in step, both of us with our hands in the pockets of our coats.

Voicing our thoughts, Renate said, "The only thing we really know is that there is an underground, that the Heidemanns are part of it, that they know whatever it is that Rudi does."

"And that they'll help him if they can."

"Yes."

The thoughts were whirligigs in my head. Luz, pregnant, and her husband, not really old; they were nice together. And the way they talked of Rudi . . .

"It's hard to imagine that she was ever married to him," Renate said. We were traveling on parallel roads.

Mother was waiting for us at home; she mounted her best. "You must be out of your minds! Going for a walk! At this hour!" And, "I demand to know where you have been." Each sentence a scream.

"But we left you a note, Mutti."

More: "Corrupt your little sister! Irresponsible!" On and on, voice mounting still.

At last she cried and Father led her into their room.

When we were once more in bed, I said, "And the way he knew the superintendent. "Ach Schaefer! *Der Kerl!*"

"Oh God, if they can only find him."

School, the next morning, was a crazy anticlimax. Even going to Christa's was. Steffi's eyes were red.

"What's the matter?"

"It's hard now that you and Christa are back in school."

It didn't seem much in comparison. I kept thinking of Renate, of how she must be feeling, waiting. She had been told not to call, not to come there again. "Our superintendent is of the same breed as Schaefer," Luz had explained when she took us downstairs to unlock the house door for us. "But I'll be in touch with you, Renate." She had taken Renate's office number too. Oh poor Reni. I forced my mind back to what Steffi was saying. Her papa was so withdrawn, he hardly talked, and they could only walk softly in stocking feet, talk in muffled tones, move dishes with exaggerated care and stay away from the windows. As far as the neighbors were concerned, the apartment was empty from nine in the morning when Herr von Adelsberg went to his office until two o'clock when Christa came back from school.

"But what do you do?" I asked Steffi.

"I sit on the bed and read."

Her face was getting small again; she had looked so pretty during the vacation. She couldn't even do the housework.

"Imagine a phantom vacuum cleaner droning in an empty apartment; the superintendent would break in to investigate," Christa said.

And they couldn't flush the toilet, or play the radio, and the chess board was always set with the endless game that Herr Levy and Herr von Adelsberg played. "Sometimes they make only one or two moves all evening," Steffi complained.

"I'll give you a chess set of your own for your birthday," I promised. "Then you can play with your father during the day."

"He wouldn't; he's too busy."

"What is he so busy with?"

"He's writing a family history."

"Hey, but that's great, that's interesting."

"I can't read it; it's in Yiddish. I mean, I can understand Yiddish, but I can't read it. Father says that it has to be written in that language. He wants it to be ready for when I leave; he talks as if he won't get out." Tears had shot up into her eyes again; I knew she was talking about the pressure both Herr von Adelsberg and her father put on her to leave on a children's transport. We all knew that sooner or later she would have to agree, but Steffi was still saying no.

On the way home to dinner I dragged my feet, afraid of facing Renate, afraid of news or the absence of news, but Renate was not at home. Mother said that she had called to say that she had to work late. Mother was also full of exciting information about a sale in town. Real Irish linen napkins, she would have to get down there tomorrow. She had apparently forgotten about last night. I joined her conversation eagerly; it was good to have busy thoughts, to chatter, to be "normal." After dinner and the dishes I hurried through my homework; I wanted to be asleep before Renate came. And I was.

I had just come home from school a few days later when Renate called from the office. "Ellen, did Mutti go to play bridge?"

"I think so. She isn't home."

I heard Renate exhale. "Thank God. Listen, Luz is coming over. I'm leaving the office now."

Standing in the middle of the salon, looking around, a feeling of . . . what? I straightened sofa cushions. The bookcase and the desk had already been picked up, and the cigar cabinet; the room looked empty. No, lopsided. I thought of the bright squares in Rudi's apartment where Luz had taken down her pictures. The thought steadied me. Walking to the kitchen to put on the tea kettle. Of course, Renate and I were simply romanticizing Luz now, we were forgetting the real facts. After all, she *had* left her Jewish husband so that she could continue to practice law—even if she was married to a nice man and not a Nazi and pregnant . . . and beautiful. I jumped when the bell rang. So soon. But the minute I saw Luz I felt better; there was always that with Luz, it must be her eyes—the honest, clear look, understanding you.

"I think we'll be able to get him out," she said quickly.

We sat down on the sofa; she continued, "The luck is that he wasn't shipped on with the Poles."

"But where is he?"

"They are still holding him at the Alexanderplatz. First we thought it was because they knew something of his activities, but it seems to be just the business of his nationality." She smiled. "Thank God for German bureaucracy."

I waited.

"It's always been a problem. Every time he had to put down his nationality there was a mix-up."

"But I thought he is an Ost-Jude," burst out of me.

"Ja. He called himself that; it tickled him. But he wasn't really. He was born in Warsaw while his father was building a bridge there or something. His mother was half Polish and half French, his father was German."

"Nationality goes after the father, doesn't it?"

"Of course. Except Rudi kept putting down Polish and French, and sometimes Turkish, on all his papers."

"Turkish?"

"He grew up in Constantinople. In any case, he finally muddled up his records; it was a big joke to him. 'I'm a saboteur of German efficiency, I'm performing a vital service to the world,' he kept saying. We fought about it for years; every time he was called before some official to straighten it out he gave them some other wrong leads."

"That's stupid."

"Yes, especially for a lawyer. He almost didn't get his degree. Which amused him also." Luz looked tired, then she shook her head. "Of course he didn't dream for it to come home to roost like this: First to get barred from practice under the law against Jewish Germans, then to get arrested as a Pole."

"Not to mention being divorced for being a Jew," Renate said from the door.

Luz and I both got up.

"I'll make tea," I said quickly, and scurried from the room.

Neither of them noticed the tea tray or me, except to wait with talking until I had left again. Later, after I had heard the front door close, I took the untouched tray back to the kitchen; Renate had slammed into our room. I put the dishes back and poured out the tea and transferred the cookies from the good platter to their tin; no sense having Mother see and ask questions. Then I walked into our room. Renate was lying on the bed, staring at the ceiling. She held out a hand to me. I sat down next to her. We looked at each other, then grinned.

"It really sounds as if they can get him out, doesn't it?" I said.

"Yes." She shook her head. "She didn't tell me anything really, just that they have contacts."

"Polish ham contacts."

"Yes."

"So what were you talking about all that time?"

Renate's face closed up.

"Did you fight?" I probed.

"At first."

"It was pretty fresh what you said, about her divorcing him."

Renate sat up, and I moved to let her off the bed. She walked up and down a couple of times before perching on the edge of the desk. Her eyes downcast, on the letter opener which she was trying to balance on her fingertips, she said, "According to Luz, that's not the way it was."

"What do you mean?"

"According to Luz, they hadn't gotten along for years." She paused.

"So?" Not getting along for years. So what? People didn't divorce for that.

"The irony seems to be that their greatest quarrel was about the fact that Rudi didn't want to practice law. He said it bored him. He wanted to go on with the car racing, or climb mountains. Luz said that he wanted to travel all the time."

I had forgotten that he had once been a race driver.

"Apparently Luz had asked him for a divorce way before all this." Renate looked up and we stared at each other.

"Do you think she was lying?"

Renate got up. "No," she said, and then hastily, "I must get back to the office. I left all the letters Dr. Klain dictated untyped."

I dreamed that night that I was walking across a bridge that swung back and forth in the wind. I kept holding on to the side where Rudi was waiting, and I knew that he had built this bridge and that it spanned the Bosporus. When I woke up the dream feelings of anger and fear were still with me. Rudi *was* irresponsible, I thought, and why couldn't Renate have fallen in love with someone else? Then I started to cry. I was crazy. Oh poor Rudi! He was sitting in prison, and here I was, mad at him because I had to worry about it.

Two days later Renate called me at Christa's to say that Rudi was home. We laughed and cried. I couldn't tell the girls about it, Just that it was good news about Rudi.

"Are they going to get married?" Steffi asked.

"I don't know," I said, startled. "I guess so." Yes, after all, probably. Because Renate loved him so much.

18

The decision was pretty firm now that Steffi would go on a children's transport to England. Herr von Adelsberg had persuaded her by explaining how much easier it would be to smuggle out a single man than a man with a child. "I promise you, you'll be reunited with your papa within a few months."

On these terms Steffi had agreed. Papers were being prepared for her, she would be Susan Adler. We practiced the name; she would probably be on a transport in January.

"What would we do without Herr von Adelsberg?" Steffi said to me once. "And what's going to happen to him?"

I shrugged. "I think that's nothing to worry about. If he can get you out and if he can get your father out, he can certainly get himself out. After all, he's allowed to travel."

Another time we talked about it with Christa.

"No, Father wouldn't leave. He'll fight the Nazis, but he won't leave his country."

"But that's dangerous."

Christa smiled cynically. "I have been telling you that for years. You're just beginning to see."

She was right.

"And you?" I asked.

"Oh I'll go. I'll go as soon as I can!" Her voice was hard.

I knew that there was more to it than Carlheinz.

And so we moved to the Pension Diamond in that hazy fall. Though, except for the few days on the balcony, it had not been lazy hazy and string-bean green. It was murky hazy and gray. We suddenly understood a great deal, which ran, a subterranean cold river, under our normal concerns.

The Pension Diamond was on the Meranerstrasse near the Bayrischenplatz. A gray, six-story apartment house, balconies stuccoed like dirty pus to the stern face. The pension occupied several floors of the building. Mother and Father's room was downstairs, mine way up on the fifth floor, Renate's on the fourth. We called theirs The Cave; it was huge and dark and full of overstuffed furniture. However, as usual, Mother soon moved all this awkwardness around, divided the room into sitting and sleeping areas, and created a nice, homey atmosphere.

"Don't start buying again now," Father warned, but she needed the round tablecloth with the fringe to hide the ugly scars on the table, and she had to have the bright vase and the colorful ceramic pots with the plants as well as a decent bedspread; he could see that, couldn't he?

In contrast, my room was bare; I thought of it as an attic cell though it was neither on the top floor nor did it have sloping ceilings. I liked its Spartan feeling—just a bed and a table and a straight chair, all of it dwarfed by a wardrobe that was too large. But mainly I liked being four floors removed from my parents.

Most of the people who lived at the pension were old, really old. They were a depressing lot, hacking away with old age coughs that drowned the sound effects of the clatter of cutlery in the dining room. Each table was adorned with medicine bottles which were always brown in those days. Ladies predominated, their silver, finger-waved heads palsied on thin necks. The few men were bald, wrinkled, and they had an abundance of moles on their creased faces. The Beauties, Father called them. At the table next to ours sat the one notable exception—a thin dark woman, about forty-five, and her son, who was tall and skinny and straight-backed. He had smooth black hair and dark eyes and horn-rimmed glasses; my interest perked up.

We met near the telephone in the fuchsia-flowered hall.

His name was Manfred Bernstein, he was twenty-one years old, and he and his mother were waiting to go to Bolivia, their papers were due shortly.

Hoping to impress him with my knowledge, I discussed living in a high altitude and the Incas about whom I had just read an enormously interesting book; they slept with llamas. I called him Herr Bernstein and he called me Frl. Westheimer; it was a fine conversation. When I reported this to my parents, Father sighed, "Here we go again!" and I said, "Don't be silly."

"Making the best of things," Mother called living at the Pension Diamond, and we all tried. But time suddenly began to drag. I would wake up sad, I would feel anxious on my way home from school, I suffered from headaches.

And then it became even worse. Renate and Mother had had another of their fights. I came into her room and found the big suitcase on her bed and Renate's drawers open, dresses flung here and there.

"What are you doing?"

"I'm packing."

"I see that."

"I've had it! I am leaving."

I sat down on the floor on a pile of sweaters. "You are eloping with Rudi, you have decided to become a racing driver and live with him in a garage."

"Don't be funny!" Renate snapped. "And get off my sweaters."

I caught her foot as she rushed by me, stopping her. She glared down at me. "Come on, tell me what happened," I said soothingly; she looked so frantic.

"What's there to tell?" But she sat down next to me, started to scratch the eczema.

"Stop it!" I took her hands.

Then her face crumbled. "Oh Ellen, I really can't stand it anymore." And the story came tumbling out.

Actually, I could see, it had very little to do with Mother, it was Rudi.

"It's so ironic—here Mother keeps yelling at me because I've been to Rudi's apartment. She keeps calling me names, saying that no one will marry me when Rudi gets through with me, that a wild young girl is not acceptable to society."

"But wild married women are!" I interjected furiously.

"Yes, but don't you see, all the time she is carrying on, I know that she is right too."

"That's ridiculous."

"No it isn't. Oh, not on the moral stuff; that's archaic. But about Rudi, she is right about him. He won't marry me."

"Did he say that?"

"Of course not. But you know he isn't honest, not even with himself. Right now he says that he isn't completely over Luz yet, to give him time."

"But I thought . . ." Yes, I had thought that when you give yourself to a man . . . Of course I couldn't say that. "I thought he loves you, he acts like it," I answered instead.

"He does. In his way he does. As long as he doesn't have to assume any responsibility. If you want to know the truth." She got up and grabbed one of the dresses and stuffed it into the suitcase. "If you want to know the truth," she repeated loudly, "he isn't in love with Luz either. He just *likes* his present life. He likes the danger. He even liked prison."

"Oh come on!"

"It's true, believe me. And he prefers an affair to marriage, he had affairs all the time while he was married to Luz, that's why she divorced him. I got that much truth out of him at last."

I lumbered to my feet, my knees felt weak. An affair. Renate had said an affair. I started to pick up scattered items of clothing. Whom was I kidding, I asked myself in silent monologue, what was I acting so surprised about; I had known, hadn't I?

Renate was saying, "I'm leaving. I called my father already, he's expecting me."

"Your father?"

"Vati, in Amsterdam."

"Are you crazy? You can't go to him."

"Why not? I told him that I was unhappy. I asked whether I could come, and he said of course."

"But we'll be going to America."

"Not me! I'm not going any place with Mother."

"Listen, Renate, you're wrong—you know she just has these attacks, she doesn't mean it."

"She does so. She doesn't love me. Maybe she loves you because you're Papi's child, but she hates me."

"She does not. And she doesn't like me any better than you—she's too busy with herself to really care about us."

"So what kind of mother is that?"

I laughed. " The kind we have."

Renate stared at me. "Don't you care?" she asked.

I thought a moment. "No," I said then. "I have you and my friends; I really don't know that it makes any difference. I mean, that's just the way she is."

"You're pretty calm about it."

Again I stopped to think. Suddenly I saw it clearly. "Don't you see," I said excitedly, "it's because I never needed her; I always had you. I mean, when I was small."

"I used to be so jealous of you; they all made such a fuss over you."

"You were? I never noticed."

"I used to hate taking you any place because you were so cute."

That's when I started to cry. Renate was really leaving; she was making a confession, she was purging herself. She put her hand on my bent neck, but she said nothing.

"I suppose you never loved me?" I sniffed, crying harder when I heard my maudlin words.

And then, as it had been so many times when I was

small, Renate began to laugh. "You cry like a little hen in tiny cackling sobs," she always said. So I had to laugh too. She hugged me. "You idiot," she said. "Of course I love you; I would have left long ago if it hadn't been for you."

"Then stay."

"No, Ellen, I have to get out of here, I'm going crazy. And you don't need me anymore either."

"But what shall I tell Mother?" I wailed.

"Nothing till ten o'clock. That's when my train leaves. Promise?" She faced me.

"When will you come back?"

"I don't know. Will you promise?"

I couldn't let her down. "I promise," I said.

She was really packing in an awfully messy way. I got up and took out the red dress she had just stuffed into the suitcase. I folded it properly, laying the sleeves in straight, putting a soft sweater in the folds where the dress was doubled. Pretty soon Renate was handing me things, and I was putting them in right. I had always been a better packer than she.

At last it was done. We both sat on the lid until the catch snapped shut. Then I watched her put on lipstick and comb her hair, and then I carried the heavy thing to the elevator. We hugged clumsily, she was carrying her handbag and an umbrella I had reminded her to take; it was raining.

"Auf Wiederseh'n Ellen; I'll write."

The elevator clanked down.

Back inside, I straightened up Renate's room.

"Where's Renate?" Mother asked when she came back from the beauty parlor.

"I don't know."

At supper in the dining room Mother talked about how impossible Renate was, staying away for meals without even calling. I could hardly eat. The awfulness grew inside of me; what had I done? And Father was at Grandfather's for skat; he wouldn't be back till late.

At ten o'clock I went to their room. Mother was sitting up in bed, her hair set in shining waves, but her eyes were worried.

"Renate has run away," I said. "To Holland, to her Vati."

Mother stared at me. Then her face fell apart. I started to cry. "I tried to stop her . . ." I threw myself next to Mother on the bed. Sobbing, I told what I knew, how she had called Herr Sokolovski: and what he had said. Mother stroked my hair and told me to stop crying. "I know it isn't your fault, Ellen," she said. Her voice was dead.

Why didn't she scream, blame me, hit me? She was always making scenes, why not now? Just that torn-apart old face. Mother, old? I cried harder.

"Go to bed, Ellen." She was reaching for the telephone.

I slunk out of her room and into my bed. Not even one, "What have I done to deserve such children?"

And had I really tried to stop Renate?

The worst thing about living at the Pension Diamond was that it was too far for me to just drop in at Christa's. It was also too far from the Friedens Temple. Father and I started to go to the Synagogue at the Prinzregentenstrasse, where I hardly knew anyone. So there really wasn't much to do around the new neighborhood except to talk to Manfred. From the beginning the friendship was under the tension of eminent separation. Such as the evening I spent with him and some friends who were leaving the next day—scattered remnant of a combo —they played their jazz softly, tootling low and warm, little teardrops at the very end of the piano. I kept a respectful silence in deference to their pain. Also in deference to my own. God, how I missed Renate. And Rudi missed her too. I had seen him on the street a few days ago, he looked positively lost. "Crazy girl," he had said about her. But he would go after her, yes, just as soon as he could get a visa.

There had been an initial telephone reconciliation between Renate and Mother, and now Renate was writing that she was helping in the hotel which her father had bought in Amsterdam.

"He's using her as a maid," Mother stormed. "He's exploiting her. Ernst, I want her home!"

Father made inquiries; there was talk of passports, papers, exit and entrance permits, visas. Then one day he came home, and his face was very white. "She can't come back, she would be arrested; she left illegally," he said.

"What do you mean illegally?"

"Her exit permit was never stamped."

"But then how did she get past the frontier?"

"God knows."

During a telephone call Renate explained, " I just kept knitting when the passport control came through."

"Just kept on knitting," Father said; he shook his head, nodded, shook it again. "To think of all the people who are trying to get out, who risk getting shot, crossing the border in the midst of night and fog."

Mother cried and stormed, "There must be something we can do!"

"Look," Father soothed, "at least she's safe. That's the main thing; she is out of here."

"That man is exploiting my child."

"It won't hurt Renate to sweep some floors; better than being arrested by the Nazis."

"You can talk! She isn't your child."

"Mother!" I yelled.

She turned on me. "You keep out of this, you . . . you helped her pack."

Later, Father said that she didn't mean it, she was upset.

One morning in November when I was leaving for school, Mother said, "I heard a lot of noise in the night. Ellen, be careful."

I kissed her and said I would be; pure routine. In all

my life I had never left my mother's presence without being told to be careful, to button my coat, to watch out crossing the street. When I was smaller, it used to annoy me, but now it had become the almost unheard ticking of the clock. As to hearing noises, Mother was always hearing things.

It was gray outside, stark branches poked black fingers into a drizzly sky, and it was chilly. I buttoned up tighter and shifted my heavy school bag from hand to hand.

The first time the fear hit me was at the corner— Cohn's Haberdashers' plate glass window was smashed. Large pieces of raggedy glass lay on the pavement—ice floats, each of the bigger ones smeared with red inscriptions: *Juden, Schweine, Dreck.* Among them floated broken arms and legs, a way off the torso and head of a mannequin, staring into the sky. Dirty underwear, lace panties with boot prints, red as with blood. "No, no, not blood; it's only paint," I remonstrated with myself. The whole display had spilled out of the window, a dirty river, and a pile of it was washed against the trunk of a trembling young elm; dogs had already visited the site.

I skirted carefully, stepping into the gutter to do so, ran blindly into a group of laughing boys who shouted, "Not so proud, little one," after me. Stepping back on the pavement, I measured the distance to the streetcar stop with my eyes. Much as I tried to neutralize my thinking, I had already seen that I would have to pass more Jewish stores. Not that I had ever known they were owned by Jews, but now there was no mistaking it—the glass, the red paint, the laughing children in front of them. I started to run; my streetcar was coming.

I sat down next to a boy I knew vaguely from school. He took my hand and squeezed it, but we said nothing. There were others I knew on the car; it was the 7:42 which we took every morning. That day there were no shouted greetings, though we touched with eyes and felt huddled together among the other passengers who did not look at us. They sat staring out of windows, pale and empty-eyed. It was really unnaturally quiet, in spite of the clanging of the bell, the screeching of the wheels in the rails, the grinding stops, and the shuddering starts. Then my neighbor whispered, "Look, look!"

I turned to the window, saw black billowing smoke and one red tongue of flame, but already we had passed the intersection of Prinzregentenstrasse. The Synagogue was burning.

It was a long ride. My thoughts jumbled, then sorted out; I tried to make an abstraction of them, draw dignity like a mantle around myself; my lips felt stiff. I sat very straight; very, very upright.

From our stop we walked the two blocks to our school in a loose herd. But the iron gates, which I had never noticed before because they had always been wide open, were locked.

The cold seeped into us, but we stood quietly. Then Dr. Schwartz came, the director. We made room for him, and he stood in our midst and spoke quietly.

"Go home, the school is closed." He paused, but no one moved. "You'll be notified." He plunged his hands into the pockets of his overcoat and said something else in such a low voice that I couldn't hear it. Then he walked away, through our ranks, down the street, becoming smaller.

"What did he say at the end?" I asked.

"He said, 'Walk proudly,' " a girl I did not know told me. I nodded; that was good, I thought. And then I wanted to get home, felt urgently that I must get home quickly, turned, and ran. Again, I just caught a streetcar. Suddenly I realized that I had gathered a lot of information—there had been raids on Jewish homes all through the night, men had been arrested, it was like the roundup of the Polish Jews. Where had I heard all this? And then the whispered snatches of talk came back, crystal clear balloons with printed talk in them. "Your father too?"— "My uncle"—"Banged on the door"; I willed the streetcar to go faster. Papi, Papi . . .

I burst in on Mother; it was only 9:30, but she was all

dressed and made up. "It's all right, he is safe," she said quickly.

They had received a call from Grandfather right after I had left. Father had gotten dressed and left. "He's walking," Mother said. "We'll meet him later; he is safe just walking."

She was right; who would suspect old Aryan-skulled Father?

Mother continued: "They came for him at 8:30, three SA men. I said he was out of town; they were quite polite."

"Manfred?" I asked.

"We warned them. He left in time too, but I didn't want Father to go with him."

I nodded. Of course not, Manfred looked Jewish.

Mother was talking again. ". . . and Grandfather said that they are watching the railroad stations; they have arrested thousands. Oh, what shall we do?" Hysteria was rising in her voice, she clasped her hands over her face.

"It's all right," I said calmly. "I know where he'll be safe; he can hide at the von Adelsbergs."

Mother's face had lighted up, but fell again. "Don't be silly, why should they take him in? It would endanger them."

"Herr Levy and Steffi have been there for weeks."

Mother stared at me speechlessly.

It was arranged. Father moved in via the back staircase. Herr von Adelsberg had said, "Well, thank God, now we can play some bridge."

And that's what they did for the week Father stayed there, every evening. Mother, Father, Herr von Adelsberg, and Herr Levy. Herr Levy learned the game the first night and beat everyone by the third.

"He's a goddamn natural," Herr von Adelsberg shouted. "Damn those clever Jews."

Late at night, Mother and I went back to the Pension Diamond. It was as if we were returning from a party.

Much as I felt guilty that I was enjoying myself at

such a time, it was wonderful to be really together with Steffi and Christa in this adventure. I kept telling myself that I would think about the Synagogue later; now there was so much to do. We cooked sumptuous meals and wouldn't let Mother into the kitchen; she mixed up the milchik and flayshig dishes. And all too quickly it seemed to me, the wave of arrests seemed to have calmed down, and it was deemed safe for Papi to come home.

My school remained closed.

Soon I began to wonder why, if vacations are such fun, I now missed school. The days ran on for endless hours; I wasn't allowed to go to Steffi in the mornings—too dangerous to go in and out—the superintendent, Herr Lustig, had made a remark to Herr von Adelsberg about the activity in his apartment since the Gnädige Frau left. Christa told me that her father had winked and nudged the man. "The ladies, ach, the ladies." but Herr von Adelsberg didn't know whether it had thrown Lustig off. Anyhow, we had to be more careful.

Mother was finishing up with the lift. Now it would have to be examined by an official, and then it would be sealed and shipped to Hamburg. Mother was nervous; she screamed at the drop of a hat; Father was always soothing her. Why couldn't she have more control, I wondered, she wasn't the only one involved; it was hard on all of us.

"Yes, but she worries," Father defended her.

"Who doesn't?"

He shrugged.

Friday nights were hardest; I missed Synagogue with an awful ache.

"Oh come on, you're not that religious," Mother disparaged.

"That's not the point!" She didn't understand a thing! And Father was a *Waschlappen*, literally "a face cloth," meaning someone limp and ineffectual.

19

Steffi was horribly gay. We all were. We talked only of boys all afternoon. Steffi would be leaving in a few days.

"Do you think that anyone will ever love me passionately?" she asked.

"You'll get someone special for waiting so long—an English earl, maybe," Christa suggested.

"Do they have orthodox earls?"

"Of course," I assured her.

Bahnhof Charlottenburg, at 7:00 A.M., February 1939.

A long line of children, orderly in rows of twos, wearing cardboard signs around their necks. Steffi's said "Susan Adler, *Kinder Transport, Numero Zwei*, London, England."

We had said good-by, we had cried. Now Christa and I stood apart. We watched the slow snake slide up the steps, vanish inside the cars. Steffi did not look back. She wore the long blue scarf Christa had knit for her—that's how we kept her fixed in view, by the bright blue scarf. Until she too disappeared—All Aboard!—and then the wailing from the group of parents.

"Where is she?" Frantically we ran along the train, peering into the windows of all the compartments. But we couldn't find her. Only when the train had started, was already gathering speed, went by us in the blur of our tears, I thought that I saw her face pressed to the window . . . but I wasn't sure. We were almost to the street before we realized that we had been clutching each other's hands. I gave another squeeze and let go; my fingers ached. Christa pulled the collar of her coat tighter and looked up at the early morning sky. Thin sunshine was filtering through bunched-up clouds. "It's trying to be a nice day," she said.

I kicked the tight wall of snow that was piled against the curb. "It's got to do an awful lot of trying to accomplish that."

At the corner we shook hands; Christa had to go to school.

And then, at the end of the month, she called me. "They arrested Papa and Herr Levy." She sounded absolutely calm, hysterically calm.

"Christa, no!"

"I can't talk, Ellen. I am at Cousin Fritz's; they are treating me like a prisoner."

"But what . . ."

"The superintendent . . . Father fought like a bear; they knocked him out. Herr Lustig told me himself. I was in school."

"Herr Lustig, the superintendent . . ."

"Ellen, I'll call you when I can." The telephone was dead.

After that Christa and I saw little of each other.

Cousin Fritz was watching her like a hawk; he felt it to be his moral obligation to cleanse her mind from the "ideological cesspool" her father had steeped her in. Christa reasoned that the only chance there was to make Fritz von Adelsberg help his cousin was to pretend to conform.

As far as she knew, her father had not been shipped to a K.Z. and was still at the *Moabit Gefängnis* at the Alexanderplatz in the center of Berlin. Christa wrote to him, but received no letters in return. Her mother, it was said, had gone into another decline.

It was one of our greatest frustrations that we had to

waste our precious minutes together by spending the time to arrange the next meeting. A sense of urgency would possess us, the clock ticking like a finger waved in warning. Once Christa managed to come to my room for a half hour before Carlheinz arrived, then I left them alone together—she only had so little time; she had to be able to account for every second. But mostly we met at street corners, Carlheinz and I strolling casually, Christa joining us, or all three of us happening to sit on the same bench at the Oliverplatz; we fed a lot of pigeons that March and April.

The first couple of meetings were almost exclusively dominated by talk about Steffi. What was I to write to her? Her letters were already frantic. In the censor-conscious language we all used, "Didn't the mailman deliver at Papa's hotel?" I was supposed to be the mailman.

Finally there was nothing to be done; I had to tell her.

"Papa is not visiting Onkel anymore. They have both gone on a trip."

From the English boarding school came the answer. "I cried and cried when I got the news that I have failed my examination," Steffi wrote.

Carlheinz felt that time was running out. He had no parents and lived alone in a furnished room. His American papers were due soon; he had cousins in the United States. But now he said he didn't want to wait any longer, he wanted to cross the border "black"—and with Christa. We made and discarded endless plans; in the end Christa always felt that she couldn't go, that she had to wait for her father to come back, had to work on Cousin Fritz. None of us said what we really knew by then, that it was hopeless, that Fritz von Adelsberg had no intention of helping. "He says, 'Why should I endanger my position by interceding for your father? He should have known better,'" Christa reported he kept saying.

"But what about your father's other contacts? He must

have known people who would help, how else did he get Steffi's papers?"

"I don't know who they are. Father never told me; he always said, 'Don't spread the risk,' don't you remember?"

Of course I did. I also remembered Judge Heidemann, his strong face. And Luz. Did she have her baby yet? I counted back; yes, she should have had it last month. Or should I ask Rudi first?

I thought of Renate's last letter; she had written about Rudi. "My pride was hurt, all those lies he had told me." But then, "When I realized that I couldn't just come back, I was absolutely panic-stricken. I knew suddenly that I had gone away to force his hand. But now, Ellen, and that is the strange thing, I find that I'm feeling better and better about what I've done. It isn't that I don't miss him, it's only that it is a pain that's getting fainter rather quickly. I guess we weren't 'fated,' as your Steffi would say."

Just the same, I would have to try Rudi.

The March drizzle, the gray fogginess, my hands in my raincoat pockets—the raincoat I wore with an extra sweater underneath because my winter coat was being lengthened, I had grown another piece after all—it all reminded me of the night Renate and I had gone to see the Heidemanns. Rudi answered the door, he greeted me naturally as if we saw each other all the time.

"How have you been, Ellen, what do you hear from Renate?"

"She's fine, we are fine."

"Good, good."

We were standing in his living room which, I noticed, had new paintings. I looked around.

"Do you like them? A friend of mine did them."

"Very nice," I said politely. Hands folded on my back, I wandered around as if I were in a museum. Wild yellow and orange swirls, black streaks; blots and splotches, splashes; I had never seen anything like it. It made my stomach ache. Or maybe it was Rudi. I turned to face him—he was wearing a white turtle-neck sweater, and the waves in his hair were glossy, and his eyes were blue and friendly. "She's good, isn't she?"

"Huh?"

"My friend. The artist."

"Oh yes. Yes, I guess so. Rudi, I need some help for someone—do you think our mutual friends . . ." I paused.

Slowly the smile died though his white teeth still shone. "Not your parents?"

"No, no. You don't know them. Do you think I could just go, or could you . . ."

"No, no," he said nervously and turned away.

I waited while he poured himself a cognac out of a bottle that stood on the round table before the sofa. "Drink?" he asked.

"No, thank you."

"No." He was still busy with the bottle, holding it to the light, reading the label. "You can't go there, they're gone."

"What do you mean?" The coldness rising from my feet.

His head tilted back, he poured the cognac down his throat. He wiped his mouth with the back of his hand. "I don't know where they are."

"But L . . ." I stopped. Maybe it was better not to say names. "But she . . . she must have had her baby?"

"I don't know, it was before . . ."

We stood silently and stared at each other. Rudi looked a little tired but otherwise he was handsome as ever. I began to rebutton my coat. On the way to the front door he had a lot to say. How he missed Renate, and how we would all be to-gether soon. He walked me to the elevator, he pinched my cheek. "Maybe I'll be your brother-in-law yet," he said when the gate rattled open.

"Maybe," I answered. "Auf Wiederseh'n."

I felt furious at myself on the way home. The melodrama, the cloak and dagger secrecy—"our mutual friends" and no names; who did I think I was? Mata Hari?

At home I found the Heidemanns' number in the telephone book and rang it up. It buzzed a long time and then a strange female voice came on. "Who is this calling please, and whom do you wish to contact?"

I hung up quickly. More melodrama.

There was nothing to do with the days. My fingernails were already manicured to perfection.

Finally Mother sent me to cooking school. A lovely Jewish lady was holding it in her apartment. That took care of two mornings. Then we heard of an ironing class—three ironing boards, standing deep in Persian rugs. And an English teacher was found for me. Herr Springer, an unworldly youth of twenty-four, a theology student from Breslau; he was waiting for his papers to England. He taught me out of *Gone with the Wind;* he said it would be easier to learn from an interesting text than a dry reader. And while he and I chewed tediously through the opening pages, I had already devoured the big, green book in my room at night. I looked forward to doing the love scenes with Herr Springer. However, I never experienced that pleasure, the pace of our lessons was too slow.

So I was busy again, anchored by routine; Mother was a believer in that.

In the meantime Father had applied for an English transit permit, a Dutch transit permit, and our passports. He wanted to leave no stone unturned. When the American visa came we should be able to leave immediately via any of these countries in case we couldn't get on a boat in Germany. Steamship bookings could not be made until one had exit permits, and a friend of Father's who had found himself in that situation had not been able to get bookings at all. His papers had become obsolete; he was still in Berlin.

Passports, on the other hand, were only issued when the consulates in question made out a certificate that stated that visas would be obtained within six months. Father had received this certificate from the American consulate, and in May we were notified to come for our passports.

When people talked of getting their passports they said, "We have been to Karlstrasse!" It was a magic term!

So we dressed up to go to Karlstrasse. I wore the new suit which Herr Phillipe had just delivered; it was to be my travel costume. Mother had these outfits all planned and hanging separately in the wardrobe, but I had prevailed upon her to let me wear the suit to Karlstrasse. In this finery I was, therefore, disappointed to be merely herded to the end of a line which came down two flights of stairs. And it was only ten in the morning. Ahead of me was a girl I knew from school, and while I hadn't known her well before that day, I soon knew all about her. And we weren't the only ones who talked freely; somehow everyone in line felt that we had everything in common; people poured their hearts out.

She informed me that she wasn't a virgin anymore because everyone in her whole crowd said why not live today while we can. "Are you?" she asked me.

I nodded defiantly. Let her think me a baby. Personally, I thought that the whole "don't want to die a virgin" thing was nonsense; we had been through that at thirteen already.

"It must be quite an anticlimax for all of you to get out of Germany alive now," I said tartly.

She wasn't angry, she laughed. "Oh well, so we are a little ahead of things. Anyhow, I am going to Sweden."

I nodded. Of course, that was different; everyone knew about Sweden.

Tired then, we inched along. It was four o'clock when we had gotten to the top step of the second floor. Mother, just behind me, was incredible; she looked perfect, her hair soft and neat, her lipstick straight, standing in that nice posture of hers. Father was pale and drawn. Ruefully, I looked down on my wrinkled suit, my blouse stuck to me. "Is it worth it?" I joked. Everyone around me laughed. Finally we arrived at the counter.

The ringing voice . . . "Westheimer, Israel Ernst."

Father stepped forward, very straight, a soldier once more. "*Jawohl!*" His voice rang too.

"Westheimer, Sarah Eva."

"Ja," Mother said evenly.

"Westheimer, Sarah Ellen."

"I am here." I wanted to sound proud, but my voice was too thin.

Stamps thumped, pens scratched, the official had a neat wreath of white hair around a brown-spotted, slightly pointed pate; he did not look at us. The passports came sliding across the counter—gray, with the swastika held in the claws of the eagle. I opened to check how my photo looked—awful of course, I looked like a child—and saw that my nationality was "stateless" now. I handed the passport to Father, who tucked it carefully into his breast pocket.

We took a taxi home.

At the pension, Father poured cognac; a small one for me too.

"America, to America!"

I had a sense of *déjà vu* until I remembered the champagne we had drunk when our affidavits had come. Only this time neither Mother nor I cried.

Having a passport lifted Mother's and Father's spirits, which was probably why the tediousness of the following weeks struck them the more painfully. Because nothing happened then, absolutely nothing. Except that I was emotionally kept in high gear by Christa and Carlheinz. Even when things were awful, they still sustained me, gave me purpose. If, in my room at night, I felt depressed, a new metal taste in my mouth and a tightness in my chest, I knew what it was about. Of course we didn't label such emotions; it was just The Times. To me it seemed that it would have been crazy to feel otherwise, which was why I couldn't understand Mother's and Father's frantic ups and downs. A couple of drinks and they were going into a mad adventure, dance into the future, reform America to *Kultur* and sexual enlightenment! But oh those early mornings when Mother sat in her bed with her cup of coffee, when Father stood morosely by the window, staring out, holding his pajama pants up with one hand. Such gloom, you could cut it with a knife.

"Do you remember when Papi lost his pajama pants when Reni and I were little?" I asked brightly one morning. I mean, they had told me the story so often, it always made them laugh. Not this time. Mother started to cry instead.

"My poor child," she wailed.

Father went on staring out of the window.

"Poor child nothing," I said angrily; Renate was perfectly all right. She shouldn't have written that she wasn't getting along with her Vati; it was all Mother needed to produce another national crisis. I forgot that I had been proud of her at Karlstrasse; she was really impossible.

In a way it was almost a relief when Tante Ruth and her Scrubber left for Shanghai; at least something was happening.

I was remembering the conversation with Nanny a couple of years earlier. What a joke Shanghai, China, had been then! Now it was a perfectly sensible place to go. Of course they couldn't wait until we were established enough in the States to send them papers. Instead we were going to send their affidavits to China. First of all, they would have a lower quota from there, and secondly, it was certainly safer to wait in Shanghai than in Berlin.

After coffee and cake in the parents' room, they got

ready to go. "Well Ellen . . . ," Tante Ruth said. Her china blue eyes staring hard, her really beautiful dark red hair in soft waves around the white face with the powdering of freckles on soft cheekbones; the pretty, stupid, dear face. I hugged her hard.

"Auf Wiederseh'n!" Tears blinding me, my God, I had never even really liked her, why this feeling of grief? It must be because I feel sorry for her, I thought; Nanny hardly ever wrote to her. She was with a Christian family in Birmingham and seemed happily submerged in their large brood.

I felt sorry for Grandfather too. It wasn't that I thought that he would miss his foolish daughter Ruth, it was just what her leaving represented.

"I can't change it!" He said in defeat and bitterness. "I tried, I planned, I worked—ach, what was the use?"

Everyone went to the station except me.

"Ellen is afraid of stations," Mother excused me.

In fact, I had argued against letting Grandfather go. "Don't let him," I had pleaded. "It's so awful."

"That's silly, why shouldn't he?" Father did not understand.

"The sounds . . ." I wasn't very articulate, I couldn't explain.

Father shrugged "He wants to go—what's the difference where? Either way saying good-by will be hard."

But when my parents came back from the station they said that they had put Grandfather to bed. "I never saw him like that," Mother said worriedly.

"I told you so!" I shouted angrily.

The next day Grandfather was himself again. He brought me a present when he came to the pension. It was unusual for him; he had never given me anything except money and the rabbit's bread he used to bring when I was small. I opened it with nervous fingers and it was a tiny, round gold watch. "To keep you from always being late," he said. It was a joke; everyone knew that I was always on time. And wrist-watches and wedding rings were the only jewelry you were permitted to take out of Germany. I embraced him—but why was he saying good-by to me already?

20

It was funny that spring. So many people were gone already. One day, on impulse, I called Romi. There was no answer. I tried again and again. Then I called Katrine.

"They left last week," she said.

"Without saying good-by?" I mean, we hadn't been that close lately, but still . . .

"She didn't say good-by to me either," Katrine said. "In fact I didn't even know that their papers had come. I just suddenly had that card from her from Rotterdam, saying that they were taking the SS *Veendam* the next day."

The same thing was happening to my parents—their friends and our family doctor were leaving. We went for a last checkup. God, he was old, the great cheeks hung down the sides of his face. His fat ear on my chest. . . .

"Breathe deeply, ah, I can hear your heart; you are in love."

The old jokes! Poking my belly. "Aha, scrambled eggs scrambling about!" And pinching my cheek, "Still Snow White!" And weighing me, "You'll never get a job as a Fat Lady in the circus!" Dopey old man, but I felt bad; he was off to Brazil. "São Paulo, they are waiting for me to correct the health standards of South America—lots of syphilis."

Mother cried. "Ach Doktor, these times!"

"Na, Eva, some young American doctor will admire these pretty—ah, lungs!" And Mother sat up straighter in the chair; her breasts were small but firm; she was very proud of them.

She told Father later, "He said I have the body of a thirty-year-old woman."

"Don't I know it!"

Carlheinz and Christa went in June. I had known that they had a plan, but they didn't tell me the details. You didn't do that. We said good-by, farewell, without actually acknowledging it. "See you some time."

"Yes, or next Tuesday on the Oliverplatz, same bench."

We touched cheeks. "Be careful!" I couldn't help the urgency.

The next week was incredible. Were they gone? I heard nothing. On Tuesday I was at the Oliverplatz. I sat on our bench for a couple of hours. Christa didn't come.

Father was notified to report to the Security Section of the Trade Ministerium, District Berlin; he was to be there on Friday. It was a form letter on blue paper. Only his name and the date and the time were typed in.

"What's the Security Section of the Trade Ministerium?" Mother asked.

"Who knows?"

"What do they want?"

"How should I know? And don't start worrying; whatever it is, it's just routine." He threw the letter across the table. "See, it's a form letter."

Just the same he was nervous. He dressed carefully in his tan gabardine suit and stood in front of his tie rack for a long, undecided moment.

"Wear the one with the blue dots," I suggested.

"If you say so—for luck."

I walked the two blocks to the bus stop with him.

"You look very handsome," I said and hung my arm through his. It was a clear day, blue and green, warm and sweet-smelling. Even the gas fumes were overpowered by the scent of the linden blossoms, and the chestnut trees had tall white candles. I waved after the bus. Then I just stood there looking after it.

I didn't know why my chest should feel so tight. Walking back home, I tried to reason with myself. I mean, what was there to worry about?

I had received a letter from Christa finally, a thin piece of air-mail stationery covered closely with her tiny script. A Christa letter, censor oriented but bubbling with joy, all about a ride in the Bois de Boulogne, happy but for the ending of ominous fear about the weather at home. Postmark: Paris, France. They were safe.

The other good news was that our Dutch and English transit permits had come; we could leave as soon as the American visa arrived; in fact, we could leave now and await the visa in either Holland or England. But the American consul had counseled against that because the transfer of files from the Berlin consulate might result in delays. We only had permission for a six-week stay in Britain and a week in the Netherlands; it might be risky. So we were sitting tight. But yet, as Father had said, much safer than before. And we had our exit permit already too. So what was I feeling so anxious about?

Of course there was Grandfather. He had said, "Your English transit permit? It came already?"

I had danced into his apartment with the news, shouting it out. I almost repeated the *already* indignantly, but I caught myself when I saw his expression. Something about his mouth reminded me of the click of his teeth in the water glass at night; he suddenly looked as if his dentures were too big. I stopped short.

But already he was normal again, smiling. "Na, that's good," he said, "that's very good. Let's have a little one to celebrate."

Walking to the liquor cabinet, his tread was firm and

youthful. He took out the cognac, measured a drop for me and took his usual hefty portion. I rolled the snifter between my palms, making the most of the moment. Yet, I felt funny.

"The sooner we go, the sooner we can get you out," I said.

"Of course," he answered in an even voice. "*Prost*, Ellen!"

"*Prost*, Opa!" I felt as if I had been spanked.

I was almost home now. I hurried a little. Herr Springer was due for my lesson. But still I couldn't throw the bad feeling.

Upstairs, Mother was pacing. "I feel so uneasy, Ellen," she blurted.

"Don't be silly."

"What can they want with Father?"

"Some more dumb papers to fill out probably."

"Why didn't they mail them?"

"Oh Mother!"

"I can't help it—I have a feeling . . ."

"Be still!" I yelled.

We stared at each other, then I started to cry. Mother put her arms around me. We stood like that for a moment. Then there was a knock; Herr Springer had come.

"Where were we?" Herr Springer asked out on the balcony.

"Where he says, 'And you are no lady.' "

Father came home at eight o'clock.

We had begun to be wild. Wild, in an icy way; frozen and lost. But there he was. Very thin, I noticed, the blue of his eyes way deep in his head. He kissed us both, solemnly, almost ceremoniously.

"What happened, for God's sakes, what took you so long?" Now Mother let the hysteria rise into her voice.

"Later," he said. "Let's start packing."

We packed through most of the night. It was a marvel, the result of Mother's organization. Everything was clean, much was prepacked, and there were lists, long prepared, that only needed to be followed. First Father's things, then Mother's, and then Mother came upstairs with me and we did mine. At four in the morning five large suitcases and three handpieces stood locked in the corridor. And while I hadn't much time to think during all this, my mind did keep going back to a blue shirt I had seen at Elsie's Blouse Emporium at the corner. It had an ascot in the same fabric, and I had thought of asking Mother whether I could buy it. Too late, too late, and it would have been so perfect with the traveling suit.

"Let's rest for a couple of hours now," Father said. "We'll call Grandfather at six and get the eight o'clock train to Amsterdam."

All three of us lay on Mother's and Father's beds for those last hours. I wanted to be close to them, and they didn't want me out of their sight. And then Father told us.

He had been accused of misrepresenting himself as an Aryan, there was a deposition against him that he had used the Hitler Salute at a customer's office.

"Krause!" Father said with certainty.

"But you have hardly been working anymore."

"He obviously wanted to make sure that I wouldn't."

Father had been drilled for hours. "Did you or didn't you raise your hand and say 'Heil Hitler'?"

"I did not, never!"

Mother interrupted to ask, "Did you?"

Father shrugged. Then he continued. "He asked me how I could be so sure that I had never done it. I answered that I just knew that I had never done that. Then he shouted, 'Don't you think that it is natural to hail the Führer?' I said, 'I know that it is forbidden to Jews to do so.'"

Over and over, under glaring lights. "Like in a damned detective film," Father said. He paused, we all lay quietly, I touched his hand; he was real. How often lately I had thought him inconsequential, but he had lived through that scene. . . .

And then the incredible luck. The examining officer, a

Leutnant Siebling, came from Nürnberg; Onkel Wolf had treated his child for pneumonia. The child had gotten well, was a strapping boy in the Hitler Youth.

"But how did you get on that subject?" Mother asked.

"For a while there he tried to jolly me, told me where he was from, that he was a family man too, that I should just sign the confession, and then I could go home. When he said Nürnberg I thought there was no harm trying, and when I mentioned Wolf he jumped out of his chair, it was crazy. He says there is no decent doctor left in Nürnberg since Wolf left. He said, 'Whatever you can say about the Jews, they are smart.' He said that he was glad when they transferred him to Berlin, away from the *Provinz*." Father started to laugh. "He spoke in the thickest Bavarian accent; I thought I was back home in Würzburg."

I cuddled closer to Father; his laughter scared me. And I felt him tense when he continued.

"Then Weber came in, and I thought I had had it."

Weber was *das grosse Tier*. He had stormed and shouted and waved his pistol at Father, but then he had said that he had to go to a meeting and directed Siebling not to be soft with the damned Jew.

"Siebling toughened up then, but I just kept saying that I was a front fighter, and that I knew how to follow orders, that I could never have done what I was accused of. In the end, I guess he believed me, but he wasn't authorized to close the case, and he was afraid of Weber. I was sure he would keep me there, except that I mentioned my regiment, and then it turned out that Siebling's brother had served in the same unit. So he told me to come back Monday. He said, 'Tomorrow is a half-day in this office, so come back Monday and bring your passport.' Then he stared at me, and then he said, 'Do you understand, Westheimer? Monday, with your passport, and eh, Westheimer, I won't be here on Monday. Monday is my free day.' I said, '*Jawohl* Herr Leutnant, I understand.' " Father sat up excitedly. "He was warning me. You see, there are still some decent Germans in our country."

"Of course," Mother agreed.

I felt as if I would choke. He thought, he really thought, that this Siebling was a decent man, a friend, just another boy from the *Heimat,* good old Bavaria. I jumped up.

"Will the stores be open before we leave?" I asked. "There is such a darling blouse at Elsie's . . ." My voice trailed off.

Mother and Father were staring at me from the bed, Father in his suspenders, Mother in a white slip with ecru lace.

"Are you crazy?" Father asked.

I got back on the bed and lay quietly; they were right, I was crazy. I only half listened as Father explained.

". . . and if they once have my passport, even if they don't arrest me—and they arrest people for a lot less—" On and on. Suddenly I was asleep, deep in a delicious black tunnel where everything was all right.

I woke to Mother's hand, soft on my face. She was all dressed in her traveling suit and the little gray velour hat with the half-veil. "Come on, Ellen, it is time." She helped me to get into my clothes as if I were a very small girl, holding the skirt for me to step into, doing up the little pearl buttons on my white silk blouse. Father had gone to get taxis. Until the jubilant morning air really awoke me as we stepped out of the quiet house, it all seemed as if I were still in the black tunnel of my dream.

Grandfather was already waiting at the station, and so was the train. Now it was I who was inside of the compartment when *All Aboard* sounded. Only Mother was still outside, her arms around Grandfather's neck. "Vati, Vati . . ."

"Make her get on, oh God, please make her get on the train," I yelled to Father.

Father jumped off again. He took Mother's arm, he

pulled her away from Grandfather, and the shuddering of the wheels and the grinding and the slam of the door—and the blurred faces, my hair blowing over my eyes as I craned out of the window, trying to keep Grandfather's tall, thin figure in sight but seeing him get smaller, smaller . . . And at the same time I was also standing next to Grandfather on the station platform and seeing the train leave, seeing the train get smaller and smaller; dip into the tunnel.

It was dark and roaring underground, not at all as in my dream, and then the train emerged into the sun and flooded the compartment with morning light.

We sat quietly in the upholstered seats of the second-class car; we had it to ourselves. Mother's lids were closed, tears lay in the tender purple of the skin under her eyes; she breathed evenly as if she were asleep. Her hat was on just right. Father sat up straight; his face stern, he was staring out of the window.

And I? I had combed my hair in front of the little mirror that hung over Mother's seat, then I had sat down. I folded my hands. I waited to feel something, but I seemed to be empty.

Hours later, the frontier at Bendheim was an anticlimax.

The customs official, accompanied by two SA men, came to our compartment. He examined our luggage carelessly, studied the passports, the railroad tickets, the transit permit, the exit permit. "Any jewelry?" he asked.

Mother held out her hand. She was wearing only her gold wedding band. The solitaire had been turned in, according to the edict. Involuntarily, my hands went to my chest, and I pressed the Mogen David against me, but then I dropped them quickly. However, no one asked me if I had any jewelry. The SA men looked bored, stood by with their hands on their backs, their feet apart.

"Everything in order," the customs official said. "Have a good trip."

I burst into tears. "I'm going to see my sister," I blurted.

"That's nice," he said.

"Heil Hitler," the SA men said.

Mother lunged for Father's right arm, said hastily, "Auf Wiederseh'n." They left.

And while we still sat, exhausted, I sniffling and trying to find a handkerchief, and of course not having one, the train started to move again. It chugged, shunted backward, lurched ahead—three times, four—then it found its rhythm and gathered speed. The station, the customs house, the black and white barrier flashed by.

"Are we out?" I asked.

"We are out. We are in Holland," my father answered. "In a free country!"

It was July 1939.

Mother and Father were in each other's arms. I stood, nose pressed against the glass. Outside, along the roadbed, flowers were growing; colors out of Montmartre.